BEFORE THE DAWN

Home to Heather Creek

Before the Dawn

Sweet September

HOME TO  HEATHER CREEK

BEFORE THE DAWN

Kathleen Bauer

Guideposts
New York

Before the Dawn

ISBN-10: 0-8249-3424-5
ISBN-13: 978-0-8249-3424-8

Published by Guideposts
16 East 34th Street
New York, New York 10016
Guideposts.org

Distributed by Ideals Publications, a Guideposts company
2630 Elm Hill Pike, Suite 100
Nashville, TN 37214

Library of Congress Cataloging-in-Publication Data

Bauer, Kathleen.
Before the dawn / Kathleen Bauer.
p. cm.—(Home to Heather Creek)
ISBN-13: 978-0-8249-4871-9
ISBN-10: 0-8249-4871-8
1. Orphans—Fiction. 2. Grandparents—Fiction. 3. Grandparent and child—Fiction. 4. Brothers and sisters—Fiction. 5. Farm life—Nebraska—Fiction. I. Title.
PR9199.3.A14B44 2011
813'.54—dc22

2010033180

Cover by Müllerhaus
Interior design by Cindy LaBreacht
Typeset by Nancy Tardi and Aptara

Printed and bound in the United States of America
10 9 8 7 6 5 4 3 2 1

Acknowledgments

I feel humbled and honored to be the first author in this new series for Guideposts. To that end I want to thank my agent Karen Solem for her hard work on my behalf, and my editor Beth Adams for her positive cheerleading and gentle guidance in bringing this book from concept to print. Thanks to the rest of the Home to Heather Creek authors for sharing ideas and expertise and for carrying on the story of Charlotte, Bob, and the Slater children.

—Carolyne Aarsen writing as Kathleen Bauer

Chapter One

So this is where we're living?" Sam eased his lanky body out of the backseat of the truck as he stared at the farmhouse, silhouetted against the blue Nebraska sky. As he tugged the earpieces of his music player out of his ears, his face, partially hidden by the hood of his sweat-shirt, showed his bewilderment.

Charlotte tried not to let the tone of her grandson's voice disappoint her. She knew that his attitude was part grief, part separation anxiety, and part sixteen-year-old boy.

"This is Heather Creek Farm. Named after the creek we crossed over a ways back. This is where your grandfather grew up."

Charlotte kept her voice upbeat and her lips formed a smile as she tucked her short hair back behind her ear. *Your mother too,* she silently added. Toby stood beside her, staring up as if wondering where Charlotte had been. The dog's tail wagged slowly, a brown and black plume, as she licked Charlotte's hand.

"This looks like a set from an old TV show," Emily, her fourteen-year-old granddaughter, said. Her long hair was pulled back in a loose ponytail that hung askew from sleeping in the car. Her eyes blinked as they adjusted to the light.

"Are we finally there?" Christopher's sleepy voice drifted out from the back of the truck.

Still clinging to the Spider-Man backpack that had been his constant companion for the past week, the boy clambered out of the vehicle and reached for his sister's hand. His close-cropped hair glinted in the afternoon sun as he yawned. He looked as bewildered as his siblings sounded.

Emily sighed. "If you want to call being out in the boonies, *there*, then yes." Emily's voice was quiet, but her words carried.

"Hey. They have a dog." Christopher crouched down and reached out to Toby, but Toby ignored him, her brown eyes still fixed on Charlotte.

Charlotte patted the dog absently, glancing over at her husband. Though she wasn't that conversant in teen-speak, she was fluent in reading Bob's body language. The way he was yanking the suitcases out of the back of the vehicle clearly showed how unhappy he was with his grandchildren's reactions.

Charlotte wanted to explain, to defend. The children had just endured a long flight from the West Coast to America's heartland, then a tiring drive through the country to get to a farm they had never visited in their lives. Bob hadn't spent a week with the children like she had. He'd had to return to the farm after the funeral in San Diego, while Charlotte had stayed to deal with the aftermath of their daughter's death. On top of dealing with guardianship issues, Denise's will, the insurance, and all the legalities that sidelined her own sorrow, Charlotte also had witnessed, firsthand, the children's grief in a way that Bob, during his brief visit for the funeral, hadn't. Denise's children barely knew their own grandparents or their family here in Bedford. Of course they would be confused, bewildered, and disoriented.

Charlotte turned away from the emotions of the people behind her and let her eyes drink in the familiar sight of the farmhouse. The white clapboard building had been Bob's home all his life and her home for the past forty-five years.

It stood solid, as it had for almost a century, edged by poplar trees. The pale green of newly budded leaves misted their branches under the achingly blue sky. A few geese honked overhead, the neat arrow of their formation pointing to a new season and a new cycle of life.

During the draining, hectic week she spent with her grandchildren in San Diego, Charlotte had longed for a quiet moment when she could allow her heavy grief some space to be released. She knew this would only come to her here, at Heather Creek Farm.

She had so hoped that the farm would be a place of healing and hope for her grandchildren too.

A light breeze teased at her hair again, and as she tucked the errant strand back behind her ears, she sent up a frantic prayer.

Please, Lord, help these children to find a space here. Help them to get over Denise's death.

She turned back to the children, a forced smile in place as she added another prayer.

Help me *to get over Denise's death.*

"So, here we are," she said.

"I'm hungry," Christopher said, his voice still hoarse with sleep.

Emily took Christopher's hand and gave him a tender look that encouraged Charlotte. The children truly cared for each other.

"I'm sure we can find something to feed you." Charlotte gave him an encouraging smile and was rewarded with a shy smile in return. "What would you all like to eat?"

"I'm not hungry." Emily's languid stare slid over her new surroundings as she toyed with a blonde strand of hair, just as her mother used to do.

Oh, Lord, how could you do this to us? To these children? How could you take away their mother? Our daughter?

Even as the questions resonated through her mind, Charlotte struggled to silence them. She had no right to question God. The only things she could do now were pray for strength, bring these children into her life, and deal with the reality of this cobbled-together family.

"But it's been such a long drive from the airport," Charlotte said, trying to catch her granddaughter's eye.

Emily was looking in the direction of the barn. "You got horses too?"

"They're your Uncle Pete's."

She tried not to let her anger with her youngest son spill into her voice. He had said he would be home when she and Bob came from the airport with his niece and nephews, but neither he nor his truck were to be seen. Because he'd had to stay home and take care of the farm, Pete hadn't been able to come for the funeral, so she had assumed he would be waiting when they arrived.

"Some of them are trained for riding. I'm sure he can take you out if you want." Charlotte latched onto the faint note of interest in Emily's voice, remembering the worn books she had on her bookshelf back in their apartment in San Diego.

"Emily just reads about horses. She doesn't know squat about riding." Sam offered this information in the same cynical voice he'd been using all week. "None of us know anything about horseback riding. Or farming." His words faded into the open air, lost in the space that separated grandson from grandparents.

A new silence surrounded them, heavy with questions and sorrow.

Charlotte knew he spoke from his own pain. She wished she knew the right words to ease it away, or the right way to usher these children from one life into another. But she could barely cope with her own emotions.

Dear Lord, please help me to forget my own sorrow, Charlotte prayed, squeezing her hands tight as if trying to contain the pain that had been her constant companion since the phone call.

"Your daughter . . . fatal accident . . . car totaled . . ." The words that had shattered her world would jump into her mind whenever she let her guard down.

She took a quick breath and started walking toward the house. They needed to keep moving, stay active.

"Let's get the suitcases and boxes inside," she said over her shoulder. "Emily, Sam, Christopher, can you help your grandfather bring your things into the house, please?"

The only sounds she heard behind her were a shuffling

of feet and the muffled rumble of suitcase wheels bumping up the cracked and broken walkway. Toby jogged alongside Charlotte until they got to the house, dropped onto the porch, and lay down, watching as everyone filed past her.

"This, of course, is the kitchen." Charlotte looked around, trying to see the familiar lines of this room through their eyes.

Wooden cupboards, painted a buttery yellow, had been new fifty years ago, but now Charlotte could see how old-fashioned the wooden knobs were. Until now, she had never noticed all the places on the Formica where countless knives had cut countless loaves of bread.

To her right, the heavy oak table, its top scarred from years of use, dominated the center of the dining area.

Charlotte guessed the stack of envelopes on the table were mostly sympathy cards, sent by people in the community. She bit her lip against a fresh wave of grief. For the sake of the children, she had to stay on top of her own emotions.

She could see dishes piled in the aged porcelain sink and on the worn counter. She guessed Bob and Pete hadn't spent much time cleaning up after themselves while she was gone.

Though she itched to tidy up and restore order to her house, she had to ignore the mess for now.

"Would you like some milk and cookies?" Charlotte whisked open the faded green curtains above the sink as she walked toward the large cookie jar squatting at one end of the counter.

Christopher's eyes lit up, then he glanced upward at his sister, who shook her head. "No. I'm not hungry anymore."

Charlotte lifted the lid and looked inside. Just as well that Christopher had changed his mind. Only a few cookie crumbs resided on the bottom of the jar. Pete had been indulging.

"Well, let me show you your rooms." She replaced the lid and kept her voice brisk, businesslike. "I'm sure you're tired."

She picked up one of the suitcases that Bob had brought into the kitchen and led the way past the pantry and down the hallway to the stairs.

While she was in San Diego, she had given precise and detailed instructions to Bob and Pete on which quilts she wanted on which beds and which furniture to take out of storage for each room. On the flight home, and then on the drive, she had imagined the children in each of the rooms.

But now, as the worn carpeting on the stairs muffled the children's footsteps behind her, Charlotte wasn't so sure. Now that they were actually here, all she could think about was that these children were hers and Bob's. All theirs.

The thought created a rush of anticipation. New adventures with these precious children awaited them, new experiences. For the first time since Denise's funeral, she felt a fragment of hope, slivering through the pain.

"This is your room, Emily." She hesitated for a fraction of a moment, memories of Denise crowding her mind, then she twisted the knob and pushed open the door.

She stepped into the room, her eyes taking quick inventory. Was the patchwork quilt, with its shades of blue and yellow, too childish? Were the pillows she'd insisted Bob put on the bed too fussy?

Charlotte had replaced the posters Denise had plastered on the wall with some old-fashioned prints she had picked up at a garage sale, but other than the matched set of Victorian girls playing with kittens, nothing else broke the expanse of blue wall.

The dresser scarf that Denise had made as a young girl hung askew on the large wooden cupboard, and Charlotte straightened it, then turned to face Emily.

"This used to be your mother's room." Charlotte spoke the words without a hitch in her voice, but her heart thundered in her chest as time wheeled backward.

Hovering in the doorway, the light from the windows silvering her hair, Emily looked exactly like Denise.

The only reply Charlotte received was a curt nod. Emily's eyes flitted around the room as she stepped inside, the wheels of her suitcase sounding hollow on the wooden floor.

Charlotte bit back a reprimand. The kids would need time.

"I'll leave you to unpack," Charlotte said as she left the room.

Christopher's room was directly across from Emily's. On the single bed, Bob had put a rust-and-brown patchwork quilt—an old one that was too large and hung onto the floor. It would have to do for now.

Ghostly imprints of long-gone pictures Bill had hung up years ago dotted the empty brown walls, and Charlotte made a note to find time to paint the room a brighter color.

"This used to be your Uncle Bill's room," Charlotte said as Christopher wandered in, still carrying his backpack. "Do you remember him from the funeral?"

Christopher shook his head. Charlotte wasn't surprised. That day had been a blank for her as well, but she had been thankful Bill had taken the time to come out.

Christopher went directly to the window above the wooden bed and looked out.

"I can see a long way," he said.

Had she imagined the plaintive note in his voice?

"Emily is right across the hall, and Sam will be around the corner," Charlotte said, glancing at Sam, who was standing behind her.

"You gonna be okay, buddy?" Sam asked his little brother, spinning the earpieces of his music player around his finger.

Christopher gave them a quick nod, then sat on the bed, looking around, clasping his backpack like a shield.

"I'll get rid of my gear and be right back," Sam said.

As Charlotte and Sam left, they met Bob coming up the stairs, boxes stacked in his arms.

"Where do these go?" he asked. His breath came in gasps as he set them on the floor.

"Just tell me where I'll be sleeping," Sam said, ignoring Bob's question. "You don't have to take me."

Charlotte glanced from Bob to Sam, then nodded. "Like I told Christopher, your room is to the left, at the end of the hall."

Sam tossed his backpack over one shoulder, picked up

one of the boxes, and without a backward glance, walked into the room and shut the door.

Charlotte looked at Bob and was about to go to Christopher when the door to Emily's room opened. She glanced at the boxes on the floor, picked up one for Christopher, then slipped into his room, shutting the door behind her.

Chapter Two

"Come, let us return to the Lord. He has torn us to pieces but he will heal us; he has injured us but he will bind up our wounds."

Charlotte let the words linger in the predawn quiet of the farmhouse, wishing they would take root in her parched and weary soul. She closed the Bible, letting her hand rest on its worn cover as she so often did when she had finished her morning devotions.

This morning, when she dropped into her faded green chair in her corner of the family room, she had been tempted to skip her regular reading. She was in Hosea, and she wasn't sure she could find any comfort in the story.

Yet, somehow, these words offered a tantalizing glimpse of comfort and hope.

"I need your help, Lord," she prayed, covering her face with her hands, stifling the sorrow that so quickly rose up since Denise's funeral. "I need you to bind up my wounds, to revive and restore me and Bob. These children too."

She believed the promise offered, but she knew the wounds would take time to heal. She wouldn't stop grieving the loss of Denise overnight. None of them would.

She walked to the window overlooking the yard. The sun broke over the horizon, casting long shadows over the ground. Pete stepped out of the barn and strode toward the house, swinging the milk pail.

She knew Pete found solace in the rhythmic swish-swish of milk squirting into the pail. Charlotte did too, but she wouldn't be milking the cow or gathering eggs for a while. The ordinary, soothing routine of her previous life would have to be foregone for the sake of the children still sleeping upstairs.

Charlotte smoothed her hands over her hair, took a deep breath, as if preparing herself for the day, then turned and walked out of the family room. She heard the comforting drone of the washing machine and the whine of the dryer. Normally she would be hanging the clothes up on the line strung out from the back porch, but she didn't have time today.

She counted the place settings once more. The table seemed too full. But no, six plates and bowls, six cups, six sets of silverware lay in a precise circle around the table, waiting for the family to gather for breakfast.

She felt a sense of anticipation. Her grandchildren were here. Under their roof. For good.

"So, where's the grublets?" Pete's voice boomed through the silence, breaking into her thoughts.

Charlotte's youngest son sauntered into the kitchen, one hand shoved into the back pocket of faded blue jeans hanging on his lanky frame, the other carrying a pail half filled with milk. His brown hair stuck out in a ragged fringe below a stained and dusty ball-cap bearing the logo of a local feed dealership.

"They're still sleeping." Charlotte put her finger to her lips and pointed upstairs. "Take off your boots."

"You going to get them up as early as we used to?" Pete set the pail on the countertop with a thunk, then pulled his barn boots off his feet and put them on the porch.

"Not this morning," she said, opening a cupboard door and pulling out a large plastic jug. "But come next week, I'll start them on a routine."

"That's our mom. Like Denise always said, bringing order to the world one list at a time."

His casual reference to his sister created a low-level ache in Charlotte's heart. Had she and Bob been too hard on their daughter? Is that why she ran away so young? She'd only been two years older than Sam was now.

In the past few years these questions had crept around the edges of Charlotte's consciousness, but since she and Bob received that late-night call from the San Diego police, the questions had moved into her mind and made a home there.

Pete rubbed the side of his nose with a finger. "Sorry I wasn't home last night when you came back."

"I was sorry too. You had said you would be here." She pressed her lips together as she yanked the straining cloth out of the drawer.

"Was out with the guys."

How could he be so casual? Charlotte clipped the cloth to the jug with quick, hard movements, then grabbed the pail and started pouring.

"Hey, slow down, Ma," Pete said. "You're going to splash the milk all over the counter."

"You couldn't come to the funeral. The least you could have done was be here when the kids arrived."

"I'm here now." Pete leaned back against the counter. "Besides, I barely know them. Would'na made no difference if I was here."

Charlotte set the pail down, her anger dissipating as quickly as it came. She didn't have the energy to chastise him about his priorities. At thirty-two, he was a grown man. Just not very responsible at times.

"So when's breakfast?" Pete asked, glancing at the clock over the sink.

"Eight o'clock."

"Wow. You're going to spoil those kids, Mom. Gettin' soft in your old age."

Charlotte ignored Pete's sarcasm as she rinsed out the straining cloth. She knew better than he did how disoriented the children had been back in San Diego. "They need order in their lives," was all she said.

"And if I have to wait that long for breakfast, I need cookies—" Pete pulled a handful of cookies out of the just-replenished cookie jar behind him.

"You should save your appetite." Charlotte deflected her disappointment with his absence last night to his eating habits. A much safer topic.

"I'm hungry now." Pete polished off another cookie and leaned ahead, looking at the pad of paper Charlotte had sitting on one end of the counter. "Whatcha writing?"

"The same thing I always write on Wednesdays. The week's menu."

"Put meatloaf on it," Pete said. "You haven't made that for ages."

"I'm sure Emily won't eat it," Charlotte said, tapping her pen on the pad. "She says she's a vegetarian."

Pete blew his breath out in a snort of disgust. "Please. Tell me you're kidding, Ma. Flippin' Californian."

"That flipping Californian is your niece." Charlotte's voice took on an automatic tone of reprimand. "You make sure you treat her with care. She's been through a lot . . ." Charlotte's words faded away as she struggled to regain control of her emotions.

Pete's only response was to shove another cookie into his mouth, looking away with embarrassment as Charlotte wiped away an errant tear.

"I know, Mom. We all have." His quiet response reminded her that though he was young when Denise ran away with her boyfriend, his sister's death gave him his own grief to bear.

"I'm sorry, Pete." She drew in a long breath. "I've got so much to deal with."

Pete got up and patted his mother awkwardly on the shoulder. "You'll do okay, Ma. You always do."

His quiet confidence should have cheered her, but somehow all it did was lay one more expectation on her shoulders.

"Will you tell your father that we'll be eating later than usual?" Charlotte said as she placed the now strained milk into the refrigerator to cool.

"Can't. He drove out to Jimmy's land. Said he wanted to see if it's ready for seeding. I told him it was, but he said he had to check for himself." Pete finished the sentence with a shrug, clearly telling Charlotte what Pete thought of Bob's checking.

Charlotte wasn't going there. Her head still ached from the tension and emotion of the past week. She didn't have room for Bob and Pete's ongoing struggle.

A squeak on the stairs caught their attention.

Charlotte looked back in time to see Christopher coming down the hallway. He wore a pair of faded blue pajamas. The cuffs were tattered, and there was a worn logo of a hockey team on the chest.

"Good morning, Christopher," Charlotte said, her voice barely breaking the quiet of the kitchen. She was going to introduce Pete, but Christopher kept his face averted, looking at the pictures hanging on the wall across from the bathroom.

Charlotte walked over to his side. "That's your mother, when she was in school."

"How old is she?" Christopher lifted his hand and touched the speckled glass covering the photograph, as if he could resurrect her memory.

"She's Sam's age."

"Did she like it on the farm?"

"She did when she was that age." Charlotte folded her arms as her mind cast back to those happier days—before the farm represented all that was supposedly wrong in Denise's life. "She had a horse she liked to ride every day."

"Do you still have that horse?" Christopher looked at her with a measure of expectation.

"Yes, we do."

"Britney's an old thing now, though," Pete put in from behind them. "No one rides her, so she just hangs around and eats hay and gets pregnant at exactly the wrong time of the year."

Charlotte shot Pete a warning glance even as she prayed for patience with her outspoken and bluntly honest son.

"What?" he asked, looking baffled. "It's true. Now we're going to get a foal in the summer. How crazy is that?"

As they looked at Denise's picture, Charlotte easily recalled that morning, sixteen years ago, when she went up these same stairs to wake up her daughter, only to find her bed made and a letter lying on her pillow. The letter told her that her eighteen-year-old daughter was already four months pregnant. She and her boyfriend, Kevin Slater, whom she had met at a summer camp, were running away to California.

"Do you have other horses?" The faint note of anticipation in Christopher's voice caught Charlotte's attention.

"We have a few riding horses, like I told your sister," Charlotte assured him. "I'm sure you could ride one of them."

Christopher smiled. "I think that could be fun."

His easy smile and the trusting way he looked at her ignited a small spark of hope. Charlotte reached out and stroked Christopher's head. The gesture seemed to loosen something in him, and his smile wobbled.

"I want to ride a horse like my mom did."

Charlotte could see he was holding his tears back. During the time she was with them in San Diego, she had never seen her youngest grandson cry.

She took a chance, knelt down, and gently folded him into her arms. Though his own arms stayed stiffly at his side, he laid his head on her shoulder, his tears seeping into her shirt.

Charlotte drew in a steadying breath, and looked up to see Pete watching the two of them. He gave her a careful smile as he sauntered over, adjusting his billed cap.

After a moment, Charlotte gently drew away. "Christopher, this is your Uncle Pete," she said, tilting her head to meet his eyes.

"Hey, munchkin," Pete said.

Christopher wiped his nose with the back of his hand and sniffed once more as he gave Pete a wary look. "My name isn't munchkin."

Pete acknowledged the comment with a slow nod. "Right. It's Christopher. And you're gonna be here awhile, huh?" Pete shifted his cap and rocked back on his heels, studying his sister's son.

"Only for a little while. Then we're going—" Christopher's eyes grew wide, then he pressed his hand against his mouth, as if he had said something he shouldn't have.

Pete shot his mother a questioning glance, and Charlotte gave him a faint warning shake of her head. Everyone found his or her own way to deal with grief. She was sure this was Christopher's.

"Yeah, well, you're here for now, buddy. Which is great. I could use some decent help on the farm."

"Help? On the farm?" This had obviously caught Christopher's attention.

"Well, yeah. I need someone to help me drive the tractor and stack bales. Feed cows. Tag calves. That kind of thing."

"Drive a tractor?" Christopher's voice was tinged with awe.

"Sure enough."

"Do you live here?"

"I got banished from the house to an apartment above the feed shed," Pete said with a wink at his mother. "It's out in the yard here. You can come visit me in my exile sometime."

She wasn't going to respond to his outrageous comment and would explain to Christopher once Pete was gone.

"Christopher? Where are you? Your GameBoy just died." Emily's sharp voice called out from the top of the stairs. She came down and stopped at the bottom, her eyes flicking from Christopher to Charlotte and Pete.

Though Charlotte had already spent a few days with her granddaughter, she could not get used to the clothes the girl wore. Today was no better. Tight black leggings hugged slim legs, and over the top of them she wore a hip-length shirt topped with a tiny vest that was more decorative than practical.

"Hey, girlie, you forget your pants?"

Emily shot him a stunned look.

"Emily, this is your Uncle Pete." Charlotte frowned at her son.

The girl gave them both a curt nod of her head, her expression becoming blank as she slipped down the stairs.

"Is Sam awake?" Charlotte asked, wondering when she should start breakfast.

Emily frowned. "I dunno." She reached a hand out to her brother. "Christopher, we need to finish unpacking."

"We're just gettin' to know each other," Pete said.

She didn't look his way but kept her hand outstretched. Finally Christopher walked toward her and together they trudged up the stairs.

"Snotty little thing, ain't she?" Pete adjusted his cap on his head, watching them go.

Charlotte waited until she heard the click of the door above her then turned to her son.

"Be careful what you say, Pete. They've had to make a huge adjustment."

"Haven't we all?" Pete sighed and gave his mother an apologetic look. "Well, I better get goin'. Thought I'd stop in and say hi. I'll be in later for breakfast."

"Okay."

"Yeah. Well." Pete adjusted his cap again, then patted her awkwardly on the shoulder again. "You'll be okay, Ma. You'll get everything working again."

"I wish I had your confidence."

Pete looked as if he wanted to say something more, but he just gave her a crooked smile and left.

Charlotte watched him go, then turned back to the kitchen. It needed cleaning.

Bob was a sporadic cook and even more sporadic cleaner. It had taken her ten minutes this morning just to get the baked-on cheese off the stove and another fifteen to scrub out the frying pan and some pots. Now she had to tackle the counters and floor and finish up the laundry that had piled up in her absence.

Twenty minutes later, Charlotte carried a laundry basket full of clean towels and bathroom supplies into the upstairs bathroom.

She worked quietly, one ear listening for sounds coming from the bedrooms, but all she heard was the muffled sound of drawers opening and Emily quietly talking to her little brother. Nothing from Sam's room.

Charlotte stacked the towels neatly in the cupboard. She picked a few towels off the floor, as well as two sets of mismatched socks, a pale blue sweater, Christopher's pajamas, and a pair of blue jeans that hung over the edge of the bathtub.

The holes in the knees of the pants and the ragged cuffs told her they belonged to Sam. She dropped everything in the laundry basket, making a mental note to talk to the children about cleaning up after themselves.

She knew, from the state of the apartment when she had arrived in San Diego, that the kids were used to order and tidiness. They needed to know that she expected the same as their mother obviously had.

Just as she left the bathroom, the door to Sam's bedroom creaked open. He stepped into the hallway, scratching the T-shirt covering his chest, his dark hair sticking up in all directions. His eyes were on the floor, and a mark on his face looked as if he had been sleeping on his hand.

"Did you just wake up?" Charlotte asked.

Sam jumped. "You scared me."

"I'm sorry." Charlotte gave him an apologetic smile and thought she had better rephrase her question. "How did you sleep?"

His answer was the same shrug she had seen all week.

"I put some clean towels in the cupboard," she continued. "In case you want to have a shower."

He frowned at the laundry basket sitting on her hip. "Those my jeans?"

"I found them on the edge of the tub. They looked dirty so I thought I would wash them."

Sam's frown made her wonder if she had overstepped some invisible boundary.

"Yeah. Sure." He gave an awkward laugh. "You don't have to, though. Mom taught us how to do our own laundry."

As she had taught Denise, Bill, and Pete to do their own.

"I don't mind, for now." Charlotte said. She was willing to relax the rules for a while. In a few days, once they were settled in, she would parcel out more of the chores, laundry being one of them.

"I need a shower, if that's okay."

"Sorry. I'll get out of your way."

He slouched past her and the door clicked behind him. Charlotte set the laundry basket down and walked to Christopher's room, then rapped lightly on the door.

Emily opened it a tiny crack. "Hi, Grandma," she said through the opening.

"Just wondering if you needed any help."

Emily shook her head.

"We're eating breakfast in half an hour."

"I'm not hungry."

She should have known. In the week Charlotte stayed with the kids, Emily had eaten breakfast once, if you could call a cracker and half a banana breakfast.

Charlotte angled her head so she could see inside the room. "What do you think of pancakes, Christopher?" she asked.

Christopher looked to Emily and, as if taking his cue from her, shook his head. "I'm not hungry either."

Checkmate.

"I'm making pancakes, bacon, and eggs for Uncle Pete and Grandpa. We'll be eating at eight sharp. So if you change your mind . . ." She let the sentence trail off, not sure what else to say. She hoped the homey scent of bacon frying would tempt the children's reluctant taste buds.

Emily nodded, gave Charlotte a slight smile, then closed the door again. Charlotte stared a moment at the door, feeling like a stranger in her own house.

The door to Sam's bedroom was open and Charlotte took a quick peek inside. His suitcase lay on the floor, open, all his clothes still inside. The box holding his personal effects, pictures and books and posters, squatted in the corner of the room, untouched. The only thing sitting out of the box was his skateboard and a soccer ball.

It looked as if he was only staying a few nights, then moving on.

Charlotte picked up the laundry basket, and as she walked down the stairs wondered what she should do. Let him keep his illusions for now, or gently make him understand?

She got the next load of laundry started, but a quick glance at the clock showed her that Bob and Pete would be coming in for breakfast in only twenty minutes. She started making the pancakes and frying the bacon, one eye on the clock.

As the sounds of bacon snapping in the frying pan filled the silence, she heard feet on the stairs. Sam's hands were shoved deep in the front pocket of his hooded sweatshirt. She glanced over her shoulder in time to see him heading straight out the door.

If it wasn't for the fact that he wasn't carrying a suitcase, she would be forgiven for thinking he was running away.

At eight sharp, Bob and Pete came into the kitchen. "Where are the kids?" Bob asked

"They're not hungry." Charlotte ignored the extra place settings as she set the plates of pancakes and bacon in front of her husband and son.

"They better not make a habit of that," Bob said as he reached for the syrup.

"Bob, you know you can't have that," Charlotte said, handing him his sugar-free syrup. Bob had recently been diagnosed with diabetes, and Charlotte was careful to watch his diet.

"I hate this fake stuff," he grumbled as he twisted the cap off. "I can't believe a little bit of syrup is going to be a problem."

"Just because you're not on insulin doesn't mean you can eat whatever you want."

Bob stabbed his pancake with his fork. "Those kids will have to eat breakfast every day. Once they start helping with chores, they're going to need a full belly to get their work done. You should make up a list, like you did with our kids."

Charlotte sat down, feeling suddenly tired. She didn't want to think about parceling out chores the same day the kids came home, but right now she didn't have the energy to argue with Bob.

Chapter Three

Can you tell me where the computer is? I'd like to check my e-mail," Sam asked as he got up from the dinner table and brought his plate to the sink.

"We're not done yet, Sam," Bob said, reaching behind him for the Bible.

Sam frowned as his glance skimmed over the occupants of the table. "Emily won't eat that chicken," he said. "And Christopher doesn't like olives."

"We usually have devotions before we leave the table."

"Devotions," Christopher asked, pushing the remnants of his salad around on his plate. "What's that?"

"We read the Bible."

Sam caught Emily's puzzled glance, shrugged, and sat back down. "Sure. Whatever."

"No need to rush to check your e-mail either," Pete said, wiping his plate with a piece of bread. "Computer connection is as slow as snail mail. The wonders of dial-up." Pete pushed the bread into his mouth.

"Dial-up?"

"You mean I can barely text my friends from the farm and now I can't e-mail them either?" Emily's mouth hung open.

Christopher ducked his head, his gaze on the olives he was stringing on the tines of his fork.

"You can e-mail. It's just slow. Takes an hour to download a song." Pete wiped his mouth with a napkin and ignored Charlotte toeing him under the table. Why was he tormenting the kids like this?

"I don't spend much time on the computer," Pete continued. "Quicker just to drive to town to connect with my friends."

"It works fine if you don't have to send big files," Charlotte said to reassure them. "You can e-mail and I'm sure you can still visit your favorite Web sites."

Charlotte wasn't entirely sure about that last comment. She only used the computer to store pictures from the digital camera Pete bought at a garage sale. They used it so infrequently that they kept it in the spare room upstairs. But there was no need to fan the flames of their discontent, like Pete was doing.

Emily sat back, her thin arms folded over her chest in a gesture that clearly underlined her frustration. "I can't believe my life right now." Just before she looked away, however, Charlotte caught the faint glint of tears in her eyes that spoke of more than a surface frustration with e-mail and friends.

Christopher bent his head further as if trying to disappear.

"You're not the only one that has it hard, Emily." Sam's voice was quiet, but his tone carried. He rocked back in his chair, staring sightlessly across the table, as if in another place. "You're not the only one whose life is less than stellar."

An awkward silence filled the room. Charlotte caught Bob's raised eyebrows, as if surprised she hadn't reprimanded them by now.

She shook her head at Bob, hoping he would get the hint. How could she reprimand or discipline these lost, hurting children? Her first priority these past few days had been to let the kids know they were loved and they were safe, and give them space to accept all the changes in their lives.

Bob's response was to clear his throat and open the Bible. The only sound breaking the heavy silence was the crackling of the pages as he flipped to his spot. He adjusted his glasses, angling his head slightly upward so he could read through his bifocals.

Charlotte felt her heart sink when he found the passage they had left off reading the last time she was home.

Bob was a traditionalist when it came to Bible reading. While Charlotte knew and agreed with Bob that all the words of the Bible are worthy of attention, she doubted the kids would appreciate the lamentation and words of retribution from the minor prophets.

Charlotte knew she was in the mood for something more upbeat and comforting, and she had hoped Bob would read something the children could understand as well.

Bob cleared his throat again.

"'Hear this, you elders,'" he read, "'Listen, all who live in the land. Has anything like this ever happened in your days or in the days of your forefathers? Tell it to your children, and let your children tell it to their children . . .'"

Charlotte glanced at the children. Christopher was staring down at his plate, much as his mother used to. Then, as she caught Sam's bored expression and saw Emily examining her nails, she doubted that they were even listening.

"What the great locusts have left, the young locusts have eaten . . . ," Bob read.

The cadence and rhythm of the language was familiar to her, but as she had done with their old and worn kitchen, she caught herself trying to understand things through the children's perspective.

What did they think of the passages that spoke of grain offerings and drink offerings? Of ruined fields and despair?

I could have used a little more comfort myself, she thought, folding her arms over her chest as she leaned back in her chair. *A little more of the love that God offers us.*

Bob was finally done. Without looking up, he took his glasses off, then gently closed the Bible and put it back on the shelf behind his head, beside the radio.

"What are locusts?" Sam asked.

Charlotte's mouth almost dropped open. She didn't think they'd heard a word.

"Grasshoppers," Bob said, folding his glasses and slipping them into his pocket. "When they come sweeping through the country, they eat everything."

"Yuck. That's gross," Emily retorted.

"The cycle of life," Pete put in.

"That doesn't sound like life to me," Emily said.

"Life is pain, princess. Anyone who says differently is selling you something," Pete said, his voice taking on a sonorous tone. His comment was familiar, though Charlotte couldn't figure out where she had heard the words before.

A faint glimmer of surprise crossed Emily's face.

"At least we don't have Cliffs of Insanity here on the farm," he said, as if testing her.

"Nothing you can say will upset me, farm boy," she retorted.

"As you wish," Pete responded.

Sam groaned. "No. Please not *The Princess Bride*."

And Charlotte remembered.

Denise had gotten the movie from a friend for her sixteenth birthday. She and Pete watched it endlessly, laughing about it over and over again. They would quote passages of it by heart.

It seemed that Emily, at least, shared her mother's love for that silly movie.

"We'll pray now," Bob said suddenly, breaking into the moment.

Charlotte caught Pete winking at Emily. Then he bowed his head and Emily followed suit.

When Bob was done with his usual mumbled recitation of the Lord's Prayer, Charlotte saw Emily slip a questioning glance Sam's way as if wondering what they had just heard.

He returned her glance with a shrug and a lift of his hands.

Charlotte made a note to teach the kids the prayer so they could understand their grandfather. She knew there was no point in asking Bob to slow down and speak more clearly or loudly. She had tried at one time, but had been told his prayer was a conversation with God and God understood him.

"Can we go now?" Christopher asked, pushing his plate away.

"Shouldn't they help with the dishes?" Bob asked, getting up from the table himself.

Charlotte hesitated. "They can go," she said slowly. "I'll do them."

Bob's frown told her what he thought of that, but thankfully he didn't push the point. He ambled to the family room, snagging the remote from an end table.

He dropped into his recliner, turned on the television, and pushed the chair back in one easy motion as the news flashed onto the television screen.

"Do we have to help?" Sam asked.

"Not this time. You can finish unpacking your suitcase."

"Can I try out the computer?"

She noticed how he avoided her suggestion, but she didn't press it. "It's in the spare bedroom, upstairs."

Emily's chair screeched over the floor as she pushed herself away from the table. She held her hand out to Christopher. "C'mon, kiddo. Let's go check out the barn. Maybe I can find a place there where I can get cell reception."

Christopher quickly joined his sister and they left, followed a few seconds later by Pete.

And just like that, Charlotte's kitchen emptied, the echoes of the children's voices dying as doors shut behind them.

Charlotte looked over the table still holding the remnants and dirty dishes from the meal. A few moments ago she'd had her grandchildren around the table, as she had imagined and longed for so many times.

Now she was alone.

Somehow, knowing that the grandchildren she had yearned to have around her table were the ones that had now abandoned her underlined her loneliness with heavy strokes.

"I THINK YOU SHOULD HAVE gotten the kids to help you with the dishes." Bob rinsed out his toothbrush and tapped it on the side of the sink. Three long taps. Two short. "You could put that on their chore list."

Charlotte didn't want to talk about chore lists and the kids. She'd just come back from settling Christopher, who had been lying on his bed, still in his clothes, holding a GameBoy that didn't work. It had taken her five minutes to convince him to put on his pajamas and another five to get him a drink of water and bargain about how far she would leave his bedroom door open. She had promised to get him some batteries next time they were in town.

Emily had only mumbled a muffled good night, which made Charlotte think she was crying. Sam was asleep.

"The sooner they get into a routine, the sooner they'll settle in," Bob continued as he slipped his toothbrush into its holder.

Charlotte knew he was right, but she had also been with them through those first devastating days after Denise's death. "I suppose, but I'd like to give them some time to adjust to all the changes in their lives."

She pulled out Bob's pill bottle from the cabinet and

shook out a pill, setting it beside his cup. Then she pumped some lotion on her hands and spread it on her face as she looked at their shared reflections in the large mirror above the sink. The unforgiving light above the mirror highlighted the wrinkles that had invaded and taken over their faces. When had they gotten so old?

These were supposed to be their twilight years. A time for quiet reflection on the past and an easing of their workload.

Were they too old to be raising kids all over again?

"I think they'll adjust better if we set out a routine." Bob filled a cup with water, took his pill, then pulled open the drawer and took out his hairbrush. "That'll help them settle into life here."

"I know, but I'm not sure how to go about it." Charlotte smoothed the leftover lotion all over her hands.

"They could learn some respect, for starters." Bob brushed his thinning hair, then smoothed his hand over his head. "I didn't like them fidgeting when I read the Bible after supper." Bob placed his hairbrush back in its own plastic box, adjusted it so it was square, then closed the drawer.

Charlotte leaned back against the counter, wrapping the ties of her bathrobe tighter, wishing she knew exactly what to do. Wishing, as she had with her own kids, that they came with a manual. A set of prescribed directions.

"I don't think they're used to Bible reading," she said. "I wonder if we shouldn't read some part of the Bible they might be interested in."

Bob's frown underlined her previous concern. "We've always read the Bible this way. From start to finish. I don't like skipping parts . . ." Bob let the statement drift off as he opened up the door of the vanity beside the large mirror, then frowned. "Where are my nail clippers?"

"You put them in the drawer last night."

"I never did."

Charlotte reached over, pulled open the drawer, and let him see for himself.

"Humph. Why did you put them in there?" He slid out one of the tools and used it to clean out his fingernails starting from his pinky. First his left hand. Then his right.

"We wouldn't really be skipping parts. Just reading them at another time."

"Our roof, our rules." Bob finished, closed up the clippers, and tapped them lightly on the sink. "We've had enough changes in our lives the past few weeks. Enough adjusting to remake ourselves." He stopped there and Charlotte heard the slightest break in his deep voice.

His muted pain echoed her own as she caught the twist of his mouth, the sorrow in his eyes.

"Oh, Bob," she said, stepping into his arms and holding him tightly.

She was enveloped by the scent of outdoors tinged with the faintest smell of diesel and dirt. She had associated these smells with him since they came back from their honeymoon to the farm. They had weathered many storms since that day. But this one—this one was so overwhelming, so huge, that it had the potential to capsize their lives.

He rested his head on hers and Charlotte felt him draw in a shuddering breath. Then another.

Tears pricked her eyes and she swallowed down the knot of pain in her throat.

"Oh, Bob. Our little girl," she whispered against his shirt.

Bob said nothing, just stroked her back with his hand again and again, but Charlotte sensed his pain.

"She's been gone so long—" His voice broke.

They stood that way for a moment, holding each other up, mute in their shared grief, then Bob drew gently away. He swiped at his cheeks, then looked down at Charlotte. The glint of moisture in his eyes cut her almost as deeply as her own pain.

Bob bent over and kissed her gently. As he straightened he touched her cheek with a callused forefinger. "I love you, Char."

"I love you too," she replied, catching his hand in her own. "I wish I knew why we had to deal with this. Why Denise had to die."

"God is faithful and will get us through this."

As Bob left the bathroom Charlotte leaned back against the counter, wishing she could share his conviction.

Where, oh death, where is your victory? Where, oh death, is thy sting?

The words from Corinthians seemed to mock her as she clutched the edge of the counter for stability.

Death did sting. It hurt; it grabbed at her and created a storm of questions that hammered at her self-control.

She tried to beat them back. As Bob had said, God is faithful.

She was about to head over to the bedroom but stopped at the doorway. On a whim, she quietly walked up the stairs, avoiding the creaking one, the third step up.

At the top of the stairs she paused and listened.

Was that crying she heard? She turned to the right, pausing first at Christopher's room, then across the hall at the door to Emily's room.

Nothing.

Very carefully she made her way back past the stairs and to the left, toward Sam's room. She leaned closer, straining her ears.

Through the heavy wood of the old door, she heard muffled sobs. Closing her eyes, she laid the tips of her fingers against the door, willing her touch beyond the solid wood to the hurting boy inside the room.

He wouldn't thank her for coming in, though her heart ached to enter, to hold him close, and to let loose his sorrow. But he barely knew her and she was still picking her way through these new relationships. Maybe someday, she thought, quietly sending up a prayer for healing for her oldest grandchild.

Watch over him, Lord. Please let him feel your comfort and presence. She waited a moment, as if to let the prayer settle.

As she walked down the stairs, she thought she heard the click of a door behind her, but she carried on and returned to her own room.

Bob was snoring by the time she slipped between the cool sheets. As she settled into the bed, her thoughts slipped to Kevin, the children's father. He hadn't been a part of their lives for years. No mention was made of him in Denise's will or by the children.

She wondered where he was, if he even cared that his children's lives had been thrown into such upheaval.

She rolled onto her side, drew a long slow breath and another, calming her tired mind.

Two days down, she thought. Many, many more to go.

Chapter Four

"This is the school?"

As Charlotte parked in the visitors' parking lot of Bedford Elementary and Middle School, she heard in Sam's voice the same tinge of dismay as on the day he stepped out of the car at the farm.

Compared to the sprawling glass-and-concrete schools the children attended in San Diego, the two-story brick building housing the elementary and middle school must have looked like a relic from the past.

"It's a good school," she said with what she hoped was a positive note as she got out of the car.

"It looks like a school you see on television," Christopher said, getting out of the car himself.

He sounded hopeful, but Charlotte could see from the looks on Sam and Emily's faces that their cup, full of disappointment with their new life, could potentially overflow today.

"Let's start with you, Sam. I've already talked to the principal and he said the guidance counselor will meet us at the front entrance."

Charlotte slipped her purse over her shoulder and walked with a confidence she didn't feel across the street to the slightly smaller, but newer, Bedford Senior High School. A few kids lounged on benches in the shade of large trees spaced out in the front of the school. They all stared at Charlotte and the kids as they walked toward the school.

Behind them Charlotte heard the growl of diesel engines as two school buses pulled in front of the school. The teachers' parking lot held a few cars already. Though Charlotte would have liked to have arrived earlier, at least they had beaten the rush.

As Charlotte pulled open the front door of the high school, she felt a sense of *déjà vu*. How often she had come here to pick up her children from volleyball, basketball, band, and cheerleading practice, always with one eye on her watch. As she drove home she would listen to their stories with one ear, her mind already leaping ahead to the work waiting.

Always in a hurry, she remembered, stepping into the building. *Rushing my children through life as I split myself in two—one part with them, the other moving, hurrying to the next chore, the next job, the next event.*

The inside of the high school smelled the same as it had then. A combination of paper and floor wax and running shoes. The door clanged shut behind them, the sound echoing in the empty hallway. Now what were they supposed to do?

A large sign hanging on the wall facing them ordered them to sign in at the office. That was new, thought Charlotte.

"Mrs. Stevenson?"

A young man with dark hair and brown eyes sauntered toward her and the kids. His blue jeans looked artfully faded and he wore running shoes, but it was the tie cinching the collar of his cotton shirt and the clipboard he held that saved him from looking like a student. As he approached them, he slipped a cell phone into the pocket of his blue jeans.

"I'm Mr. Santos. Jeff Santos. Sorry I'm late." He held his hand out and Charlotte shook it, relieved that he was here.

"We just got here ourselves. This is Sam Slater, my grandson. He's a sophomore."

Sam shook Mr. Santos' hand with little enthusiasm, then looked past him down the long, narrow hallway.

"I'm sure this is different than the school you went to before," Mr. Santos said with a smile. "We're a bit podunk but proud of it. I'm your guidance counselor. I'll be showing you around and filling you in on what's available here at Bedford High. Are you interested in sports?"

Sam's eyes lit up. "I played soccer back in San Diego. Defense."

Mr. Santos shook his head with a look of regret. "Sorry. We just have football in the fall, then basketball, track, and golf."

"Golf." Sam spoke the single word with a faint edge of contempt. It was obviously not a sport he would participate in.

"We've got a great track program, if I can brag up our team. Last year we won the state championship," Mr. Santos said.

Sam gave a listless nod of acknowledgment, and Charlotte could see he was losing what little bit of interest Mr. Santos had kindled in him.

Mr. Santos glanced down at Sam's worn and tattered shoes.

"Nice kicks. You skate?"

Sam nodded.

"What's your setup?"

"I ride an Alien Workshop with Thunder lows and Spitfires." Sam brightened again.

"Nice. That's a good little kit. Workshops have a nice shape."

Sam's smile grew as Charlotte watched the exchange, completely mystified. "What are they talking about?" she asked Emily.

"Skateboards. That thing that Sam always had cluttering up the hallway back home."

"Of course." She remembered seeing Sam with his friends, zipping up and down the road in front of the apartment on the wheeled boards, going up ramps and jumping and turning. The whole exercise seemed pointless, but it was the only time she'd seen him smile.

"I'll take care of Sam from here," Mr. Santos said, giving Charlotte an encouraging smile. "If you don't mind giving me his transcripts . . ." He held out his hand for the envelope that Charlotte had brought with her.

Charlotte gladly handed over the papers. She had envisioned spending time with Sam and his teachers while Christopher and Emily hung around, but it would seem they were done.

"Sam, do you mind coming with me?" Without checking to see if Sam was following, Mr. Santos walked down the hall, his shoes squeaking on the gleaming floors.

Sam took a few steps, then glanced back at Christopher, who was clinging to Emily's hand. "You gonna be okay, buddy?"

Christopher nodded, but Charlotte caught the faint sparkle of tears in the little boy's blue eyes. He was trying hard to be brave, and her heart melted at the sight.

She touched his head lightly, but he burrowed deeper into Emily's side.

Sam waved, then jogged to catch up to Mr. Santos, his backpack bobbing as he went.

"So, I guess he's taken care of." Charlotte pulled open one of the large double doors leading outside. "Let's see about you two."

A light breeze had sprung up and Charlotte shivered, pulling her coat closer. Though winter had long released its grip on southern Nebraska, now and again a bit of cooler weather returned, as if waving one last chilly good-bye.

"It's freezing out here," Emily complained, hunching her shoulders against the breeze.

"I'm sure it feels cold compared to San Diego," Charlotte agreed. "But you'll get used to it. Especially if you dress a little warmer."

"What's wrong with what I've got on?" Emily asked.

Her skimpy skirt and blue tank top were warm enough for California, but here, where sweaters could be worn almost year-round, her clothing was hardly adequate.

"You might want to consider taking a sweater with you tomorrow," Charlotte suggested, keeping her tone gentle and avoiding any reference to the suitability of her clothes. That confrontation was for another day. Makeup? Another month. Pacing. It was all about pacing.

"I hate wearing sweaters," was Emily's terse reply. "So what do we do now?"

"We'll get you set and then take care of Christopher."

"Why don't we find his class first," Emily said. "I'll feel better if I know he's okay."

"Of course."

Christopher clung to Emily like he was about to go to an uncertain doom. Better that they get him settled while Emily was still around.

Charlotte caught Christopher's frightened gaze and gave him a reassuring smile. "The kids in the school are nice."

Even as she spoke the thinly comforting words, her conscience accused her. What did she know of the kids in this school? She hadn't put one foot inside either of the buildings since Pete quit going to high school.

By the time they found the front office, students were trickling in, gathered in animated groups, laughing and joking.

Charlotte caught Emily watching, a look of longing haunting her heavily made-up eyes. But as soon as she caught Charlotte's gaze, it was as if someone had erased all expression from her features.

Charlotte prayed that her granddaughter would find a friend who would help her adjust to her new life.

"Here we are," Charlotte said with false cheerfulness as she pulled open the office door.

Inside, a young woman sat at a desk situated behind a waist-high counter dividing the work area from the public. A dark headband held back her auburn hair. The navy blazer she wore over her white shirt created a look of crisp efficiency. A plastic nameplate on her desk told Charlotte that this capable-looking person was Lisa Grienke.

Charlotte cleared her throat and Lisa looked up, raising her plucked eyebrows. "Can I help you?" she asked, placing the papers she'd been working on in a neat pile on one side of her large wooden desk.

"My name is Charlotte Stevenson. This is Emily and Christopher Slater."

"Oh yes. The Slater children." Lisa frowned as she glanced from Charlotte to Emily and Christopher. "You're their grandmother?"

"Yes."

"And you're taking care of them?" Lisa asked as she plucked a file folder from a basket on the far side of her desk.

"Yes." Was Charlotte imagining the faint surprise in Lisa's voice?

Lisa flipped it open. "Christopher, you're in classroom 7 with Miss Hutchens. Emily, you're on the second floor, 8B. Mr. Levenger."

After Sam received such a warm welcome, Charlotte had hoped the same would happen to the youngest children, especially since Christopher looked so lost and forlorn.

"Are those from their previous school?" Lisa nodded toward the envelopes Charlotte still held.

"Yes. Their grades and other papers I was told you might need." Charlotte handed them across the counter still dividing them.

Lisa skimmed over the contents of the envelope and then let loose a soft sigh. "Would have been nice to get these a bit sooner."

Charlotte felt as if she had been reprimanded, but before she could form a reply, Lisa walked away.

She reappeared through the door dividing the counter from the office and jerked her chin at Christopher. "Follow me."

Emily clutched Christopher's hand as he moved closer to her. Neither of them moved.

Lisa glanced back, a slight frown pinching her forehead. "Well, come along, Christopher."

The determined set of Emily's chin did not bode well for Lisa's abrupt command.

"I don't want to go," Charlotte heard Christopher whisper to his sister.

"There's nothing to be afraid of," Emily whispered back. "It'll be okay."

But from the way Christopher still held back, his backpack dragging behind him, Charlotte could see he didn't share Emily's optimism.

Lisa waited by the door, the look of impatience on her face creating a low-level tension in the room.

She was about to say something when the office door burst open and someone charged in.

Charlotte's first impression was of a woman too short for her width, wearing crisp new blue jeans, a bright-colored T-shirt, and hooded sweatshirt.

Charlotte recognized Melody Givens, who was laughing out loud and looking over her shoulder as she came into the office. As the door shut behind her, she held up a brown paper bag. "Hey, Lisa. Special delivery for you," she said.

Melody owned Mel's Place, a café downtown, and was one of those boisterous people who boosted the energy level of a place simply by showing up.

"What should I do with it?" Lisa asked, looking at the lunch bag as if it held a swarm of snakes.

"It's Ashley's lunch. I don't have time to go scouting around for her. She's probably hanging out in the bathroom, putting on makeup I said she couldn't. Just page her. Tell her it's here. She'll come and get it."

Melody set the lunch on the counter, and before Lisa could voice the protest Charlotte could see forming on her perfectly painted lips, Melody had turned to Charlotte.

"Hello, Charlotte," she said, glancing from Charlotte to Emily and Christopher. "Hey kids." Her expression softened, and Charlotte saw Emily recoil from the sympathy in Melody's face.

"I was sorry to hear about your mom. Made me cry. I went to school with her. We were on the cheerleading squad together." Melody glanced down at her stout figure and laughed. "Though you'd never guess it now." Melody's mercurial expression now showed a deeper sadness.

Her straightforward attitude and self-deprecating humor warmed Charlotte's heart.

"Thank you so much for your letter," Charlotte said. "Your memories of Denise were precious to me."

While many people had sent cards, Melody had filled three lined pages with scattershot memories of Denise, as if she had scribbled them down as they occurred to her.

The cards now lined the mantel of the fireplace in the living room, but the letter was tucked away in Charlotte's Bible, the breezy memories now precious beyond price.

"I missed her when she left, that's for sure." Melody turned back to Emily. "So, you must be about the same age as my Ashley? Fourteen?"

Emily nodded, her expression growing wary.

"Don't you worry. I know you're thinking, 'Great, this is the place where the mother tells me we'll be best of friends,' and then you're thinking, 'This lady is nuts.'" Melody laughed. "I am. But hey, Ashley is a lot cooler than me. Or so she keeps telling me."

Another belly laugh punctuated that line. "I know she thinks she's too cool to eat her lunch. That's why she left it behind. I'm onto her."

Lisa cleared her throat, catching everyone's attention.

"You bringing these kids to their classes?" Melody asked.

"That was the point." Lisa's voice was cool, calculated. Charlotte almost shivered.

"I can take Emily if you want. That way I can introduce her to my Ashley. And I can give Ashley her lunch."

"I'm afraid I can't do that."

"Now, Lisa, no need to be afraid. I'm as harmless as vanilla pudding. As jiggly too." Melody added a grin to her comment, but Lisa didn't seem to see the humor in the remark.

"Principal Harding specifically asked me to make sure I accompany the Slater children to their classrooms."

"Then I'll do some accompanying too."

And before Lisa could protest, Melody opened the door and Emily followed, Christopher clinging to her hand.

"We'll take care of Christopher first," Lisa said, striding briskly down the hall, ignoring Melody and the various staring children they brushed past.

Charlotte felt suddenly conspicuous and cast a concerned glance at her granddaughter.

Emily looked neither left nor right, her mouth set in a determined line. She looked like someone going to her execution.

Charlotte had never had to start over in a new school and had no idea how Emily felt. She remembered a few "new" children who would come to school from time to time. Sometimes they fit in, other times, not.

The group dodged a few staring children, then turned a corner and came to an open door.

"This is Christopher's classroom," Lisa said, indicating with her hand that Christopher should enter.

Charlotte glanced into the room. Laughter and noise bubbled from inside. A few children were tapping on the glass of a hamster tank sitting on the window ledge. As she looked farther inside she saw brightly colored posters of animals and letters lining the walls. Pictures drawn by the children papered one bulletin board.

The room felt comfortable and inviting.

"I'll wait with him," Charlotte said, reaching out her hand to take Christopher's.

Emily shook her head and clung to her little brother. "No. I will."

"But you have to go to your own class," Charlotte said.

"I won't leave him alone with someone he hardly knows." Emily pressed her lips together in a line of defiance that Charlotte wasn't sure how to cross.

"We don't have much time," Lisa said, tapping her manicured fingers against the sleeve of her jacket. "You need to get to your class, Emily."

"I'm not going." And without looking at any of them, Emily marched into the room, taking Christopher with her.

"She needs to come with us," Lisa said to Charlotte, as if Charlotte had any control over Emily.

"Let her be with her brother," Melody said quietly.

"And what about her teacher? What am I supposed to tell Mr. Levenger?" Lisa's frown deepened as if she couldn't see past this contretemps.

"Tell him Emily will be coming when she's sure her little brother is okay." Melody shrugged. "Not rocket science, Lisa."

"I realize that." Lisa gave Melody a tight smile. "But we simply can't let students do whatever they please."

"Don't sweat it, Lisa," Melody said. "I think Mr. Levenger will understand."

Lisa huffed, then turned and strode back to the office, her back stiff with disapproval.

Charlotte felt suddenly unsure of herself. She would never have let Denise publicly defy her like Emily just had, but she had been disciplining Denise since she was born.

Emily came ready-made with her unfamiliar attitudes and ideas that Charlotte was still learning about.

"I suppose I could let Emily stay with her brother," Charlotte said, thinking out loud.

"Of course you could," Melody assured her. "It's not a big deal."

Charlotte shot another concerned glance into the room. Emily leaned against the wall, Christopher beside her. Neither of them spoke to anyone else in the class.

"I wouldn't fuss about it," Melody continued. "If having his sister with him makes that little guy feel better, let it be. Christopher's teacher is a sweetheart. She'll understand their situation and make allowances."

Melody patted Charlotte on the shoulder as if comforting her. "And I wouldn't get too bothered about Lisa. She's a good person at heart, just a tad caught up in rules and regulations."

Melody's easy acceptance of the situation eased Charlotte's misgivings. Charlotte nodded, then with one more look at her grandchildren to assure herself that everything was, indeed, okay, walked back down the hallway.

"What time does school get out?" she asked Melody. "I told them I would pick them up this afternoon."

"Three thirty. You won't be able to park in front of the school between three fifteen and three forty-five because the school buses line up on the street. But you can park around the corner on Goldenrod and wait for the kids at the front of the school."

"But Sam is in the high school."

"The kids all go to the same row of buses. Just wait by them. They'll find you."

"Thank you. And thanks for your help this morning."

Melody flapped her hand in a dismissive gesture. "Not to worry. Us parents need to stick together." She glanced at her watch. "And now I gotta run. Need to deliver this lunch and relieve my helper who's covering the early-morning coffee rush. All those old retired farmers need to get themselves fortified before they go touring the countryside checking out spring planting."

Charlotte laughed and for the first time since she had taken over the care of her grandchildren, felt the tension in her neck loosen.

When they came to the stairway going upstairs, Melody stopped.

"I didn't want to say too much in front of the kids, but I want to let you know how sad I was to hear about Denise. She was a lot of fun. I just wish—" And then, to Charlotte's surprise, Melody's voice broke. She bit her lip, shaking her head as if embarrassed at her lapse.

"And that's the last thing you need, isn't it," she said, her voice wobbling, "me crying."

She took a quick breath and swiped the tears from her eyes with the heel of her hand. She gave Charlotte a quivering smile. "I want you to know that Russ and I are praying for you and Bob and the kids."

Charlotte felt her own emotions tremble at the thought that people she barely knew were praying for her family. But she couldn't let herself indulge in tears. Not in this public place.

Her quiet thank-you was almost lost in the unyielding drone of the buzzer marking the beginning of a new class. She gave Melody a careful smile, then left before her emotions got the better of her.

As she walked to her car, she took a steadying breath and sent up a prayer for the grandchildren she had left to cope with this new and strange place.

Chapter Five

Darkness. The kind of darkness that pushed down. Like in a coal mine.

Emily lay on her bed wondering how a place could be so completely dark. Back in her bedroom in San Diego, she could almost read a book in the light coming in her window from the streetlamp outside.

But this?

She swallowed down a knot of fear and sorrow. The day had been lousy. She had spent the whole morning with Christopher and then, when she went to find her class, got lost. The school wasn't even that big.

Emily sighed and rolled onto her side. She missed her school, she missed her home, but most of all, she missed her mother. And, as always, when she thought of her mother, the tears came.

A creepy howl split the night.

Emily jerked to a sitting position, all her nerves tingling as she wrapped her blankets tightly around herself.

There it was again, followed by another coming from another direction, then another.

Then Toby started barking.

Shivers crept up her spine, chilling her heart.

Werewolves? Some kind of crazy animal that ate people? What did she know? She grew up in the city. The only sounds she ever heard were the wails of sirens, horns honking, people yelling. Ordinary stuff like that.

Would that silly dog be able to protect them? She wasn't big.

Emily clutched the blankets closer, wishing she could have shared this room with Christopher. At least she'd have company. She wondered if her little brother was afraid, but she was too scared to go check on him.

All she saw out the window was dark sky spangled with stars. Kind of pretty, if you weren't scared half to death.

Whenever she had nightmares she would crawl into her mother's bed. Sometimes, when she was younger, her mother would sing her a song. Something about a shepherd and Jesus.

Her heart jumped. There was that howl again.

Emily stuffed her fingers in her ears, thinking about her first day at school. Thinking about how scared Christopher had been until two little girls said they would be his helpers for the week.

When she finally found her class, some girl named Ashley introduced herself. Said she was Melody Givens' daughter, the lady that met up with Grandma and Christopher and her.

Ashley seemed kind of cool. Bouncy. Friendly. Liked to laugh.

But she wasn't Bekka.

Emily reached down beside her bed for her phone. It was

charging up. Somehow the battery went dead really fast out here. Sam had lost his charger so until he got a new one, he was out of luck. Good thing he didn't ask to use hers or it would go dead even faster. She flipped it open and to her surprise, saw one bar beside the reception. One tiny bar.

Would it work? She'd been trying to phone her friends since she got here, but no luck.

She frantically punched in the speed-dial number for her friend, then carefully brought the phone to her ear so she wouldn't disturb the fragile connection.

The phone crackled, but she heard one ring. Then another.

"Please pick up," Emily breathed, desperately needing the connection with her friend and her real life.

"Hey, Em. Wow. Haven't heard from you in ages. Whatcha doin'?"

Emily smiled at the sound of her friend's voice coming through her phone. "Listening to the dog barking at some creepy animal howling outside."

"What? What kind of place is that?" Bekka's voice sounded crackly.

"According to my Uncle Pete, it's a farm. Like I didn't know. Honestly, he's so lame." Emily curled up on her side, pulling the blankets over her head and creating a cocoon for herself. The light from her phone created a comforting green glow.

"What's your grandma and grandpa like?"

Emily had to think a moment. "Grandma's okay. She's kind of uptight. Grandpa doesn't say much. Uncle Pete, well, he's kind of weird." She knew that wasn't true. He was actually kind of fun. But she couldn't tell Bekka that.

"How old is he?"

"Old. I think he's thirty or something like that."

"*Eeuw*. Really old." Bekka's voice faded away and in the background Emily heard laughter, then Bekka saying, "Yeah, sure. Just a minute."

"Who's over?" Emily asked.

"Tamrah, Natalie, and Stephanie."

Jealousy shot through Emily. When she lived in San Diego, Tamrah had desperately wanted to be part of their "group." But it had always been Nat, Steph, Bekka, and her, Emily. They'd been best friends since elementary school.

Now she was gone, and Tamrah had stepped into her place.

"Whatcha doin'?" Emily choked down her jealousy. She couldn't afford to make Bekka mad. Grandma hadn't let her take her cell phone to school, even though town was probably the only place with decent reception. So she had to make the best of this precious moment of phone connection.

"Tamrah brought a movie, but it's some lame cartoon show."

"My turn to say *eeuw*." Emily felt a gentle glow at Bekka's criticism of Tamrah and she cheerfully piled on her own.

"Tamrah's okay. Just likes weird movies . . ." Bekka's voice trailed off again, then Emily heard her laughing. "You should see this, Em. Tamrah was playing a part of it backward."

How could her friends have fun without her? They had

cried when she left and said they would text each other all the time. But they didn't.

"So, when you coming back, Em?" Bekka was asking.

"I don't know. Grandma thinks we're staying here, but I know we just need to wait for my mom's insurance money to come. Then we can go where we want."

"That'd be awesome. You can come home."

"Sam said maybe our dad will come and get us." Emily didn't want to think about what would happen if neither happened. Their plans made staying here bearable.

"So what's school like there?"

"Lame. And the kids are real hokey. One kid wore a cowboy hat to school. And cowboy boots."

"Oh, grossville."

Bekka's loud laugh encouraged Emily. She told her some more hokey school stories. So maybe she exaggerated a little bit. Maybe she shouldn't have poked fun at her grandparents and Ashley the way she did. But she was so far from her friends and she was lonely, and as long as she and Bekka kept talking, she felt like she was back in San Diego. She could pretend she and Bekka and Nat and Steph were going to the mall tomorrow. She could pretend she was going to borrow Nat's new pants and Steph's coat.

She could pretend she was in her apartment. She could pretend her mother was sleeping down the hallway, and if Emily wanted to, she could crawl into bed with her mom and everything would be even better.

Chapter Six

"Christopher needs to go home, Mrs. Stevenson." Lisa leveled Charlotte a sharp glance from beneath her carefully shaped eyebrows as her manicured fingers flew over her keyboard. "The school nurse isn't working today, but this little boy is definitely ill."

Christopher sat beside Lisa, huddled on a metal chair, his arms folded over his stomach. The toes of his sneakers barely grazed the floor, making him look even more vulnerable.

Charlotte knelt down in front of Christopher, touching his arm, wondering why she hadn't noticed that he was feeling bad this morning. "Where does it hurt?"

"Right here." He pressed his hand to his abdomen, then winced.

"We don't want anything spreading. Best if you take him home." Lisa pushed her chair toward the printer and plucked a paper from it. Her eyes skimmed over it before handing it to Charlotte. "Sign this please."

"What's this?"

"For our files. We need to have documentation when a child leaves the premises."

Charlotte scribbled her signature on the bottom, feeling

like she was signing out a library book instead of taking home an ill grandchild. "Will you need anything else from me?"

"No." Lisa glanced at Christopher as if to make sure he wasn't breathing potential germs into her immaculate office. "Thank you," she added belatedly.

Charlotte held her hand out to Christopher. "Shall we go?"

He didn't look up or take her hand as he slid off the chair. He bent over to pick up his backpack, then followed her out of the office, his shoes squeaking on the shining hall floor.

The halls were eerily quiet, and Charlotte felt as if she was breaking some law, taking Christopher back home this time of the day.

"Can Emily come too?" Christopher asked, as Charlotte pulled open the large double doors leading outside.

"No. She has to stay at school."

For a moment Charlotte questioned the wisdom of sending the kids to school so soon after their arrival. But she and Bob had decided that it was best to establish a routine for the children as soon as possible. Comfort lay in predictability.

Had they made a mistake?

"When did your stomach start hurting?" she asked Christopher as she pulled out of the visitors' parking lot and onto the street. It was only his second day.

"Before lunch," was Christopher's mumbled reply.

Charlotte avoided looking at the digital clock on the dashboard of her car while she drove through the quiet streets of town. She didn't want to think of the hastily opened bills that she had dropped onto the desk when Lisa had called.

Too much work and not enough time, and in two hours she would be making this same trip, but in reverse, to pick up Emily and Sam.

One thing at a time, she reminded herself as she unclenched her fists on the steering wheel.

"Did you eat any lunch?" Charlotte asked as she turned off Main Street onto the highway leading home.

In her peripheral vision she saw him shake his head. "I'm not hungry."

He leaned against the window of the car as if pulling into himself. She hoped he wouldn't throw up, but they made it home without incident.

Charlotte parked the car by the house. No sooner had she shut off the engine than Christopher scrambled out of the door and ran up the walk. Charlotte jumped out of the car, following him.

But instead of running to the bathroom, Christopher scooted down the hallway and up the stairs.

Charlotte waited at the bottom, ready to go up and help him. But all she heard was the click of his bedroom door shutting and then, nothing.

Half an hour later, the creak of the dining room floor behind her alerted her to Christopher's presence.

Charlotte turned from the table that served as her desk tucked into a corner of the family room. Christopher stood in the opening between the two rooms, his hands shoved in the pockets of his blue jeans, his head down. The afternoon light coming from the window over the kitchen sink gilded his cropped light hair, making it shine.

"Can I go outside?" he asked.

"Are you feeling better?"

He nodded.

"Maybe I should go with you," she said, pushing her chair away from the desk. He didn't know the farm well enough to go exploring. Pete and Bob were working on the tractors, which meant they would be moving them around. "I have to get eggs from the chickens and feed the cats anyway."

She also had to vacuum the upstairs and find the time to get the garden ready for planting and make up a chore list for the kids.

She pushed down the low-level panic that seemed her constant companion recently, held out her hand to her grandson, remembering all the times she had imagined precisely this moment when Denise lived so far away.

But Christopher only gave her a shy smile and walked ahead of her to the porch and out into the sunshine by himself.

Earning his trust was going to take time, Charlotte reminded herself as a way of smoothing over the faint hurt his rejection gave her. As she followed him out the door, she mused at how he managed to get over his sore stomach so quickly.

"CAN YOU CHECK MY TIE?" Bob asked, standing in front of Charlotte, his brown suit coat draped over his forearm.

Charlotte wiped her hands on the tea towel sitting on the countertop, then adjusted the gold-and-brown-striped tie, making sure the knot was perfectly centered on his white shirt.

The scent of coffee and toast from breakfast lingered in the air. Charlotte had stacked the toast that Bob had made on a plate, doubting whether the kids would eat it when they came down, but she didn't have the heart to throw it away.

"Is Pete coming to church?"

He always asks, Charlotte thought as she shook her head.

Bob shrugged his suit coat on but didn't button it up. He hadn't been able to get the buttons to meet for years. Charlotte wasn't sure she should mention his weight gain, but she'd discreetly been trying to change his eating habits instead.

"Are you sure you should stay home from church with the children?" he asked, fiddling with the buttons as if tempted to give them yet another try.

Charlotte wasn't sure. She'd been second-guessing her decision all morning.

"Ever since I brought Christopher home from school with a sore stomach, I've been wondering if I should have sent the children to school so soon." Charlotte voiced her doubts with some hesitation. She and Bob hadn't disagreed over how to raise their own children and it was foreign to her to have this happen now.

"Routine—"

"—is good. And I know that." She smoothed the lapels of Bob's suit jacket, fussed with the hanky square tucked in the pocket. "But I think, today, I'm going to keep the children home."

An hour ago, she had started trying to wake the kids. Emphasis on trying. Every time she went back upstairs to rouse them, she had had to listen to a thinly veiled litany of complaints from Sam and Emily about how early it was and how they always slept in on Sunday mornings. She hadn't pushed the issue too hard, knowing how exhausting grief could be.

Bob frowned. "People will wonder where you are. What should I tell them?"

"That I'm staying home for the sake of the children." The confidence with which she spoke was undermined by her own concern about what people would say and second thoughts about the propriety of staying away from church.

"Okay." Bob's sigh clearly expressed his opinion, but he didn't push the issue. "But next week?"

"Next week we'll be in church because I'll have an entire week to prepare Emily, Sam, and Christopher. I want them to come with us too. I just don't have the energy to get it done today."

Bob nodded, dropped a light kiss on Charlotte's forehead, then turned and left.

Even as she heard the car door slam, questions about her decision lingered. She couldn't remember the last time she had missed a church service. Now more than ever, surely she should yearn to be in God's house?

But the thought of facing the concern and questions from well-meaning friends kept her in the kitchen, listening as the sound of the car's engine receded into silence.

Plus, she still hadn't managed to get the kids out of bed.

When the counters were wiped clean, the floor swept,

and the braided rug centered in front of the sink again, Charlotte wandered over to her chair and opened her Bible to the place where she had last left off.

If she wasn't going to go to church, the least she could do was spend some time on devotions. But when she lowered her head to pray, the only emotion swelling in her heart was anger.

She pushed it down and struggled to find the peace she often felt when she read the Bible, but her struggle was in vain.

"Why, Lord?" she whispered, her hands clenching into fists. "Why did you take her away before we had a chance to reconcile with her?"

She stopped, wondering if she was going to be punished for her anger, but nothing happened. There was just silence broken by the faint tick of the kitchen clock, the hum of the refrigerator, and the far-off honking of geese, returning to nest to start their new families.

"ARE YOU SURE those boots fit, Christopher?" Charlotte leaned back on her heels as her grandson wiggled his foot. "I want to make sure they won't fall off."

Though the rubber along the top of the old boot was cracked and worn, the rest was waterproof enough for a walk around the yard.

The kids had been up for a few hours, and they'd just finished the big Sunday dinner Charlotte had made to compensate for staying home from church. Now Bob was having his usual afternoon nap in the recliner and Pete was in his apartment. Chilling out, he had told her.

Charlotte stood up and handed Emily an old pair of her boots.

"Can't I just wear *my* boots?" Emily asked.

Charlotte thought of the suede, sheepskin-lined boots Emily wore the other day and shook her head. "They would get too dirty, honey."

Emily sighed and slipped the rubber boots on, grimacing as she did so.

"No one is going to see you." Sam stood up and pretended to snap an imaginary pair of suspenders over his voluminous hooded sweatshirt. "Ready to rock and roll, Grandma," he said.

"I thought we could head out to the chicken barn first." She snagged an empty ice-cream bucket from a pile inside the porch, then led them outside. Toby had heard the door slam and came running to them, tongue hanging out, eyes wide with anticipation.

"We'll go for a walk another day, Toby," Charlotte assured her dog, bestowing a quick pat on her head.

"So what are we going to do at the chicken coop?" Emily asked, glancing at Toby, who trotted along beside Charlotte.

"Gather the eggs." She'd purposely waited on this morning chore so she could show the kids. "One of you will be taking over that job in a few days." She was thinking this would be a good job for Emily.

Emily frowned at her but continued walking, Sam and Christopher trailing along behind.

"What's in the window of Pete's place?" Christopher asked, pointing to the garage across from the large red hip-roofed shed that dominated the yard.

"That's his suncatcher." Charlotte looked up at the bank of windows along the top of the building. "He bought it at a garage sale."

"Can we see inside his place?" Emily asked.

"Not right now. I don't want to intrude on his privacy." This wasn't entirely true. There were many, many times Charlotte had to restrain herself from climbing up the long flight of stairs, breaking in and cleaning up. Respecting Pete's privacy was a secondary consideration. The first was the fear of the mess she would find once she got in.

"There's the chicken coop," she said, pointing past the shed to the smaller building, its wooden plank siding faded to a silvery gray by the sun and wind. "Usually the chickens are out in the yard this time of the day, but I kept them locked up so we could gather the eggs together."

"Yea, us," Sam said in a world-weary tone.

Charlotte ignored it. "You want to open the door slowly when they're locked inside. They tend to squawk and flap around." As Charlotte carefully pushed open the wooden door, Emily pulled a face.

"That smells raunchy," she said, plugging her nose.

"It's just chicken smell." Charlotte sniffed, wondering if they smelled extra bad today. Nope. Just smelled like chickens.

The chickens, thankful for their freedom, squawked, then hopped out the entrance, raising dust as they immediately began scratching in the dirt.

Toby sat on her haunches, watching them, her head tilted forward as if there was nothing she wanted more than to get the chickens running, but she'd had enough run-ins with broody hens to know to leave them be.

"Come on inside," Charlotte said, leading the way into the barn.

Christopher followed first, his head swiveling as he took everything in. Sam followed, but he clearly wasn't as interested as Christopher. Emily stayed by the door, pinching her nose with her thumb and forefinger.

"The first thing I always do is change the water." Charlotte picked up the bucket beside the feeder and caught the puzzled look on Christopher's face.

"That bucket was lying on its side," he asked. "How come the water doesn't run out?"

Charlotte brought the pail over so Christopher could have a closer look. "It has a solid top, except for this little half-round trough coming off the top. So the water stays in and as the chickens drink it, more comes into the trough. That way we can give them a full pail of water and they don't spill it."

"That's kind of cool."

Charlotte smiled and pointed with the toe of her boot toward the bin hanging on the wall. "This is where the feed goes." She glanced at Emily, who was now standing inside the doorway.

"And where do the eggs come from?" Emily asked, scowling.

"The chickens usually lay them in the nest boxes lining the walls, but you have to check the corners of the barn as well. Sometimes one chicken will lay an egg there and the rest will follow."

"Are there real eggs in those boxes?" Christopher sounded puzzled.

"Yes. You can go see if you want."

He looked at Charlotte to see if she might tell him she was kidding. Then he walked cautiously across the straw-covered floor of the chicken coop. He looked into the first box, then the second. He pulled back in surprise.

"Hey. You're right." He picked up one of the eggs and looked back at Emily and Charlotte, his eyes wide. "These are real."

"That's what chickens do," Charlotte said with a smile.

"I know. But . . ." He sounded puzzled, as if he was trying to reconcile the eggs in the chicken coop with the Styrofoam containers that his eggs had always come in before. "I've just seen eggs in the store."

"It's a good idea never to come to the coop without a pail to put eggs in," Charlotte said, handing Sam the plastic bucket. "We'll go fill up the water and you can put the rest of the eggs in this."

"Just call me Farmer Sam," he groaned.

She took Emily and Christopher to the feed shed beside the barn and showed them how to change the water. "We keep the chicken feed in that bin over there." She opened the lid of a large plastic container and scooped out some feed. "This goes into that metal container you saw hanging just above the floor of the barn."

"You really want *us* to do this every day?" Emily asked.

"One of you will."

Christopher took the full feed pail and ran out the door of the shop, a smile on his face.

Step by step, Charlotte thought, pleased to see him interested in something.

As Charlotte refilled the water pail, Emily wrinkled her nose and shuddered. "I'm not too stoked about this whole chicken-chore thing."

"I'm sorry, Emily, but it needs to get done." Charlotte led the way to the chicken barn, wondering how to break the news to Emily that she had her in her mind for the job.

Sam came out of the barn holding out his pail. "I got thirteen eggs, Grandma. Look, Emily."

Emily humored her brother and peered into the pail he held out to her. Emily held up her hand. "I don't even want to know what is on those eggs."

Charlotte chuckled. "Yes, we usually have to wash the eggs before we use them."

They were headed back when Toby spun away from them to greet a truck pulling onto the yard. The driver parked by the barn and got out, waving her arm. "Hey, Charlotte," she called.

"Who's that?" Emily asked.

"Hannah Carter, a dear friend. She lives down the road from us."

As Hannah walked toward them, the late morning sun highlighted the gray strands that threaded through her auburn hair. Today she wore a pale pink sweatshirt with a faded imprint of a goose wearing a ribbon around its neck.

She remembered when Hannah found that sweatshirt and how much she loved it. Pete had teased Hannah unmercifully the first time she wore it. He said the day a goose allowed anyone to put a ribbon around its neck would be the day he would take up ballet.

Now Hannah was standing in front of her, and with the ease of old friendship, she slipped her arms around Charlotte and held her close.

"Oh, Charlotte. I'm so, so sorry," she murmured. "I'd hoped to see you at church, but Bob said you stayed home."

As Hannah drew back she held Charlotte's hands in hers, her gray eyes locked with Charlotte's, as if delving deep into Charlotte's pain. "I've worn out the knees of my best jeans praying for you."

With every person she met after Denise's funeral, it seemed she had to deal with the loss of her daughter anew. But she couldn't break down in front of the kids. A crying grandmother wasn't much of a support.

"Thanks, Hannah." She swallowed, composed herself then turned to the kids. "Sam, Emily, Christopher, I'd like you to meet Hannah. As I said, she is a close friend."

Hannah looked like she was about to hug the children, but Charlotte saw Sam edging away so she discreetly put her hand on Hannah's arm to hold her back.

"We just finished gathering the eggs. I was going to show the kids around the rest of the farm."

"I've got a casserole in the truck that should go in the fridge. You just wait here. I'll be quick as a wink." Hannah held up her hand to forestall Charlotte, but she felt the obligation of Hannah's generosity pull at her. She followed her friend to the truck, Sam in her wake, still holding the pail of eggs.

"I can take them," Charlotte said, sensing that he would prefer to be with his little brother, possibly even his sister, rather than spend time with two older ladies.

Toby stood between them, looking from the kids to Charlotte, and then turned and followed her to Hannah's truck.

Charlotte took the box Hannah gave to her. The bottom of the box was warm from the casserole dish inside, and as she moved it, she caught the scent of onions and hamburger.

"I've made a banana loaf and a couple of pies too," Hannah said as she pulled another box. "I hope the kids like apple."

"I don't know. I haven't made them apple pie yet." Charlotte tossed a quick glance over her shoulder and saw, to her dismay, that Emily was heading in the opposite direction of her brothers. The kids were scattering.

"Well, they can try mine and if they like it, they'll for sure gobble yours up." Hannah strode toward the house with her box and Charlotte reluctantly followed. "Yours are always the best."

Once inside, Charlotte's innate sense of hospitality fought with her desire to be with her grandchildren. Hannah loved to linger and an hour visit was, by her measurement, a short one.

"So, you managing?" Hannah asked as Charlotte put the box on the counter.

"It's been hard," she said quietly. "It's like a dream still."

"I feel so helpless," Hannah said, her deep voice reverberating through the quiet of the house. "I wish I could do more for you. Such a blow. Denise was always such a pretty little thing. I loved having her come over. I remember showing her how to tie her shoes, teaching her to bake bread . . ."

The silence surrounding them was born of a shared sorrow. Charlotte's mind skittered past the memories Hannah had resurrected like a swallow catching flies.

It puzzled her how she could so easily evoke the picture of Denise at age seven, twelve, or eighteen, but no matter how hard she tried, she could not recall what Denise looked like the last time she saw her.

The refrigerator hummed to life, and Charlotte heard Sam calling to Emily from outside. Charlotte walked to the porch to see if they were in sight.

Hannah fidgeted a moment, tapping her fingers with their chewed-down fingernails on the counter.

Charlotte glanced past Hannah to the family room. All she could see of Bob was his stocking feet on the footrest of the recliner.

Hannah followed the direction of her gaze.

"I think we should go outside," Hannah said.

Charlotte gave her a grateful smile. "Thanks. I really did want to be with the kids. I feel like I have so much catching up to do with them."

"How are they doing otherwise?" Hannah asked as she slipped her coat on. "How is school for them?"

"Hard to say. I think Emily met up with Melody's daughter, Ashley. She phoned here yesterday. Sam still complains about the lack of a soccer program. And Christopher—"

Charlotte let that last sentence drift off as they stepped outside. She still didn't know what to do about Christopher. He trailed Sam around the farm like a little wraith.

Toby jumped up again and followed them, her tail wagging like a plume.

Hannah picked up the thought. "He's probably missing his friends. I know it's not all fun and games for young kids starting in a new school."

She slipped her hands into the pockets of her oversized jacket. "These days kids have it harder. Every movie and television show is about kids getting picked on and all the cliques. In that show *Room 222*, new kids always had a hard time. Especially if they were a bit square." Hannah was an avid television watcher, even though her favorite shows were the older ones.

"Don't let Sam hear you. He won't understand."

"I'm sure I could make that groovy talk cool again."

Charlotte laughed, surprised she could.

"That's a nice sound," Hannah said, reaching over to pat her friend on the arm. "You looked so down in the dumps when I came, I wondered if you would ever laugh again."

"I have wondered too." Charlotte craned her neck again, looking. She was so sure she heard the kids but still couldn't see them. Where could they be?

"I'm sure they're fine," Hannah said as they walked toward the sound Charlotte had just heard.

"I still like to check."

Hannah laid her hand on Charlotte's shoulder. "If I could take on even a portion of your sorrow, I would. You'll just have to make sure you stay positive. Those children need a smiling face in their life."

With each gentle pat of Hannah's hand, Charlotte felt her burden grow. Positive. Smiling face. Not so easy to do when your own heart was as fragile as ice in spring.

"You go see if you can find those kids," Hannah said, "and I'll mosey along. I promised Frank I would make him a supper that would stick to his ribs. But I want you to know I'll be praying for you."

"Thanks so much, Hannah," Charlotte said. She hesitated a moment, then covered Hannah's hand with her own. Hannah was a dear friend, and Charlotte had a feeling she would depend on that friendship more in the coming months.

"Remember, keep smiling," Hannah said, smiling herself as she got into her vehicle.

The dust of Hannah's truck still hung in the air when Charlotte resumed her search for the children. Toby ran ahead toward the storage shed and Charlotte followed her.

Christopher was leaning against the side of the shed watching Emily, who was sitting on a fence, holding her cell phone in the air.

"Still nothing," Charlotte heard her say.

The kids hadn't seen Charlotte or the dog yet, so she quickly stopped on the other side of the shed. They wouldn't know that Toby always followed her around, so they might not clue in to the fact that where Toby was, Charlotte wasn't far behind.

Emily dropped her phone onto her lap and stared off into the distance. She blinked quickly a few times, then drew in a quick breath, as if pulling herself together again. "Well, Christopher, we should probably find Grandma," she said, her voice tinged with irony. "See what other exciting things she's found for us to do on the farm."

Charlotte felt a tinge of resentment at Emily's words. She was trying. She really was. She didn't know how to entertain kids that had grown up with a television with hundreds of channels available twenty-four hours a day. They were used to malls, rec centers, and video stores all within walking distance of their home.

"I want to go home," Christopher said quietly. "I want Mom."

"So do I." Emily replied with a hitch in her voice. "But we're stuck here for now."

The unspoken sorrow of their words struck at Charlotte's own pain. But she pushed it down, sent up a quick prayer for strength, fixed a smile on her face, and stepped around the shed.

Christopher had spied Toby and was kneeling on the ground, fondling the dog's ears. "You're a pretty doggy," he said. "Do you like living on the farm?"

"He's a dog. Of course he does," Emily said, climbing down from the fence. She stopped when she saw Charlotte.

"Shall we go see the calves now?" Charlotte asked.

"Actually, I'm not feeling very good. I'd like to go back to the house," Emily said.

"And what about you, Christopher?"

"I wanna go with Emily."

And that was the end of the tour of the yard, Charlotte thought as she led them back to the house.

Chapter Seven

Charlotte eased the porch door open, grocery bags hanging from her arms and straining at her hands, just in time to hear the telephone ringing.

The insistent tones created an annoying urgency she knew she should ignore but couldn't. She eased her bags of groceries onto the porch floor, kicked off her shoes and ran.

Lisa Grienke was on the other end.

"Christopher isn't feeling well," Lisa said in her clipped voice.

Charlotte bit her lip, wondering what to do, then made a decision.

"I can't come and get him." She tried to sound sure of herself. Tried to ignore the second thoughts creeping at the edges of her mind. She had to be firm.

On Tuesday she had run to school for the same reason. But, as he had done the Friday before, Christopher magically got better as soon as he got to the farm.

"But he says he feels horrible."

So did Charlotte right about now. "I'm sorry. He's fine. I know he is."

"Okay, then." Lisa's heavy sigh was like a light reprimand. "If that's how you feel. I'll send him back to his classroom."

"Thanks for calling, Lisa," Charlotte said. Then, before guilt could make her give in, she hung up.

She leaned against the wall beside the phone, looking down at the bags of groceries spilled out on the floor.

I did the right thing, she thought, pushing herself away from the wall. *I did the right thing.*

She had to stay the course, as Bob would say.

The past few days had been hectic. Monday, halfway home from school, Emily realized she had forgotten her homework. By the time they got home, Charlotte barely had time to get supper going and the laundry done for the day. As the work piled up and decisions got harder to make, it was getting tougher and tougher to follow Hannah's advice and keep wearing a happy face.

"Who was that on the phone?"

Charlotte sucked in her breath and spun around.

She hadn't seen Bob lying in the recliner in the family room. "What are you doing here?" she asked, pressing her hand against her chest, trying to hold in her heart.

"I was just a bit tired." He snapped the footrest down and slowly pushed himself out of the chair. "Pete's working on the John Deere and claimed he didn't need my help."

"Are you okay?"

"I'm fine. Just needed a rest." Bob waved off her concern as he gave Charlotte a quick smile. "I better go make sure Pete didn't decide to do an engine overhaul."

Charlotte watched him leave, suddenly anxious in spite

of his easy dismissal of her disquiet. The last time Bob lay down in the middle of the day was when he was diagnosed with pneumonia ten years ago.

Charlotte went to the porch, watching as he slowly made his way down the drive toward the machine shed at the end of the yard. He walked with his hands in his pockets, his head down.

CHARLOTTE TURNED OFF the rototiller, her ears still ringing from the drone of the machine. She had a moment of satisfaction as she surveyed the fresh dark dirt of the garden, waiting for seeds.

Toby, lying in the sunshine, yawned and stretched out, enjoying the spring air.

The muffled honk of geese flying high above her added a gentle counterpoint to the breeze rustling the leaves of the trees beyond the garden. Spring was here; she could feel it in the warmth of the sun on her cheek and the scent of dirt in the air.

This spring, more than ever, she needed the reminder of God's promise to Noah, that as long as the earth endured, seedtime and harvest would never cease. She needed to know that God was faithful and would remain faithful through this difficult time. She thought again of Bob napping on the recliner and felt another nip of anxiety.

"Hey, Ma. Time for a coffee break."

Pete's voice rang across the yard and Charlotte glanced over her shoulder to see her husband and son walking toward the house. Bob strode a few steps ahead of his son, his head down. He was walking faster than he had the other day. He seemed fine, Charlotte thought with relief.

Right now she didn't need one more thing to juggle. Trying to get the three grandchildren settled in while, at the same time, dealing with her own sorrow and questions was all she could handle. She hadn't even made an appearance at the last Bible study and prayer group she usually attended.

Charlotte pulled the rototiller to one side, then went to join Bob, but he didn't give her a smile.

She read anger in the set of his jaw and the way he had his hands jammed into the pockets of his twill pants.

From the way Pete was whistling an off-key rendition of some country-western song, Charlotte guessed the two of them had gone head to head once again.

She guessed it had to do with the tractor that had come limping into the yard this morning. They were supposed to be seeding, but it looked as if they'd had a breakdown, which always made Bob cranky.

In the kitchen, she washed her hands, then filled the coffeemaker. She had planned on putting out a plate of vegetables, cheese, and crackers with coffee but could tell Pete would need something sweeter to lighten the atmosphere. She pulled out fruit and the banana loaf Hannah had brought the other day.

"I don't see what the problem is. We've got enough land," Pete was saying as he followed his father out of the bathroom adjoining the porch.

"We've got cows to feed. That's the problem." Bob pulled

the chair out from the table, its legs screeching over the worn linoleum.

"So from the hundreds of bales that we put up, we can't spare a few more for the horses." Pete dropped into his chair. "You're being ridiculous."

"You got enough of those hay-burners."

Charlotte felt like rolling her eyes. Not again. Every spring Bob and Pete discussed, with bare civility, Pete's horses. Pete liked the challenge of buying them as two-year-olds, training them, and then selling them once they were broken in.

"I sold two of them. And made a few bucks. And what about Britney? That's a horse not paying her way."

"Britney is another story. She's been here for a long time."

"Britney should have gone down the road long ago. Now she's going to have a foal and she's pushing the upper age limit for that. We'll have to change her name to Sarah."

"Wasn't her fault that Swinton's stud broke through the fence." Bob reached up and turned on the radio sitting on the shelf above his chair to drown out his son's argument.

"I'm sure she didn't lure him in," Pete said, raising his voice over the early morning market report. "I just hope having that colt doesn't kill her. If it doesn't, she really needs to go down the road."

"That horse is not going off this farm." And from the hard edge in Bob's voice, Charlotte knew that Bob would not budge one inch from that decision.

Charlotte set the plate in front of the two men, hoping that food would calm them.

"How much money did you make on those horses?" Charlotte asked as she poured them both a cup of coffee, steam rising in tendrils from the mugs.

She knew exactly how much Pete made. She did the bookkeeping and had deposited the check. Even she had been surprised at the amount. But she thought it wouldn't hurt for Bob to hear it as well.

"More than enough to pay for my time and for their feed," Pete said, looking directly at his father as he did.

Bob pulled out his farm paper and rustled it open, signaling that the conversation, for now, was over.

Charlotte gave Pete a surreptitious smile, but her son only shook his head and helped himself to a piece of bread. He glared at nothing in particular.

"And how are the repairs coming?" Charlotte asked, resting her elbows on the worn table, glancing from the newspaper hiding Bob's face to Pete.

"Okay."

"Will you have the tractor ready to go by Saturday?" If she was late putting in the garden, the men were even later putting in the crop. Their county had been blessed with an unusual amount of rain this year, which had held up the seeding for the first time in a long while. But now it looked like they would be held back even more.

"We will. Of course we won't be able to roll a wheel until Monday, because the next day is Sunday, after all, and the Lord doesn't appreciate us doing work on Sunday."

It was going to be one of *those* coffee breaks. The kind when she wondered why Bob and Pete even bothered coming inside. They could squabble in the barn as easily as in the kitchen, and it would mean she wouldn't have to moderate or choose sides.

Charlotte stood up and got the list she'd started this morning after breakfast. This week she had realized more than ever that Bob was right about the kids being best off with structure and regularity. Creating a schedule would help them all get their feet under them. Help restore order. And chores for the children were a part of that.

"Will you be able to help us in an hour or so?" Pete asked. "I'm not going to get done fixing that seed drill. I was hoping you could feed the cows."

"Can't your father?"

"He's got to go to town for parts."

Charlotte mentally calculated how much time she had available to her. "I can go in and pick up the parts. I want to get the kids from school anyway."

Bob lowered his paper. "You're not driving them to school all next week as well, are you?" The faint censure in Bob's voice only underlined the dilemma of her concern for the children versus the orderly life she needed more and more.

"No. They're taking the bus come Monday. I know I need to get back into my own routine. I haven't milked the cow for two weeks."

"That'd be good. Pete makes too much noise when he's milking her. He doesn't get the same amount you do."

Pete ignored Bob's comment.

"And what about driving the grain truck to deliver seed? Will you be able to do that next week?"

"I might, but I'm not sure, Bob," Charlotte said as she

picked up her pen to rework the chore list. "Things are going to be different for us for the next little while."

She refocused her attention back to the list. It took all her concentration to balance the work out, yet make sure each of the kids had a job that had some merit.

For a few moments, quiet reigned in the kitchen. The coffeemaker hissed as droplets of water oozed down the side of the pot onto the hot plate. The late morning sun shone through the speckled windows, promising a warm, spring day. And reminding Charlotte of yet another job that needed to be done.

She added washing windows to her own list.

"What you got there, Ma?" Pete asked, leaning closer.

"Chore list for me and for the kids. Do you two have anything you want them to do?"

"What *can* they do?"

"Probably not a lot. We'll have to teach them."

"Right. Like I got time for that." Pete dropped back in his chair.

"You seem to have time to train those lousy horses," Bob grumbled from behind the newspaper.

Charlotte frowned at the gray paper and spoke up before Pete could. "On Sunday I showed them how to take care of the chickens. Christopher or Emily could do that."

"Well, yeah. They can't mess that up." Pete's reply wasn't heartening, but Charlotte added the job to the list.

"I thought Sam might be able to help you two somehow."

"How?"

"That's what I was hoping you could tell me." Charlotte

gave her son a firm look. She wasn't in the mood for his antics.

"I dunno."

"Bob, do you have any ideas?"

Bob's reply was another shake of his paper.

"All right. If you two don't tell me, then I'm sending them all out there as soon as school is over, and you can figure out what to do with them."

Bob sighed and lowered his paper. "I suppose Sam could help us get the equipment ready. Come summer, there'll be enough for all of them to do when we need to move pipes."

"We wouldn't need to move pipes if we had a pivot," Pete said.

"We won't need pivots if we've got three extra hands."

Charlotte suppressed a smile. Bob didn't often get one over on Pete.

Bob turned a page of the paper, and the room was silent for a moment. "I also think we should have Bill and Anna and the kids over for dinner soon. We haven't seen him since the funeral."

Charlotte's mind flashed back to that day. Though she had tried to bury those memories, they would be seared forever on her mind.

Emily sobbing as the casket was lowered; Sam crouched down on the ground beside the open grave, his hands clutching his head; Christopher clinging to Sam. They wouldn't leave the grave, wouldn't talk to anyone afterward.

Then when they went back to their apartment, they

retreated into silence. Charlotte had tried to talk to them about their mother, tried to get them to verbalize their sorrow, but it was as if they had shed their tears at the funeral and were moving on. They had obediently packed their things—sorting which were to be shipped and which they would take with them on the flight to Nebraska. But all the decisions of what to keep and what to give away had fallen on Charlotte's shoulders.

Denise's furniture, Denise's clothes, all the things that were a part of her daughter's life, disposed of . . .

Enough. Put it aside.

"I don't mind having them over, but—"

"I do," Pete put in, grinning. "Those kids of Bill's are even spookier than Christopher. I don't think they've ever had a snotty nose or dirt under their fingernails. And if they did, I'm sure Anna-banana would have them sterilized and put in isolation."

Charlotte stifled a smile. Pete made no secret of the fact that he didn't care for his sister-in-law.

"Anna is meticulous. That's all." Bob frowned at his son. "Bill is lucky to have her."

"And the males of the world are lucky he does." Pete winked at his mother, cradling his coffee cup between his hands. "Saved some other poor guy from spending half his life rearranging furniture and putting up swags and shelves and knickknacks."

Bob shook his head and returned to his paper. Charlotte was thankful Bob didn't resort to his usual, "You're just jealous." There were times Charlotte thought that too.

Not jealous the way Bob thought Pete was—jealous of

Bill's house, his fancy car, his well-paying job, and the respect he had in the community. No, there were times that Pete's jealousy ran deeper.

He was often jealous of the easy rapport that Bob and Bill shared. How Bill could make his dad laugh instead of frown. Charlotte knew parents shouldn't play favorites, and she and Bob had spoken about precisely that from time to time, but she also knew that Bob didn't see how he tended to favor Bill. He preferred to think he was simply proud of his older son, which often made Pete think he wasn't proud of the younger one.

"Bill phoned yesterday when you were picking up the kids from school and said he wanted Anna and the girls to meet their cousins."

"That's sweet of him, but Sam, Emily, and Christopher are still adjusting to some huge changes in their lives," Charlotte said, tapping her pencil on the paper. "They're not even used to us yet."

"I'll say. Christopher won't even talk to me." Pete reached over to the plate and grabbed another slice of banana loaf. "He seems kind of spooky."

"Pete! He's not spooky, he's afraid. And lonely, and sad," Charlotte said.

"I caught him hanging around the barn yesterday when he was supposed to be sick. He wasn't doing anything. Just sitting on an old straw bale, staring off into space." Pete tugged a grape free and examined it. "Like I said, spooky."

"At least he's venturing out of the house more and more. Emily and Sam have been retreating to their rooms."

"Emily find cell phone reception?"

"No. But they did manage to access something called Facebook, and have been spending quite a bit of time on the computer checking it out."

"So what should I tell Bill?" Bob asked, bringing everyone back to the topic. "The sooner they meet them, the better."

Charlotte wanted to agree but was still hesitant. Bill was a kind and giving soul, but she wasn't sure how the grandchildren would respond to Anna, who prided herself on her honesty, which really meant occasional bluntness.

"How about they come after church for lunch?" she said, trying to find a balance that would satisfy Bill and give the kids some leeway.

"Why not supper too?"

"That's too busy for me," she said, which was truer than she cared to admit. She always felt an unspoken tension around Anna, whose own home was a showpiece, whose children were adorable and well behaved, who was always immaculately turned out, and who could cook like a gourmet chef.

Which reminded her. She jumped up and pulled a package of hamburger out of the freezer to defrost. She put it in the microwave and keyed in some time.

"What do you mean? We can have soup and bread. Nothing fancy," Bob said over the hum of the microwave as he got up to head to his recliner.

Right.

Pete grabbed a toothpick and leaned back in his chair. "Aw, let's stick with lunch." He scratched his jaw. "I don't know how long Emily can go without saying at least once that her life sucks. I don't think we should subject Anna to such indelicacies."

Charlotte caught Pete's wink and had to press back a smile. She pulled out her old, worn recipe box and flipped through it, trying to find a magic combination of food that would work for Emily as well as the rest of the family.

"You shouldn't encourage that kind of talk."

"I don't, Ma. She comes out with that sort of stuff all by herself."

"When were you talking to her?"

"She was hanging around the horses." Pete leaned forward, his chair legs thumping the floor. "There. If you're making up a chore list, you could put her down for feeding them. She seems kind of interested."

Charlotte walked over to her list, scratched out one of the chores under Emily's name, moved it to Sam's.

"Why are you spending so much time on that anyway?" Pete asked. "You've been scribbling on that list for the past few days."

"I discovered with you kids that making up a chore list requires a steady hand and keen mind. I have to keep it balanced so no one will think I'm being unfair." Charlotte tapped her pencil on her lip, looking the list over with a critical eye.

"Doesn't matter what you do. Someone will say it isn't fair. All you need to do, Ma, is make up the list, hand it out, and show no fear."

Pete gave her a cocky grin as he pulled an oil-stained paper out of his pocket and laid it on top of her chore list.

"By the way, if you're going to town anyway, do you mind picking up these things? Just some O-rings, grease, and a mineral block for the horses."

She took the paper and tucked it into her shirt pocket, making another note on her own chore list.

"And I better get back at it," Pete said. "Sounds like Dad is down for the count."

Charlotte leaned back to look into the living room. Bob lay back in his recliner, a gentle snore emanating from his mouth.

"I'll let him sleep for a few more minutes, then I'll get him up," Charlotte promised.

"Don't rush. I wouldn't mind having a half an hour to get some work done on the tractor without him breathing down my neck, telling me I'm doing everything wrong."

Charlotte didn't bother to respond. The two of them did not always work well together, but Bob was anything but useless, as Pete implied.

She finished up the chore list, made three copies, and put them up on the refrigerator. Then she scribbled out a quick menu for tonight.

There. Structure. Order. Just the way things should be.

Chapter Eight

Saturday morning. Breakfast done. Dishwasher going. Check, and check. Charlotte glanced around her neat kitchen. One day she was going to replace the faded green curtains hanging above the sink. Another day she was going to repaint the pale yellow cupboards. Around each knob she could see a darker ring, remnants of years' worth of hands grasping the handles to open or close the doors.

But not yet.

Charlotte took a breath, readying herself for the next thing on her list, then strode up the stairs. She knocked on the door of Sam's room, then opened it.

"I'm going to town. Do you want to come?" As she asked the question, Charlotte stayed outside Sam's door. Pete, who used to have this room, always had a sign on the door declaring the room off-limits to sisters, brothers, fathers, and mothers, with a heavy line underscoring mothers. After dealing with approximately five thousand dirty diapers, runny noses, and torn blue jeans, she usually walked straight in, presuming she had earned the right to ignore Pete's warning.

Sam didn't need a sign, however. Charlotte felt the boundary as if he had put up a wall.

Sam lay on the bed, tossing his soccer ball up and down, up and down. "I'm good," was all he said.

Charlotte took that to mean no. "When I come back, we'll go over the chores."

"Goody," he returned to tossing his ball without another word.

Before she closed the door, Charlotte glanced around his room. Nothing hung on the walls and his suitcase still lay on the floor with all his clothes in it, even the ones she had washed and folded.

His skateboard stood propped in one corner of the room, useless out here on the dirt and gravel roads.

She gently closed the door.

Dear Lord, she prayed as she walked down the hallway, *help him to accept us and accept this place. I know it's hard for them, but soften their hearts to their new life and us.*

She stopped at the bottom of the stairs and closed her eyes, clutching the banister. *Heal their pain,* she prayed. *Heal* our *pain,* she added.

She waited a moment to release the prayer. Then she picked up her purse from its usual spot on the extra kitchen chair, grabbed a jacket from the porch, and changed her shoes.

She found Emily and Christopher strolling across the yard. The cool air had forced Emily to put a denim jacket over her tank top. She had her head down, looking at something in her hand. A cell phone probably. Charlotte had to give that girl credit for persistence.

Christopher poked his stick into the ground from time to time. His pale blue T-shirt had a streak of dirt across it, where he had wiped his hand over it.

"Emily, Christopher," she called, "I'm going to town. Do you want to come?"

Emily's head shot up. "Yes. Absolutely."

Charlotte didn't know what surprised her more, the enthusiasm in Emily's voice or the fact that she wanted to come along.

"C'mon, Christopher. Let's go." She slipped her cell phone into the pocket of her low-slung blue jeans, grabbed Christopher's arm, and almost dragged him across the yard.

"Wait. I dropped my treasure," he said.

Emily stopped while Christopher bent over and picked something up and put it in his pocket. Charlotte didn't bother asking. She made a mental note to check all the pockets of Christopher's pants when doing laundry.

Charlotte said nothing about Christopher's dirty shirt or Emily's exposed navel. She was thankful enough they wanted to go along with her.

"I'm taking my car," Charlotte told them as she walked toward the garage. Emily veered right and arrived before Charlotte did, then waited by the door.

"You can get in," Charlotte said, pulling her keys out of her purse.

"Isn't it locked?"

"No. We don't lock the doors when we're home." In fact, Charlotte seldom locked the car when they were in town. Pete was always haranguing her to be more careful.

"Weird." Emily held the back door open for Christopher, who climbed in, stick and all.

Charlotte climbed in the front, feeling like a taxi driver. "What do you have to do, Grandma?" Emily asked as Charlotte reversed out of the driveway.

"I have to pick up some parts for Uncle Pete and some groceries. Did you need anything?"

She shook her head. "Nope. Just wanted to see something different than a barn and cows and—" She stopped.

Toby watched them go, then plopped down on the edge of the driveway, where she would stay until they returned.

"Is there anyplace you want to go, Emily?" Charlotte asked, glancing in her rearview mirror at her granddaughter.

"Is there a, uh, like, a mall in town?" Emily kept her gaze focused on the trees slipping past the window.

"No."

"Well, a place that sells clothes?"

"I have to go to the tractor dealership first and then get groceries. We can stop at Brenda's Boutique after that."

"You can just drop me off, Grandma. I can find it on my own."

"But you don't know Bedford that well."

"It's not the city, Grandma," Emily said with a light laugh.

"Can I come with you?" Christopher asked, tapping his stick on his knees.

Emily shook her head and ruffled his hair. "Remember that time Mom and me went shopping for a dress? You were totally bored. You lay on the floor and played with your cars. I was so embarrassed."

"But you and Mom took so long."

"Mom wanted just the right dress for me—" Emily's voice trailed off, and Charlotte wondered if she was reliving that day. She wondered how long ago that was. Weeks? Over a month?

Christopher stopped tapping his stick and in the mirror Charlotte saw his features shift and his eyes stare off as if seeing something that only lived in his memory.

The rest of the drive to town was quiet. Charlotte parked the car at the grocery store across from the tractor dealership, and to her surprise, Christopher and Emily tumbled out of the car behind her.

They walked across the street, and as they neared the building, Christopher stopped in his tracks, staring at the tractors parked in a row by the parking lot.

"Those are bigger than Grandpa's tractor," he said, a tinge of awe in his voice.

"That they are." Charlotte had to smile. He had the same look on his face that a younger Pete had had every time he saw these tractors. Like uncle, like nephew.

They followed her into the office and were greeted by Brad Weber, a tall, heavyset man whose hair looked like it could use a brush and whose chin carried a two-day stubble. Brad was the kind of man who made Charlotte want to bring him home, feed him, and clean him up.

"Hey, there, Miz Stevenson," he drawled, pushing himself upright. "What can I do for you?"

"I've come to pick up that part Pete ordered, and I need some O-rings. Here's the sizes."

Brad took the list from her, scanned it quickly, then with a nod, ambled off to get what she needed.

"Grandma, can I have a quarter?" Christopher asked.

They were standing by the candy dispensers in one corner of the dealership. Charlotte had her doubts about the freshness of the contents. She was sure the level of those candies hadn't changed since her own kids were pestering her for quarters. She shook her head. "No, honey. We don't waste our money on things like gumballs."

"Sorry, Christopher. If I had a quarter, I'd get you some."

Did Charlotte imagine the judgment in Emily's voice?

As Charlotte watched the two children, so like Denise and Pete long ago, nostalgia brushed at Charlotte with a heavy hand. What would it have hurt to give out a quarter now and again instead of seeing the disappointment in her children's faces? Had saving those quarters made such a difference in their lives?

Charlotte dug into her purse and pulled out a handful of quarters. "Emily, Christopher. Here."

Emily took the money, frowning, wondering why her grandmother changed her mind.

"And here's your stuff, Miz Stevenson." Brad dropped the parts on the counter and punched the numbers into the computer.

"You put that on Bob's account, Brad?" Charlotte said as he bagged up the parts.

"You'll get the damages at the end of the month." Brad leaned one elbow on the counter; lowering his six-footsome frame to Charlotte's level and looking like he was getting ready for a chat. "How's that tractor working for the guys?"

"Good. They've been doing some work on the engine."

Charlotte told him what she could, but she also knew this was simply a warm-up to the more serious conversation that would come in its own time.

Brad frowned as he pulled a can of chew out of his back pocket. "I told Pete that they had to call us if they have trouble. We could have sent a mechanic out."

"You know Bob. He doesn't like to bother people and he prefers to do things himself."

"Well, I told Pete the other night that if Bob fiddles with that motor, the limited warranty won't cover it." Brad tapped the lid of the can, then opened it. "So, how are things going otherwise?" As Pete's good friend, Brad was privy to many of the goings on at the Stevenson farm.

"Busy but pretty good." Charlotte was fully aware of Emily and Christopher behind her at the candy dispensers. She was also aware of kids' internal radar intuitively picking up on any shift in the conversation that might have anything to do with them.

"I was sorry to hear about Denise," Brad said. "Must be tough."

Charlotte simply nodded. She knew she ran the risk of bumping up against people's condolences everywhere she went.

She glanced back at the kids, but they were crouched over the dispenser, digging the candy out with their fingers.

"Well, I should get this part back to the farm." She took the bag. "Don't be such a stranger, Brad. Come over sometime and I'll replace that missing pocket for you," she said, pointing to the dark patch on one side of his shirt outlined by bits of loose thread.

Brad pulled his head back to see where she pointed, then flashed her a grin. "I lost the original."

"I'm sure I could find something to patch it with." Charlotte then turned back to her grandchildren. "Emily, Chris. We should go."

Christopher frowned at her as he popped a gumball in his mouth. "My mom always calls me Christopher."

His casual referral to his mom in the present tense stopped her from reprimanding him for talking back to her. Instead she said, "I'm sorry, Christopher."

"Where do we have to go next?" Emily asked.

"The grocery store." Charlotte put the parts on the front seat of the car and closed the door. "Then the fabric store."

"I think I'll head down the street."

"I would prefer going with you."

Emily frowned. "That's okay, Grandma. I'm just going to look around." Her voice, though not outright defiant, held a faint edge that made Charlotte uncomfortable.

"Why don't you wait a moment and we can go together."

Emily caught her lower lip between her teeth, as if biting back another reply, then, to Charlotte's relief nodded her assent.

As they walked across Lincoln Street, Charlotte wondered what had been accomplished. Emily didn't seem happy with her, but Charlotte knew she had to be firm. She didn't like the idea of Emily wandering around Bedford on her own.

Christopher ran ahead to the large glass doors of the grocery store. He stepped in front of the electric eye and waited, grinning as the doors swished open and stayed there. "Hurry up, Emily," he said. "I'm holding the door for you and Grandma."

"Then we better hurry," Charlotte said, playing along as she picked up the pace. She stepped through the doors and dropped her purse into a nearby cart.

"C'mon, Emily. I can't wait here all day," Christopher called out to his sister.

Emily took her time, as if letting everyone know that though she was here, she would prefer to be somewhere else.

Don't worry about her, Charlotte reminded herself as she pushed the cart past the cashiers. *She's just testing you.*

Christopher seemed content to walk alongside Charlotte as she consulted her list and filled her cart. They lost Emily once or twice, but soon enough she would catch up. Soon Charlotte stopped checking for her.

"Can we buy Froot Loops?" Christopher asked as they reached the cereal aisle.

"No, honey. They're not good for you," she said. Instead she picked up her usual cereal and added a bag of oatmeal and ground flax for Bob.

Christopher solemnly nodded.

Three aisles later, Charlotte realized Emily no longer followed them. She stopped by the canned vegetables, pretending to be taking her time deciding, glancing back once in a while but after a minute, still no Emily.

Where could she have gone? Had she decided to take off and walk around town anyway?

Charlotte turned around and had come to the end of the aisle when another set of questions beat at her.

If she thinks you don't trust her, you'll be in deeper trouble.

She wouldn't outright defy you. Would she?

Charlotte pressed her lips together, frustrated with all the second-guessing she had been doing lately. What had happened to her? Yes she had much to deal with, but sooner or later she had to exert her authority over these children.

She stopped at the end of the aisle, tapping her fingers on the cart, wondering, when she heard someone around the corner and out of sight say her name. She waited, and against her will, listened. She didn't recognize the voices, but she clearly heard what they were saying.

"Charlotte is going to be busy, that's for sure . . ."

"My Lily is in the same class as the girl, Emily. From the way Lily talks, Emily sounds like a handful. I wonder if Charlotte will be able to handle her . . ."

Charlotte recognized the one voice. Allison Cunningham, a woman she knew only in passing, but who seemed to know much more about Charlotte than Charlotte knew about her.

"If she can't, she might have another teenage runaway on her hands."

"Like mother, like daughter. What do you think about this cake mix?"

The voices faded away, leaving Charlotte feeling angry and humiliated. How dare they talk about her like that?

About Denise? How dare Allison act as if she'd never had any problems with her own daughter?

Charlotte clutched the handle of the grocery cart, hoping, praying she could get her anger under control.

"Why do you have your eyes closed, Grandma?" Christopher was asking.

She sent up a quick prayer for strength and patience, then gave her grandson a gentle smile. "I'm just thinking."

"Are you thinking about Froot Loops?" he asked hopefully.

"No, honey. I'm thinking about Emily." The irony of the situation wasn't lost on her. She had just overheard two women discussing her ability to take care of her granddaughter while said granddaughter was missing.

"Why are you thinking about her, Grandma?"

"I'm thinking we need to find her." She drew a slow breath and started backtracking. Maybe Emily was dawdling in one of the aisles.

And maybe she's developed a deep fascination with Froot Loops too, Charlotte thought as the wheels of her cart clattered noisily over the floor. Christopher trotted alongside her, looking around as well.

But Emily wasn't by the cereal, or the endless pop and chips aisle, or the paper and plastics aisle, or the frozen food. Charlotte stopped her headlong rush through the store and forced herself to think rationally.

Where would a girl of fourteen possibly want to spend any amount of time in a grocery store?

She had a thought, did an abrupt about-face, and headed for the book and magazine stand at the other end of the store. But when she got there, no Emily stood paging through the fashion or beauty magazines.

Relax, relax. She can't have gone far.

"There she is," Christopher said, pointing toward the produce section lining the walls.

And there, leaning against a bin of bananas, cell phone pressed to her ear, stood Charlotte's runaway granddaughter.

Chapter Nine

"I wanted to talk to my friends," Emily said as she closed the cell phone and slipped it in the front pocket of her jeans.

"Why didn't you tell me?" Charlotte asked.

Emily looked down at her feet, and raised her shoulders in a slow shrug. "I dunno."

"You shouldn't have run off from me," Charlotte continued. "I was worried."

Emily's look questioned Charlotte's sincerity.

"I doubt Charlotte can handle her."

Charlotte dismissed the accusing voice. Emily was just a girl, lost and alone. She needed guidance and boundaries. That's all.

Something she hasn't been getting since she came.

But how could she have done things otherwise? Their lives had been turned so topsy-turvy they didn't know which way was up anymore.

"I have to pick up a few groceries yet, Emily," Charlotte said, a new firmness entering her voice. "I would like you to help me."

Emily nodded and followed her and Christopher back to the aisle where Charlotte had left off. Where Charlotte had heard those women questioning her ability to take care of these children. Did they know how many times she wondered that too?

Was she too old? Too set in her ways? She thought of the kids and the gumballs, then made a quick detour down the grocery aisle and without looking at Christopher, tossed a small box of Froot Loops into the cart.

"Did you still want to go to the clothing store?" Charlotte asked as the kids helped her put the groceries into the car.

"Yeah. We could check it out." Emily sounded hopeful.

"We can walk there," Charlotte said. "It's just down Lincoln."

Emily perked up at the thought and as Charlotte closed the door, her granddaughter was already heading out of the parking lot.

Charlotte slung her purse over her shoulder and followed. She hadn't been to Brenda's Boutique for over a month and wouldn't mind seeing what new spring fashions she'd brought in.

Emily paused at the window, looking at the mannequins in the display. A few had chipped fingers and one had a broken nose. They had been in use since Brenda's mother owned the store.

"Retro," was Emily's succinct pronouncement.

She pulled open the door and strode inside, her eyes flitting over the racks and the other mannequins Brenda had set out.

"Can I help you?" Brenda, the owner, approached them, her thinly plucked eyebrows portraying perennial surprise, her bright red lips a harsh slash against her plump face.

"Do you carry blue jeans?" Emily asked, still looking around.

"Not very many." Brenda's crimson lips widened. "The ones I have are in the back."

Emily nodded as she flicked through a circular rack of pastel blouses. "What about jackets?"

"Any particular kind?"

"Bomber style. Fake fur on the collar?" Emily was now perusing another rack of long trench coats, her hands moving faster, her expression growing more panicky.

Brenda frowned. "No. Nothing like that."

"So you just have these old lady clothes?"

"Emily." Charlotte's reprimand was automatic. But as she glanced from Emily's skintight jeans and baggy vest to the polyester dresses on display, she realized that her granddaughter's tastes and Brenda's inventory were a world apart.

"We cater to a specific clientele," Brenda said, her lips prim.

"Yeah. Not my style." Emily sighed, pushed her hands in the pockets of her pants and glanced at Charlotte. "We can go to that material store now."

"Okay." Charlotte felt suddenly sorry for Emily. The poor girl had been so excited when they left the farm but now looked as if she'd received a lifetime sentence.

"We'll go get the car and drive. It's not far, but we won't need to backtrack if we do." Charlotte held the door open for Emily.

Brenda stood in the center of her store, her arms crossed over her ample bosom, her eyebrows pinched together, her mouth pursed in disapproval.

"Thanks, Brenda," Charlotte said, hoping to appease her.

But Brenda flounced away, the rustle of her silk dress her only answer.

Thank goodness Charlotte didn't have to do any clothes shopping for a while. She doubted she would receive much of a reception at Brenda's.

The spring breeze played with the newly budded leaves on the trees lining Lincoln Street as they walked back to the car. From the light posts, flags rustled and flowed with the teasing wind. The promise of warmer weather danced on the breeze, and as the sun shone down on them, Charlotte got a foretaste of summer.

As they parked the car in front of Fabrics and Fun, Charlotte felt a gentle lilt of anticipation. Her sister-in-law, Rosemary Woodsmall, owned the store. Rosemary was like the sister she'd never had. She was always ready with a listening ear and a practical outlook.

"Christopher, are you going to stay in the car or come into the store with us?" Charlotte asked, looking in the rearview mirror.

"I'm coming." Christopher scrambled out of the car.

Emily stayed put, reaching into her pocket. "I'll stay here, Grandma." *No doubt trying to call her friends again,* Charlotte thought.

Charlotte slung her purse over her shoulder and walked into Rosemary's store. Above her a bell tinkled, announcing their arrival, then tinkled again as the door closed.

"That's neat." Christopher looked up, smiling as the ting of the bell subsided behind them, absorbed by the bolts of material lining three walls of the shop, filling the shelves, and covering the floor space.

Sun slanted in through the wide windows facing the street, lighting up the display of cloth and quilts in the window.

Two women stood by the cutting table tucked into one corner of the shop, chatting with Rosemary, whose short steel-gray hair framed her narrow features. As she cut from the bolts of material piled on the table, the women fingered the cloth, commenting on what they would do with it.

Rosemary looked up then and smiled. A measuring tape hung around her neck and a few strings from material clung to her beige slacks. She must have been working in the back of her shop, where she held sewing classes.

"Be with you in a flash," she called out, waggling her fingers at Charlotte. Then, as her hazel eyes slipped past her sister-in-law, Charlotte saw Rosemary's quick smile shift into an expression of subdued sorrow. She had seen Christopher.

Charlotte gave her a quick nod. As the women Rosemary was helping glanced her way, she caught the same look on their faces.

She couldn't bear three sad faces, so she turned her attention to the cloth beside her. She allowed herself to be distracted by the feast of colors and patterns as she slipped her fingers over the tight bolts of material.

Rosemary had arranged the fabric by color; shelves of red to gatherings of purple, lightest to darkest on each shelf. Small bookcases broke up the shelves and on these resided fabric pieces called fat quarters, folded and arranged in fans of contrasting hues.

A hexagon-shaped table runner covered an end table, and below the table, Rosemary had tucked a basket holding the kits with various swatches of cloth needed to complete the runner. The cloth was tied up with a ribbon, a paper pattern tucked behind it.

The entire place held the promise of completed projects, or at least the thrill of adding to one's stash of fabric.

As always, being here brought a sense of peace to Charlotte's soul.

"What is this store?" Christopher asked.

"A fabric store. The owner is Grandpa's sister, and she sells material to make quilts and other things."

"There's a lot of colors here." His voice held a faint note of reverence that called to Charlotte.

"I love being in this store," Charlotte said, pulling out a bolt of deep red fabric covered with tiny leaf shapes outlined in black. "I spend a lot of time and, according to your grandfather, too much money here."

"What do you do with the stuff you buy here?"

"I make quilts. Like the one on your bed." Charlotte laid the bolt of material on a nearby table and kept looking.

"The quilt on my bed has forty-eight light blue squares and twenty-four white squares," Christopher said. "I forget how many red, yellow, and brown squares there are."

His simple reply cut at her heart. Charlotte easily imagined this young child, sleepless, hunched over a quilt, counting squares in the watery light of the moon.

Though Christopher seldom instigated contact, and at times shied away from it, she still reached over and stroked his hair. He flinched only a little bit this time.

Rosemary had rung up her other customers' purchases, and the two women, their bags rustling, scurried out of the shop as if they could hardly wait to get home to begin cutting and sewing and creating. No other shoppers were in the store.

"Hullo, my dear girl." Rosemary walked up to Charlotte and gently grasped her hands while studying her sister-in-law's face as if seeking evidence of the huge change in Charlotte's life. "How are you?"

Her question was quiet and laced with the deep concern of a family member.

Charlotte glanced down at Christopher still looking around the shop, his hands shoved in the front pockets of his blue jeans. She knew she had to temper her words.

"We're doing okay. A few challenges . . ." Charlotte felt her voice tighten as the sorrow she hadn't dared release pushed upward. She heard again the skeptical voices from the supermarket and felt her own confidence waver.

Rosemary shook her head gently, as if in commiseration, then gave Charlotte a quick hug. "I've been praying so hard for you, as has the entire prayer team."

"I'm going to need those prayers."

Her eyes slipped to Christopher. "Hello, Christopher. My name is Rosemary Woodsmall. I'm your great-aunt."

Christopher pulled his hand out of his pocket and held it out to her. "I'm glad to meet you, Mrs. Woodsmall."

Rosemary angled Charlotte a wry glance as she took the young boy's hand. "My, you are a polite young man. You can call me Aunt Rosemary, if you like."

"Thank you," he said.

Rosemary squatted down. "And what grade are you in?"

"Four."

"Miss Hutchens is a good teacher. Did you make any new friends yet?"

He shook his head. "No, ma'am."

Rosemary pressed her hands against her knees and pushed herself to a standing position. "Bedford is a pretty friendly place, Christopher. I'm sure you'll find some new friends in no time flat."

Charlotte glanced out the window to her car parked in front, a figure still sitting in the back. Emily was still around but who knew how long she would tolerate waiting?

"I got your flowers," Charlotte said. "Thanks so much. They're still so fresh and cheerful."

Rosemary waved away her thanks as if they were of no consequence. "Such a little thing to do. Times like this a person feels so helpless." Rosemary held Charlotte's gaze. "I want to tell you, though, that what you have done is a loving and special thing. Taking in these children. I'm sure there'll be a special place in heaven for you and Bob. That's quite a sacrifice . . ."

Her voice trailed off as she glanced down at Christopher, still standing beside them. Her hand came up to cover her mouth as if trying to retrieve the words that had slipped out. Then she turned to Christopher.

"There's a box of books and toys in the back of the shop,"

Rosemary said. "You can go see if there's anything there you might be interested in."

He nodded, then wandered off in the direction Rosemary had pointed, his footsteps muffled by the shelves of fabric stacked up between them and the back of the shop.

Once he was safely out of earshot Rosemary drew Charlotte aside. "I can't believe I said that right in front of him. He's so quiet, it's like he's not even there." She fluttered her hands, obviously distressed.

"He doesn't say much. I have to confess, I'm worried about him."

"Of course you are. And I didn't help matters any. Here, sit down." Rosemary pulled a quilt off a nearby chair and draped it over a table, removed a basket from another chair, drew it up beside Charlotte, and grasped her sister-in-law's hands between hers. "Do you want some tea?"

"No. You've got a shop to run. I'm sorry I just—" She stopped. She wasn't used to feeling so shaky.

Without a word, Rosemary got up, walked to the door, and flipped the *Open* sign to *Closed*. "There. The shop is out of order for now," she said as she sat across from Charlotte again. "Now. Tea?"

"I'd love to, Rosemary, but I've got Emily waiting in the car. I can't stay too long."

Rosemary leaned back in her chair and crossed her arms. "Long enough to tell me how you really are."

Charlotte sighed as she mentally took stock. "Tired. Confused. Sad." She raised her one hand in a gesture of helplessness. "Wondering if I've done these children any favors. I feel so incapable."

Rosemary shot her a warning glance. "Don't talk that way. You're their grandmother. They belong with you."

"There was a young mother who offered to take them, a friend of Denise's who lived in the same apartment block. The kids were staying there when I came. She had two young children, seven and nine years old." Charlotte sighed, rubbing her temple with her forefinger. Why did she have a headache now? She never had headaches. "She was living with her boyfriend."

Rosemary harrumphed. "Hardly an example for the older two. Sam and Emily must be about sixteen and fourteen by now?"

Trust Rosemary to remember the ages of children that had been only a distant set of names in her life. But if they were family, Rosemary would remember every tidbit of information passed on to her. "Neither Sam nor Emily were crazy about the idea. And of course, neither were Bob and I."

"I can see why."

"I thought the farm could be a place of refuge for them. I thought they would be so excited to come. But they seem to be biding their time until something else comes along."

Charlotte thought of Sam and his suitcases, still packed. Of Emily constantly in touch with her friends back home. Of Christopher, often in another world. "And now I'm wondering if we're the best people for the job. After all, Bob is sixty-five, and I'm sixty-four. And then there's the mistakes we made with Denise—"

"Don't even think that, Charlotte," Rosemary said, leaning

forward, her hazel eyes blazing with intensity. "Denise made her own decisions."

The logical part of Charlotte's mind knew that, but the comments she overheard had dug up her own insecurities and exposed them to the cold light of day.

"I know. I've always wondered why Denise left, though. We never got close enough to her to talk about it."

"Even if you did, do you think it would solve anything?"

"I guess it doesn't matter, does it? We won't know now." She got up to see where Christopher was. But all she saw of him was his head in the back of the shop. She turned back to Rosemary. "Right now my priority is my grandchildren."

"Don't worry about the children. They will learn to like the farm," Rosemary said. "How could they not? You and Bob are such warm, wonderful people. But you need to take care of yourself too, my dear. You've taken on quite a bit, as I said. But you've also lost a daughter. You need to give yourself time to mourn."

And how did that fit in with Hannah's advice to put on a happy face? To be a positive influence on the kids?

The pressure on Charlotte's temples seemed to grow with each person she spoke to.

Charlotte walked to the door of the shop and looked out. Emily was still in the car. Still talking on her cell phone. Charlotte looked back at Rosemary, who was watching her, an enigmatic expression on her face.

She didn't want to talk about the kids anymore. They were such a huge part of her life right now, but she needed to connect with the other parts of her life.

"How was prayer meeting?"

"Good. Quiet because of spring work. A lot of the women couldn't come."

"I feel bad that I've missed a couple of meetings," Charlotte said, returning to the bolt of fabric she had been looking at before. "I'll be back as soon as possible."

Rosemary squeezed her arm in commiseration, then let go. "You don't worry about coming back just yet. Take care of what you need to. Take care of yourself. Like I said, give yourself space to grieve."

"What I need to do is get back into my own routine," Charlotte said, fingering the material.

Rosemary released a gentle sigh that Charlotte recognized but didn't acknowledge. This one was her long-suffering, be-patient-with-my-stubborn-sister-in-law sigh.

"You might be right," she finally said, much to Charlotte's surprise. "Now, how much of this do you need?" Rosemary dropped the bolt of cloth onto the cutting table, effectively shifting the subject into safe territory.

"Just one yard," Charlotte said as the bell behind her tinkled.

Emily stood just inside the doorway, looking around. Charlotte doubted she'd find anything she liked here either.

Christopher heard the sound and got up, peering around a table full of bolts of fabric. To Charlotte's surprise, however, he joined her at the table.

Rosemary set a long plastic ruler down on the material, and with one quick movement ran the rotary cutter along its edge neatly slicing the fabric off the bolt.

"Why don't you use scissors?" Christopher asked.

Rosemary folded the fabric into a tidy square. "The rotary cutter is far more accurate. And neat."

"Really neat," Christopher echoed, misunderstanding Rosemary's intent.

Emily sauntered up, her hands slung up in the pocket of her jean jacket. "Hi, Grandma," she said, her eyes flitting from shelf to shelf. "Lots of stuff in here. No wonder you were taking so long."

"Rosemary, this is Emily. Emily, this is Grandpa's sister, Rosemary Woodsmall."

"Hey." Emily inclined her head in what Charlotte presumed was a greeting, then wandered over to a quilt displayed over a chair in the back corner of the shop. "Did someone make this, Mrs. Woodsmall?" she asked, glancing over her shoulder.

"You can call me Aunt Rosemary, dear. A good friend of mine made it. She buys her material here, makes the quilts, and then I sell them here. Sort of like recycling," Rosemary answered, slipping Charlotte's material into a plastic bag. "Except with new material."

Charlotte glanced over at Emily, now wandering along the bolts of cloth, touching them lightly, pulling a few out as if to take a closer look, just as Charlotte had.

She felt a flicker of anticipation. Denise had never been interested in sewing, but from the way Emily fingered the material and inspected the baskets of patterns, Charlotte wondered if her granddaughter might have some interest.

She caught Rosemary's glance and knew she thought the same thing. "By the way, Bill, Anna, and the kids are coming for lunch after church tomorrow. Do you want to join us?"

"Sorry. I'm going on a quilters' tour tomorrow." Rosemary folded the material and smoothed it out, laying it down on the table. "Maybe another time?"

"Anytime." Charlotte hid her disappointment. She really wanted Rosemary to come. She would be a buffer. The way she felt right now, she wasn't sure she wanted to face Anna alone.

"I'm also tied up the following Sunday, but I can come after that, and I'll bring dessert." Rosemary called out, "Emily, what kind of dessert do you like best?"

Emily turned, frowning. "Dessert?"

"Yes, I'm coming for Sunday dinner in two weeks and bringing dessert."

Emily shrugged, then smiled as if a memory surfaced. "Cheesecake? My mom always made this yummy cheesecake that had chocolate in it and tasted like almonds."

"I believe I know exactly which one that is. I think she might have gotten the recipe from me."

"Really?" Emily's pert mouth curved into the tiniest of smiles. "That's kind of cool."

"Oh, very," Rosemary said with a quick wink. "I guess I'll see you again."

"And we should get going," Charlotte said. "We need to talk about your chores when we get home."

Emily gave Charlotte a puzzled look. "For serious?"

"Yes. For serious."

"Okay." Emily slouched out of the store, her posture telling Charlotte as much as her single word did.

Her granddaughter was not amused.

Chapter Ten

"I don't want to go into that stinky chicken house with those freaky birds flapping around." Emily made a face as if she would sooner go to school in overalls than feed chickens.

"But you just love chickens, Emily," Sam said, a faint edge of sarcasm threaded through his voice as he checked over his own list. "I mean, you won't eat them."

"Isn't there something else I can do?" she asked, pulling the juice pitcher out of the fridge and pouring herself a glass.

"You just have to feed them and gather the eggs like I showed you," Charlotte said.

Sam held up his list. "What does this mean, help Grandpa and Uncle Pete? Help with what?"

"Whatever they might need help with." Charlotte's mouth grew tired from the forced smile she kept in place while she went over the lists with the kids.

"Like drive the tractors?" A hopeful note entered Sam's voice.

"Maybe."

"Cool."

Though his long dark hair fell down over his face, hiding his expression from her, Sam's faint note of enthusiasm heartened Charlotte. She wasn't going to put a damper on his hopefulness. Let the men do that and deal with the repercussions.

"I have to feed Toby and the cat, but I didn't see him anywhere." Christopher wiped the milk mustache from his mouth with the back of his hand.

"Him is a she and she hangs around the barn when Uncle Pete milks the cow. Otherwise, she's pretty elusive. She has a litter of kittens, so even more so these days."

Charlotte's smile came easier with Christopher. He didn't express his sorrow through quiet obstinacy as his older brother and sister did, which made it much easier to connect with him. "She catches mice, but she needs cat food as well. We usually just put out a bowl and she comes and helps herself. I'll show you where everything is."

Christopher scratched his arm while he looked over the rest of the list. "And what are pipes?"

"Laying out the irrigation pipes is a summer chore. You don't have to worry about that yet, but I wanted to let you know it was coming," Charlotte said. "So let's go outside and I can show you what you need to do. Sam, Emily, why don't you come too, so you can see how it's done?"

The children followed her to the door. As they stepped out of the house, Toby leapt to her feet and walked behind them.

"How come Toby only goes with you?" Christopher asked.

"I guess because she's my dog," Charlotte said, patting Toby's head absently. "Grandpa gave her to me many years ago as a puppy and I take her for walks almost every day. She also comes with me when I do the chores, so she's used to me."

"I tried to call her, but she wouldn't come with me." Christopher sounded disappointed.

"She needs time to get used to you," Charlotte said. "And once you start feeding her, she'll realize that you're a good friend."

"Maybe." Christopher looked longingly at Toby, then sighed.

"I keep her dog food in the porch and her bowl is on the step." As Charlotte showed them, Toby stuck her head in the bowl as if expecting some more food.

"I think she's hungry now," Christopher said.

"No. She's an optimist."

"What's that?" Christopher patted Toby on the head, then followed Charlotte past the garden waiting to be seeded.

"Someone who always thinks the best thing is going to happen and not the worst."

"Mom always told us to keep on the sunny side," Christopher said. "Is that optimist?"

"Yes, honey. That is being optimistic." Charlotte smiled as his words resurrected a memory: Denise singing "Keep on the Sunny Side" at the top of her lungs. "Hannah—that's Mrs. Carter—taught your mother that song," Charlotte said as they walked toward the horse and milking barn.

"How does it go?"

Charlotte felt suddenly self-conscious, aware of Sam and Emily watching her. So instead of singing she recited the words. "It starts something like this, 'There's a dark and a troubled side of life, there's a bright and a sunny side too. Though we meet with the darkness in strife, the sunny side we also may view.' And after that comes the chorus, which is about keeping on the sunny side of life. Your mom used to sing it all the time when she was little."

As the words came back, they seemed prophetic. She hoped, for the children, and herself, that the storm the song spoke of in the second verse would indeed pass away in time.

"You'll have to get Mrs. Carter to teach you that song," Charlotte said to Christopher as they walked toward the smaller barn. "She can sing much better than I can."

"Our mom liked to sing when she was driving," Christopher said. "She would sing with the radio."

"But she could never remember all the words," Emily put in.

Charlotte remembered that as well. How Pete and Bill would tease her about her fractured versions of the songs she sang along with.

Her throat constricted and she swallowed angrily. When would she be able to think of her daughter without feeling this pain?

"You okay, Grandma?" Emily asked.

Charlotte blinked, then got her emotions under control.

"Of course." She cleared her throat as she led the way to the back corner of the barn. "This is where we keep the cat food, Christopher." She opened the door, releasing the smell of leather tack and the pungent smell of horse emanating from the heavy blankets resting on top of the saddles.

"I've put the food in a container so mice don't get at it." Charlotte showed him the plastic pail, half-full of cat food, tucked in one corner of the barn.

"Wow. Look at all those saddles," Emily said with a note of awe in her voice. "Are these for the horses?"

"Yes. We'll go over the chores for them next." She turned to Christopher. "Do you understand what you need to do?"

"Yeah. But I still don't see the cat." His eyes flicked around the barn as if looking for the elusive animal. Charlotte followed the direction of his gaze, but the only thing she saw was slivers of light slanting into the barn, dust motes dancing in the beams. There was no sign of the gray-striped tabby that flitted in and out of the barn during milking time.

"The cat will find the food if you put it out," Charlotte assured him as she led them out of the barn.

Christopher glanced over his shoulder once more, then trotted to catch up to them.

The spring sun warmed Charlotte's hair as they walked across the yard. Swallows swooped and soared around them, catching bugs. It was a beautiful day and she was finally spending some ordinary time with her grandchildren on the farm.

As Bill, Denise, and Pete had grown older, she had looked forward to times like this—only in her imaginings she held the hands of cute little toddler grandchildren with a dog following them. Instead she led slouching teenagers around the yard with Toby slinking along behind her as if resenting the time they were taking from Charlotte.

You take what comes your way, she reminded herself,

thankful for this new chance. Thankful for the presence of Denise's children.

"Is that him? Is that the cat?" Christopher grabbed her hand and pointed.

Charlotte turned back and sure enough, there was the cat, trotting across the yard.

"What does he have in his mouth?" Emily asked.

"Looks like a mouse," Charlotte said.

"Gross. That is so disgusting." Emily shivered. "I hate it that cats kill mice."

"I bet you would hate a mouse crawling up your pant leg more," Charlotte said as the cat slipped into the barn.

"*Eeuw*. No way that happens."

"Happened to me. I was driving the grain truck and all of a sudden I felt something crawling up my pants."

"Oh, that would freak me out," Emily said. "What did you do?"

"I reached down to grab it so it wouldn't go up any further, but as I grabbed it, it bit my leg." Charlotte laughed at the memory. "I swerved and almost put a loaded grain truck into the ditch." The kids started to giggle too.

"So how did you get the mouse out?" Sam asked

"As I was still holding onto the squirming mouse I slowed the truck down and pulled over, jumped out of the truck and started dancing and screaming and shaking my leg. I was doing the hokeypokey all by myself."

"The mousey pokey," Christopher said. His little joke made her laugh.

"Did the mouse get out?" Sam asked.

"Not right away. He was hanging on to the inside of my

pant leg, but finally, after I just about shook my leg out of joint, he fell out on the road. Then he scooted away as fast as his little legs could carry him."

"Bet he never got into a grain truck again," Emily said, smiling.

"I don't know. Mice aren't too bright. They think with their stomach, not their brain. I'm sure all that free grain was a temptation he couldn't resist again. But for months afterward I kept my pants tucked in my boots when I drove."

As they walked toward the corral, the horses heard their voices and whinnied. Charlotte went to the fence and leaned on it, smiling as the horses trotted toward them.

"What are their names?" Christopher clambered up the fence to stand beside her and wrapped his arms over the upper rail.

"That black one is called Shania. The bay with the star on his forehead is Ben. The sorrel is Princess, and the dun mare is Britney. She's pregnant. And the bay with the blaze is Tom."

"How come the male horses have the boring names?" Sam asked.

"I don't know. You'll have to ask Pete. Except for Britney, he's named all the horses."

"Britney isn't named after the singer, is she?"

"No. Britney was born way before that girl's time. I think Denise had read the name in a book and just liked it."

"Mom named her?" Emily perked up.

"Yes. Grandpa said if she helped him with the chores for the winter, she would get her foal in the spring."

"Our mom did chores too?" Christopher asked.

"You bet. All the kids did."

Britney whickered gently and was the first to walk to the fence. She went directly to Emily and nuzzled her arm.

Emily reached over and petted Britney on the nose. "Aren't you a pretty girl?"

"She's very friendly," Charlotte agreed. "Especially if you bring a carrot."

"Do we have some?"

"We have a few old rubbery ones from last year in the root cellar. They'd be good enough for the horses."

Emily climbed up one more rung on the fence, leaning in a bit closer to stroke Britney's head. Her smile brightened her face and lightened her eyes. Charlotte felt a warmth blossom in her chest at the sight.

"You're so pretty," Emily cooed. "Tomorrow I'll bring you a carrot."

"Hey, Sam, Grandma got you tied up?" Pete's voice called across the yard.

Sam spun around, looking for his uncle.

The huge overhead doors to the shop were open and Pete stood just outside, waving to Sam. "Could use your help over here," he called again.

Sam glanced at Charlotte as if asking permission.

"Go ahead," she said, smiling.

As Sam jogged away, Charlotte felt a measure of relief. One less person she had to placate. Let the men do that.

"Well, Emily, the chickens await."

"I really, really don't want to do the chickens, Grandma." Emily turned to Christopher. "How about you help out your sister and feed the chickens for me? I'll love you forever if you do that, okay?"

Christopher bobbed his head in quick agreement. "Sure."

Emily turned back to Charlotte and gave her an *I-told-you-so* look.

Emily's quick assumption that her brother would cover for her bothered Charlotte.

"Well, that's kind of him, but Christopher has his own jobs to do." Charlotte held Emily's smug gaze, watching as it faded.

"But he said he would."

"It's your job, Emily." Discipline and order, she reminded herself. Children function best with discipline and order. Stay firm.

Keep on the sunny side.

Be easy on yourself. Take care of you.

Keep your spirits up. Put a smile on your face.

"But I don't want to do it."

All the well-meaning advice she'd been getting the past few days didn't help her face down her now-belligerent granddaughter.

"It's your job, Emily. From now on you have to do your share."

Emily's face tightened and her eyes narrowed. "No, I don't. Not for long! Soon, soon—" She pressed her trembling lips together.

"Soon what? What are you talking about?"

Emily looked away and shook her head.

Charlotte was about to press the point when a jangling tune sounded from the pocket of Emily's snug blue jeans.

Emily turned her back to Charlotte, flipped open the phone, and pressed it to her ear, her finger in her other ear.

"Hey. Steph—just wait, I'm losing you. Hey, I'll call you back." She snapped the phone shut.

She started to walk away, but something suddenly occurred to Charlotte. She put her hand on Emily's arm, forestalling her departure.

"Emily. How do you pay for your cell phone?" Charlotte asked.

Emily glared at her. "Mom always paid it. Sam has one too."

"I've arranged for mail sent to your address in San Diego to come here, so I'm thinking we can expect a bill sometime soon?"

Emily addressed her question with a slow shrug.

"Do you know how much it costs?" Charlotte didn't have a cell phone, but she knew they could be pricey.

"I'll pay it myself." The muted defiance in her voice caught Christopher's attention. "So you don't have to make me do chores to pay for the bill, if that's what you're going to say."

Christopher hunched his shoulders as if making himself smaller and invisible. He edged away from them.

Charlotte gave him an out.

"Christopher, could you see if there are any more eggs in the chicken barn? You're not afraid to check them, are you?"

"No. No, I'll go." He ran off, thankful he didn't have to witness any more conflict.

Charlotte waited until he was out of earshot, then turned to Emily. "Emily, I don't think you should be using your cell phone anymore."

"I said I'd pay the bill!"

"You don't have enough money to pay the bill. And if you're not willing to do chores, then we're not going to pay it either. Why don't you put it away until we see how much it costs?"

Emily flipped her cell phone open and closed. "What about the insurance money? From my mom. I'll use that to pay the bill."

"What insurance money?"

"Sam said Mom would have had life insurance. From her job. Working as a waitress. And that we should get it."

Her mind flashed back to Sam's suitcase, packed and ready to go. A wave of grief washed over her.

Charlotte frowned. "Honey, the only insurance money your mother got from her work was barely enough to pay for the funeral." In fact she and Bob had to put in some extra themselves. "There was nothing else."

Chapter Eleven

Why did she feel so cold?

Emily shivered as she stared at her grandmother, trying to figure out if she was fibbing to her.

"But—how—" She couldn't find the words she wanted. Couldn't figure out what to say.

Emily felt like the air was closing in. Like the ground was coming up and the sky was coming down and she was getting squashed between them both.

She backed away from her grandmother, then turned and started running.

Vaguely she heard Grandma call her name. But she couldn't stop. She had to find a place where she could breathe. Where she could think.

Down the driveway. Onto the road. Then up the hill. Faster. Faster. Keep going. Don't stop.

She ran until she felt a stitch in her side and then she ran a bit farther. Her chest hurt and her stomach hurt, and when she finally stopped, she bent over, her hands on her knees, sucking in air.

When she caught her breath, she turned around.

She had come to a rise in the road, and from here the

fields sloped away from her on and on until they came to the horizon.

Too much land. Too much space.

In spite of how long and hard she had run, she could still see the place she had run away from.

She'd have to run for miles and miles and miles before she got away from the farm.

Until something changed, she was stuck here.

She dropped down in the grass on the side of the road, sweat pouring down her face. Her heart thumped heavily in her chest and she could hear a roaring in her ears.

She didn't belong here. She didn't want to be here. This wasn't fair. A knot thickened her throat and she swallowed it down. She wasn't going to cry. Not out here in the middle of nowhere.

She took a deep breath, trying to keep herself calm.

She pulled her cell phone out of her pocket, thankful to see that it hadn't fallen out while she was running. Flipping it open, she felt relief sluice through her.

She got reception. She could call Steph back.

Her fingers were trembling as she punched in the numbers. But there was no answer. So she sent a text message, and when she was done, checked her inbox. Nothing. Where could she be?

Maybe they couldn't send messages to her when she was out on the farm. Maybe because she couldn't call them, they couldn't send her anything.

That was why, Emily thought, slowly standing up. They were her friends. Of course they wanted to get hold of her. They had been friends for so long.

As Emily looked down the road, she saw a dust cloud coming toward her. A crazy thought occurred to her.

What if she started hitchhiking? What if she just ran away?

"And then what?" she said aloud, as if to remind herself of the reality of her situation. "You got no money and you got no extra clothes. You just got your useless cell phone."

Her connection to her friends and her other life.

The cloud came nearer and topped the rise, silhouetting a large pickup truck.

Grandpa was driving. He didn't look too happy.

Emily's heart sank. Why couldn't it have been Grandma driving? Though she still felt like she barely knew her, she felt more comfortable around Grandma than Grandpa.

He pulled up beside her and Emily climbed up into the truck and sat against the door, staring straight ahead.

Grandpa didn't say anything as he turned the vehicle around, then headed back to the farm. The only sounds in the cab were the radio playing some whiny country-music song and the pinging of gravel from the road.

Emily kept waiting for him to get mad. Whenever she did what she wasn't supposed to at home, her mom would always yell.

But Grandpa didn't say anything. When he pulled up to the house, Grandma was nowhere to be seen.

Grandpa cleared his throat. "I know you don't want to live here, Emily. But please promise me you won't do that again." That was all he said. He turned to her. "You made us worry."

She waited for him to start yelling, but all he did was sit there with his large hands resting on the steering wheel, staring ahead.

"I'm sorry, Grandpa." She couldn't imagine living here the rest of her life, so she couldn't promise him anything more. She just got out of the truck and walked up the sidewalk.

Except for the humming of the refrigerator, the house was quiet. Emily walked slowly into the kitchen, then past the pantry.

Just outside Grandma and Grandpa's bedroom door, she paused. What was that noise? Sounded like someone was coughing.

Emily quickened her steps and jogged quickly up the stairs before Grandma could come out of the bedroom.

She dropped onto her bed, too many thoughts spinning through her head. They were stuck here.

Grandma had been mad at her.

And somehow that last thought made her feel almost as bad as finding out that she, Sam, and Christopher weren't going to be leaving here anytime soon.

Chapter Twelve

"Is this okay to wear to church?"

Charlotte turned to her granddaughter fidgeting in the doorway to the downstairs bathroom.

She would have been okay with the pink and brown plaid shirt Emily had put on over the skin-tight pink tank top but it was the thigh-high denim skirt that gave her pause.

Emily looked down at her clothes, tugging on her shirt. "What's wrong?"

"The skirt is a bit short."

"I thought you'd say that," Emily replied, turning away and walking back up the stairs.

If she knew it was too short, why did she wear it and then ask for my advice? Is she deliberately trying to goad me into a fight? Or should I have kept my comment to myself?

As she brushed her hair, her mind scurried from second to third thoughts. Since the overheard comment in the grocery store and the confrontation over the cost of Emily's cell phone, uncertainty had dogged Charlotte.

Were they too old to do this? Too set in their ways to handle all the emotional stress and fuss that came with teenagers?

What if they repeated the mistakes they had made with their own children?

But what else could she have done? There was no way she could have left her grandchildren behind. Not after all the years that she and Bob had been separated from them.

"Grandma, I don't have any socks."

Christopher's quiet voice drew her mind back from speculation to reality.

Her grandson stood in the hallway, one set of bare toes covering the other, his hands tucked in the front pockets of a pair of pale brown corduroy pants.

She frowned. "They should be in your drawer."

He shook his head.

She glanced at the clock as she headed to the laundry room just off the kitchen. In fifteen minutes they would have to be out the door. The children had eaten breakfast in their pajamas, which Bob had frowned upon but which Charlotte didn't have the energy to deal with. Now they were running around trying to get ready.

A laundry basket rested on top of the washing machine, still full of the children's clothes.

"Sorry, honey, Grandma must be losing it." She handed him a pair of socks. "Are Emily and Sam ready to go?"

"Sam is hogging the bathroom again and Emily is—" He stopped, looking away.

Probably texting or talking on her cell phone, telling her friends about her uptight grandmother who wouldn't let her wear a skirt skimming her bottom.

"Could you tell them we'll be leaving in fifteen minutes?" she asked.

Christopher scampered out of the room, eager to do this small chore.

Charlotte felt like a coward sending Christopher to do her dirty work. But the reality was they listened to him without complaint and couldn't argue with him.

A few minutes later she stood at the bottom of the stairs calling up to the kids. "Emily, Christopher, Sam. Time to go."

"Coming," Emily called from her room.

"Grandpa is waiting outside," Charlotte said as Christopher met her at the bottom step.

She waited another full minute for Emily and Sam. Why weren't they coming? Should she call again? Would they think she was being a nag?

Even as the questions collided with each other in her mind, Charlotte knew she never went through this much indecision with her own children. She simply did the next thing that needed doing without all this second-guessing.

She was about to call their names again when she heard doors opening upstairs. The clock ticked off a few more seconds, and then finally Emily and Sam came down.

"I said we were coming," Emily said, a light frown creasing her forehead when she saw Charlotte waiting.

Instead of making excuses or apologizing, Charlotte led the way to the car. Bob and Christopher were already inside and a few minutes later they were heading down the road to church, five minutes late. Thankfully, Bob didn't say anything.

"SO THESE ARE YOUR GRANDCHILDREN?" Nathan Evans' wire-rimmed glasses glinted in the overhead lights of the church fellowship hall as he glanced over Charlotte, Bob, and the kids. "Glad you could come to our service."

"This is Sam, Emily, and Christopher. Children, say hello to Pastor Evans."

As Charlotte introduced them, she cradled the cup of lukewarm coffee she had been holding for the past fifteen minutes. Since she poured the cup for herself, she'd been hugged, patted on the back, and given condolences. The children had been on the receiving end of many of these well-wishes as well and now looked as if they would sooner be anywhere than in the hall, which was buzzing with the usual after-church conversation.

Sam politely shook Pastor Evans' hand. Emily, holding Christopher's hand, simply nodded. Christopher kept his eyes trained on his shoes.

"I'm sure you're still adjusting," Pastor Evans said as he unbuttoned his corduroy blazer and loosened his tie. "Moving from San Diego to Nebraska has got to have created some major culture shock."

Charlotte was surprised at his breezy tone. Nathan was known to be a caring and compassionate man. That he didn't address the loss of the children's mother seemed odd to her.

"I know it will take some time before you feel at home here," he continued, still talking to the children, "but I hope you can feel God's love and caring through your grandparents."

Sam muttered a barely audible "Thanks" as if he was uncertain this was the right answer. Emily fiddled with the hem of her blouse, a sure sign that she felt ill at ease. Charlotte didn't blame her.

"It's been a difficult few weeks for all of us," Charlotte said. "But we are managing."

"If you ever need any help, or need to talk, I'm always available." As he spoke, his gaze took in Christopher, Emily, and Sam—as well as Charlotte.

Just as Charlotte was about to thank him, Melody Givens came bustling up, her daughter Ashley following behind.

Charlotte couldn't help but blink. Melody wore a sapphire blue gauzy shirt over a lime green fitted dress with a pink and green scarf wound around her neck. Charlotte felt drab and dull beside this lively, colorful woman.

"Hey, Charlotte, so good to see you." Melody paused as her eyes held Charlotte's. Charlotte read compassion and caring in their depths. Melody waited as if making sure her unspoken message sank in, then turned to the girl behind her.

Though they went to the same church, Charlotte didn't always pay much attention to the younger kids, so she was surprised to see how old Ashley had become. The freckles that had dominated her face had faded to a pale sprinkle across a pert nose and the once carrot red hair that spiraled out of control had softened to a deep auburn, curling loosely over her shoulders.

"Charlotte, you remember my daughter. Ashley, say hello to Mrs. Stevenson, Emily's grandmother."

As Ashley shook Charlotte's hand, her hazel eyes held the same unspoken compassion as her mother's had.

"I'm so sorry about your daughter," she said.

"That's very kind of you." Charlotte was about to introduce

Emily, as she had already done a dozen times this morning, when Ashley flashed her granddaughter a grin.

"Hey, Emily, good to see you here," Ashley said.

"Wasn't really my idea." Emily lifted one shoulder in a "What-can-I-do?" shrug.

"In Bedford, there's not much else to do on Sunday morning but go to church." Melody said with a hearty laugh. "Besides, I'm pretty sure your grandparents just have farmer vision on the television so there wouldn't be much to watch on the tube at home."

"Farmer vision?" Emily asked, obviously unfamiliar with the term.

"Reception by way of antenna," Melody said.

"We can't get cable at the farm." Charlotte felt as if she had to make excuses for her grandchildren's lack of viewing options.

"All that cable does, and satellite too, for that matter, is give you more bad options of what not to watch." Melody laughed again. "You kids aren't missing much."

Sam's look told Charlotte that he didn't agree, but thankfully he said nothing.

"So what do you like watching, Sam?" Melody asked. "Sports? Comedy? Reality shows?"

Sam looked puzzled, as if surprised this woman would want to talk to him. "I like hockey and soccer."

"Which hockey team's got your loyalty?"

"The Kings."

Melody shook her head. "You poor soul. You should have stuck with the Ducks."

This elicited a reluctant smile from Sam. "Well, they didn't do that bad last year."

Melody rolled her eyes in mock horror. "You *are* a faithful fan. They didn't even make the playoffs. Of course, I should talk. I'm stuck with cheering for the Predators and, let's face it, where've they been the past few years?"

"In the basement," Sam said with a light laugh.

Charlotte felt a small rush of envy at Melody's easy manner with her grandkids. This was the first time she'd seen Sam laugh.

"Hey, Sam," Ashley said, breaking into the conversation. "I was telling Emily about youth group. We've got a social thing going tonight. Do you want to come?"

"What's youth group?" Sam asked.

"Come talk to our youth leader. He'll give you the skinny." Ashley wiggled her fingers in a follow-me gesture. Emily glanced at Charlotte as if seeking permission to go along.

"You go ahead, Emily." Charlotte gave her an encouraging smile, thankful to see Emily making a few connections in the community. "We'll find you later."

Christopher looked from his departing brother and sister to his grandmother as if unsure where he should be.

"C'mon, Christopher," Emily said, and the decision was made.

"We've got a program for boys his age too," Melody said as Christopher trailed after his sister and brother. "It doesn't start for another couple of weeks, but I can give you some information on it."

"I've heard of the program. Doesn't Alfred Wodarz run it?" asked Charlotte.

"He hasn't done it for ages. Jason Vink does now."

"Okay, I officially feel old."

Melody laughed again and clapped Charlotte on the shoulder. "Hey, no worries. You'll soon be catching on to the schedules and rhythms of having kids in the house again."

"I wonder." She glanced across the busy hall, taking in the young children running between their parents' legs, older children gathered in little groups along the wall or in the corners. At the far end of the hall she saw Ashley introducing the kids to Jason, the youth leader. "There are times I feel every day of my sixty-four years. I remember when Jason was a young kid standing on the stage at the Christmas pageant, pretending he was a rabbit."

Melody's belly laugh caught the attention of the people close to them, but she was oblivious.

"I never heard that story."

"Not everyone saw it." Charlotte smiled, trying to reconcile the memory of a goofy little boy hopping across the stage with the tall young man holding a baby on his hip and talking animatedly to Emily, Sam, Christopher, and Ashley.

"What are you and Bob doing after church? Would you like to come for lunch?" Melody asked.

Charlotte felt a moment's regret at the plans she and Bob already had in place. She would have loved to go to Melody's place. Melody had an easy air about her and seemed comfortable with the kids.

"I'm sorry. We've got Bill and his wife and kids coming over today."

Melody waved off Charlotte's apology. "No worries. We'll catch you and Bob again sometime."

While she talked, Hannah and a fellow friend from their prayer group, Celia Potts, joined them. Melody stayed around long enough to chat a moment, then left Charlotte with her dear friend.

Hannah took the cup from Charlotte's hands and set it on a table nearby. "I've been watching you and I don't think you've taken more than a sip from that cup since you poured it for yourself."

"I'll get you a fresh cup," Celia offered.

"No thanks. I should get home."

"You look tired, Charlotte." The concern etched on Hannah's face came through her voice.

Charlotte couldn't stop the sigh escaping from between her lips. "I am. Everyone means well and I appreciate the sympathy—" She hoped she didn't sound ungrateful.

"But you just want to go home and put your feet up and rest." Hannah's gentle smile told Charlotte that her friend understood. "Grief is tiring. You should go."

"I think the kids are arranging something for tonight," Charlotte said, glancing across the hall. Ashley was chatting with Emily. Sam seemed to be listening as well.

Please, Lord, let them find some friends here at church, she prayed as she watched. *Let them find a place here.*

"Are they starting to settle in?" Hannah asked.

Charlotte turned her attention back to her friend, then waggled her hand in an uncertain gesture. "Too early to tell."

Celia shook her head, her dark hair swinging around her youthful face. "I think it's so amazing that you and Bob took them in," she said. "That's quite a commitment. I mean, how old is the youngest?"

"Christopher is ten."

"That young?" Celia's incredulous voice underlined Charlotte's own insecurities.

Just what she needed.

"And teenagers." Celia shuddered. "I was so glad when our kids grew out of those teen years. And for you it will be especially hard. Those poor kids, losing their mother in a car accident. Where was Denise going when it happened?"

This was just getting better and better.

"All the police told me was that she was driving alone and she apparently swerved to avoid something. She rolled her car. The kids were at home." And she officially did not want to think anymore about Denise or the accident. "Oh, there's Bob. And the kids. I should go."

Charlotte said a quick good-bye to Celia and put her hand on Hannah's shoulder, hoping her friend understood her sudden departure. "I should go. Bill, Anna, and the kids are coming for lunch and I want to be ready."

"Of course. Have a good visit, and tell Bill I said hi." Hannah's smile granted her absolution and Charlotte promised herself she would call Hannah as soon as she had a moment.

Charlotte intercepted the kids and left the hall, her insecurities trailing behind her.

Chapter Thirteen

"Of course much of our success this year will depend on how well we manage our budget, which, as mayor, is my next challenge."

Uncle Bill looked around the kitchen table, frowning as he spoke, as if everyone gathered around the table was as worried about his problems as mayor of River Bend as he was.

Trouble was, Emily didn't have a clue what he was talking about. Nor, she suspected, did Grandpa.

He sat at the end of the table, his arms folded over his chest, his head down. Once in a while he leaned forward and took another sip of his coffee, so Emily knew he wasn't sleeping even though it looked like he was.

"How are you going to solve this, Bill?" Grandma asked, tucking her arm around the shoulders of Madison, Bill and Anna's little girl. Madison scrunched in closer, like she did this all the time. Emily didn't care.

"Bill's quite inventive," Anna sounded kind of smug. She smoothed her hand over her dark hair, a pale blue scarf holding it away from her face. The same pale blue as her eyes. If it weren't for her thick, dark lashes or the thin, plucked line of her black eyebrows, Emily would have thought she dyed her hair.

She looked like she'd stepped out of one of those fashion magazines for older ladies, with her white silk shirt, collar turned up, and blue suede jacket decorated with complicated stitching and leatherwork. Huge silver hoops dangled from her ears and when she moved her hand, Emily was almost blinded by the rock she wore on her finger. Fancy, schmancy.

"We need to think out of the box," Bill was saying.

"I think out of the box all the time," Pete put in. "Mostly because I hate sitting *in* a box in the first place."

"The reality of River Bend's situation is very dire, Pete. I hope you appreciate that."

"I would think what happened the past few weeks is a whole lot more dire than your town budget," Pete said.

The conversation stalled. Emily guessed Uncle Pete meant Mom.

"I realize that. Of course. Denise was a part of all our lives—" Bill said. Then he started talking about grief and loss, and Emily shut him out. Every time Emily thought about her mom, her stomach got sore.

"I think we can talk about something else," Grandma said.

Emily was glad Grandma tried to change the subject, but sometimes she wondered if Grandma even missed her mom. She glanced down the table at Bill and Anna's two little girls. Madison, the older one, sat like a little statue on one side of Grandma, in Christopher's spot. Jennifer sat on the other, where Emily usually sat.

They looked like they had stepped out of one of those mail-order catalogs with the mom, dad, and all the kids dressed nice and matching. The headbands in their dark hair matched their mom's, and so did their blue corduroy jackets. Since they had come into the house, the only thing Emily had heard from them was "Thank you, Grandma." "Yes, please, Grandma." "No, thank you, Grandma."

Maybe they're wind-up toys, thought Emily, wondering how normal kids ended up so polite.

She felt a sudden urge to yawn, and struggled to stifle it.

"Did you stay up too late last night, Emily?" Anna asked.

Emily felt her face redden and she looked down at the piece of lemon pie Grandma had served up. She didn't want to see Grandma frown at her again.

A nudge in her side made her look at Uncle Pete. His eyes shot from Anna back to her as he leaned a bit closer, speaking only loud enough for Emily to hear.

"I think she means no . . . *harm.*" His voice took on a Spanish accent and he put extra emphasis on the last word.

She snickered. Pete was doing it again. Quoting *The Princess Bride.*

She whispered, "She's really very short on . . . *charm.*"

"You've got a gift for rhyme."

"Some of the time," she shot back, grinning now.

"What are you two talking about?" Anna sounded annoyed.

Emily pressed back a snicker as Pete widened his eyes, pretending he was really surprised.

"No more rhyming and I mean it," he said.

"Pete, what is going on?" Grandma asked, sounding a little peeved.

"Emily and I are talking about movies." Pete took a bite of pie with one hand and nudged Emily with his elbow.

Emily sputtered again but picked up her fork.

She'd been waiting all through lunch for this pie. She tried not to eat too much fattening food, but this looked too good to pass up. It sat on the plate in front of her looking like something out of an advertisement. It made her mouth water, but all she could think about was how her Uncle Pete, who was kind of a hick, knew lines from *The Princess Bride* by heart.

"What kind of movies do you like, Emily?" Anna asked.

Emily swallowed the bite of pie so she could reply, barely getting a good taste of it.

"All kinds." She wasn't sure if Grandma and Grandpa would approve of all the movies she watched, so vague was a better way to go.

"Horror, romance, suspense?" Anna pressed.

Emily nodded, taking another bite of the pie, determined, with this mouthful, to really enjoy it.

"So, all of them."

Another nod. Her mouth was still full.

"Well, that precise answer covers a lot of ground." Anna's voice took on a sharp note that made Grandma's gaze turn to Emily. The frown on her face didn't look good.

"Actually, it covers a lot of film," Pete put in. "Trouble is, poor Emily here won't be able to indulge in her movie habit with farmer vision as her only option."

"She could rent movies," Anna said to Pete, leaving Emily to enjoy the scrumptious pie.

Sam put his fork down and picked up his plate. "Can I be excused, Grandma?" he asked, already standing up.

"Of course."

"What about the dishes?" Grandpa asked.

Sam glanced from Grandpa to Grandma, and Emily groaned. Were they supposed to hang around until everyone was done and then do the dishes? She had every intention of scooting out of here and checking out the horses.

"I think Mom and Anna need some bonding time over dishes," Pete said, getting up.

Anna frowned at Uncle Pete, but he only gave her a quick wink. That only seemed to make her frown more.

"Great idea," Emily said, licking off her fork as she jumped to her feet.

"Yes. It is." Anna's frown turned to a thin smile. "All the kids can go out together. Jennifer. Madison. Finish up. You can go outside with your cousins."

Why did she feel like her little revenge on Anna had backfired?

Five minutes later she, Sam, and Christopher were heading out the kitchen door with Bill and Anna's two perfect little girls trailing along behind.

"Just a minute, my dears," Anna was saying, pushing her chair back from the table. "You should put on your hats. There's a bit of a chill wind out there."

Emily wondered what she was talking about. It had to be at least sixty-five degrees outside, but when Anna followed them to the porch, she figured out what Anna wanted.

"Now, I know you kids will take good care of my daughters, won't you?" Anna said, tugging a cute little hat over Madison's curls. She smiled, but Emily could see her smile got only as far as her lips. Almost like she didn't trust them.

She wasn't going to look at Sam because she was pretty sure he would make a face.

"If you have any problems, make sure you come back here right away, okay?" Anna said to Madison. "And, Madison, you make sure you take care of your little sister."

"Of course, Mommy." Madison let her mother kiss her forehead, took her little sister's hand, and headed out the door followed by Emily, Christopher, and Sam.

Toby lay on the step outside and, as usual, she stayed put. Toby never accompanied them when they went out in the yard without Grandma.

"So, did you find out anything last night?" Emily asked her brother as they strolled down the sidewalk. Christopher and the girls had run ahead, so they had a few minutes to talk.

Sam shook his head. "It took forever to download the program. By the time it was done, Grandma was checking up on me. I could check at school if I can get on a computer."

"Do you think it will work?" she asked.

Sam shrugged. Emily wanted to hit him. Since Mom died, that was his answer to everything. This lame, annoying shrug.

As Emily glanced at her older brother she felt the question pushing against her chest. Asking it would make him mad, but she couldn't hold it back. She couldn't talk to Grandma or Grandpa about it. She barely knew them. Only Christopher and Sam understood. Really understood. She took a breath and took a chance.

"Do you miss her?"

It was as if the words fell between them like a rock.

Sam pulled his hood farther over his face and hunched

his shoulders. "Why do you want to talk about Mom? She's gone." He sounded mad.

"I miss her." Emily swallowed the lump that always came in her throat when she thought about her mother.

"Well, crying about it won't bring her back and it won't get us away from here."

"I thought you liked it here. You act like you do."

"It's not home." He looked away from Emily. "No matter what happens, it will never be home."

He was right. But where would home be? She angled her head away and quickly swiped away a tear that slipped down her cheek. She didn't dare ask him the question.

"Sam? Sam?"

The sound of someone calling her brother's name distracted her for the moment. Sounded like Uncle Pete.

"What does he want?" Sam sounded ticked off, but these days that was pretty normal.

"Get yourself over here now, sonny," Pete's voice called out from somewhere by the shop.

"He's standing by some old truck," she said, pointing.

Sam started jogging, leaving Emily behind.

"Wait for me," she yelled.

"You got to take care of the girls," Sam called out as he ran past Madison and Jennifer, who stared at him.

Emily wasn't impressed, but she knew she would get into trouble with Grandma and that scary Anna woman if she left the kids alone.

Madison and Jennifer were watching her so she sucked in a long, slow breath then asked, "So, what do you want to do?"

"I wanna see the baby calves." Jennifer flashed Emily a quick smile. "Grandpa said they had some new ones."

"Is that okay with you, Christopher?"

He nodded, so they walked toward the corrals.

Just a few of the calves lay close to the fence. They had their eyes closed as they sunned themselves beside their mothers, their ears sporting bright yellow tags with black numbers written on them. A few lifted their heads, staring at the newcomers with a mixture of curiosity and concern. One jumped to its feet, its head weaving back and forth as if trying to figure out what they were.

Emily laughed at the sight. The first time she saw the calves, she was surprised at how cute they were. Sam was lucky he got to work with them.

They watched the calves awhile, but then Jennifer started walking away. "Where you going?" Emily asked.

"I want to see the cat and her kittens," Jennifer said.

"We can't find them." Christopher had found a stick and was making designs in the dirt.

"They're really hard to find. I'll show you." Jennifer let go of her sister's hand and ran toward the barn.

"Jennifer, you're not supposed to run," Madison protested. "Come back here."

But Jennifer kept going. "You're going to get your Sunday shoes all dirty," Madison cried, sounding more desperate. "Mommy won't like that."

This stopped Jennifer in her tracks. She looked down at her patent leather Mary Janes already covered in dust.

Who brings a kid to the farm in fancy clothes, Emily wondered, and why did Madison care now?

"It's okay," Emily said, trying to console the younger girl. "We can wipe them off before we go back to the house."

Madison wrinkled her nose as she considered this possibility.

"I want to find the cat," Christopher said, tapping his stick on the ground. "Grandma said she's around somewhere and I can never find her."

"She likes to hide in the barn," Jennifer said. "I found her under the straw bales upstairs, way in the back, behind a door in the wall. I'll show you." Jennifer shot Madison a warning glance.

Madison hung back, obviously still not convinced of this new adventure.

Emily looked at the girl's blindingly white socks and shiny black shoes and had a brain wave. "Why don't we take your socks and shoes off, and then you can go in your bare feet."

"But my feet will get dirty."

"But we can wash them and that way your socks and shoes will stay clean." Emily sat down on the ground, tugging on Jennifer's shoes. "Hey, Christopher, let's take our socks and shoes off too."

Madison watched them, then dropped to the ground beside them.

Minutes later they were all walking in bare feet toward the barn. Emily liked the feel of the cool ground under her feet. In San Diego the only time she and her brothers went barefoot was the few times their mom took them to the beach. Her favorite was La Jolla.

She wiggled her toes and grinned.

Jennifer was already in the barn, calling for them to hurry. She was clambering up the vertical ladder to the loft as quick as a monkey. It didn't take any urging for Christopher to follow. The straw on the wooden floor tickled Emily's feet as she followed Christopher.

Madison, however, hung back.

"C'mon. Don't you want to see the kittens?" Emily asked, grabbing the rough wood of the ladder.

"Yeah. I do."

"Then c'mon."

Jennifer stuck her head over the edge of the loft floor, pushing bits of straw over the edge. They floated down through the air.

"She never comes up here, 'cause she's scared," Jennifer said in a matter-of-fact voice. Then she disappeared again.

"You don't need to be afraid," Emily assured the little girl. "I'll go up behind you."

Madison sneezed as she glanced up at Jennifer. Emily could see she wanted to go up but didn't dare.

"I found them. I found the kittens!" Jennifer said.

How did she do that so fast? Emily knew Christopher had been looking for the cat for the past few days and here this little Miss Priss finds them in a few minutes.

Jennifer appeared in the opening again, holding a squirming little bundle of fur. "Here, Emily. Come see the kitten."

"I want to see the kitty," Madison whined. "I want you to go up and bring it down."

Oh right, Miss Majesty. "You can climb the ladder. You're a big girl."

Still Madison hesitated.

"The mommy is getting mad," Jennifer cried. "You have to come before she hides the kitties again."

"I got one," Christopher called out.

"Okay. You stay down here then." Emily scrambled up the ladder. She wanted to see the kittens. The straw in the loft itched her stomach as she scrambled onto the floor. She had never been up here before, and she looked around, grinning. This place was huge!

"Here. You can have her."

Emily took the wiggling bundle of fur from Jennifer and to her surprise the kitten squirmed once more, then settled against her chest.

She touched its tiny ear with her fingertip, amazed at how perfect it was. This was the cutest thing she'd ever seen in her life. Jennifer scampered off again, dove behind a bale and came up with another kitten, not caring about the bits of straw and hay clinging to her hair and clothes.

Emily laughed and cuddled the kitten closer. Just then she heard the opening notes of her cell's ringtone. She clung to the kitten with one hand, finagled her cell phone out of her pocket and glanced at the display. Bekka.

"Hey, girlfriend, guess what I'm holding right now?" Emily said. The little bundle of kitten snuggled closer and started purring. "It's the cutest little kitten you ever saw."

"Doing—farm—" Bits and pieces of Bekka's voice came through the static. *Oh brother.* The reception was cutting out, and frustration pushed away the momentary pleasure.

"I wanna come up!" Madison wailed from below.

"You stay down there," Emily called out to Madison,

then turned her attention back to Bekka. "Say that again?" Emily pressed the phone closer to her ear, trying to drown out the little girl below. "I can't hear you." She got up to try to find a better spot. In the background she could hear Madison crying.

"Can't hear—call back—" And then the phone went dead. Emily glanced at the screen. The call was lost.

Lousy farm with its lousy reception! She thought of the last time Bekka tried to call her and how Grandma said she wasn't going to pay the bill.

Dread hung in her belly. What if she couldn't use her cell phone at all?

She closed her eyes and clung to the kitten with one hand, her useless cell phone with the other.

"What's the matter?" Christopher asked, juggling two kittens. Though he seemed concerned, his grin just about split his face.

"Nothing," she said, slipping the cell phone back in her pocket.

"That's like my mommy's phone." Jennifer said. "She talks on it all the time too."

"I'm coming up," Madison howled from below. Emily glanced over her shoulder. Madison had climbed halfway up the ladder and was swaying, barely hanging on with her tiny hands. The little stinker was going to fall.

"Just stay there until I come down," Emily said, quickly putting the kitten down. She shouldn't have left her alone.

"I'm scared."

"Just wait. I'll be right there. Don't move."

Madison was crying now with huge gulping sobs. Emily

felt guilty. She should have been paying better attention to her.

"I can't hold on," Madison screamed. "My hand hurts."

"Settle down. Just keep holding on." Emily glanced down, but before she could take another step, Madison let go of the ladder and plunged to the ground below.

Chapter Fourteen

I have to say, you and Dad Stevenson are very brave, doing your duty by those kids."

Anna brushed a nonexistent piece of lint off her jacket and gave Charlotte a careful smile. "I know I would have a hard time taking someone else's children. I'm sure not many people would be able to take care of two teenagers and a young boy. Especially when you've got so much grief to deal with."

Charlotte wasn't sure she was able either, but at the same time she couldn't help feel a small stab of resentment at Anna's choice of words. *Duty.* As if she and Bob had no choice.

"We chose to take them in," she said carefully, trying not to read too much into Anna's phrasing. "They're our family. And I pray every day that God will give us strength to love and care for them." She finished rinsing the dishes and re-filled the sink with soapy water.

"Of course they're family, but you haven't seen them much, have you?" Anna hastened to add, seeming to understand how tactless she'd been. "Bob said that when Denise ran away, she never wrote anyone, never called."

Charlotte twisted the tap shut and slid the plates into the sink, almost spilling water onto herself. "She called us."

"But not very often?"

Charlotte pressed her lips together, stifling her reply. Anna's undiplomatic words were a stark reminder of their estrangement from Denise and her children.

"Do you prefer that I wash or dry, Mother?"

Why did that always make Charlotte feel like a nun? But she simply gave Anna a quick smile. "If you could dry, that would be great. The sooner we get done, the sooner we can check on the children."

Anna frowned as she slipped her beautiful jacket off and carefully hung it on the back of a nearby kitchen chair. "Are the girls okay with them?"

"They're fine," Charlotte assured her, rinsing the soap off the plates. "She and Sam are attentive to Christopher so I'm sure they will take good care of Madison and Jennifer." She was surprised herself at the defensive tone that crept into her voice. Though they had been here less than two weeks, Charlotte already felt protective of her other grandchildren.

"Oh, I'm sure Emily is fine with the girls. And Christopher too." Anna's hasty reply told her otherwise, but Charlotte let it pass. "Madison and Jennifer were very excited to come. They missed coming last week." A note of resentment crept into Anna's voice as she carefully rolled her sleeves up. "I hope it won't be as long until our next visit."

Until Denise died, Sam, Emily, and Christopher were simply shadowy figures—children of a woman Anna barely knew. Madison and Jennifer had always received all the attention as the most visible grandchildren in the family.

"Of course not. But I'm glad the girls can finally meet their cousins." As Charlotte stacked the rinsed plates on the drain board, she wished Anna could understand that right now Emily, Sam, and Christopher needed her more.

"I just hope everything is going okay. I mean, my girls barely know what Denise's children are like."

The awkward silence was broken by the dripping of the tap and the swishing of water over the dishes.

Anna wiped the plate she held with slow methodical strokes. "I always wondered why Denise never came to visit with the children," Anna said after a while. "I know my parents would have helped me out if I couldn't afford it."

"Denise was a very proud young woman," Charlotte said, loosening her grip on the brush. "She didn't want our help." In spite of that, she and Bob sent Denise what money they could from time to time.

"But that meant you didn't get to see the children much." Anna sighed as she laid down the towel, picked up the plates, and set them in the cupboard. "I'm so thankful my girls have had so much contact with my family. I know I would just die if my mother couldn't see the girls so often."

Charlotte wrung the water out of the cloth with more force than necessary. "Well, I have to say I'm thankful that we are able to still be a part of their lives now."

"Yes, but it's not the same as seeing them grow up from little, like you were able to do with Madison and Jennifer."

"It isn't, but having Sam, Emily, and Christopher living with us gives us a chance to be fully involved in every aspect of their lives now," Charlotte asserted, dropping the cloth into the water and rinsing it out again. She found a tea towel and helped Anna finish drying the dishes.

She was eager to get outside. In spite of her assurances to Anna, she wanted to see for herself how the kids were getting on.

"I think we're done here," Charlotte said, glancing around the kitchen. "Let's go find the children."

The sun beckoned, and as Charlotte stepped outside, she lifted her face to its welcome warmth, letting the life-giving rays wrap themselves around her.

"I don't suppose you're putting your garden in?" Anna asked as they walked down the sidewalk, Toby right on Charlotte's heels. "You probably don't have time."

"Emily and I will be putting it in this week." Charlotte pushed her hands into the pocket of her worn sweater and pulled it close around her. The blissful silence of the afternoon eased away the busyness of the morning. She felt more magnanimous outside and for a moment felt a touch of regret that she couldn't seem to find common ground with her daughter-in-law. "Come and look at the apple trees. I've never seen so many blossoms on them as this year."

"I don't see the children."

Charlotte glanced around the yard, listening. "I hear Madison's voice coming from the barn. Jennifer probably found the kittens."

"I'm always surprised your dog doesn't accompany the girls when they go outside."

"She doesn't go with Sam, Christopher, or Emily either."

"I still don't hear the kids," Anna said, a frown wrinkling her smooth forehead.

The trees were, as Charlotte had promised, a pinkish white mass of blossoms that seemed to glow from within.

"Don't they look like brides?" Charlotte marveled, touching the white and pink petals clustered along the branches.

"They are beautiful," Anna agreed, but she sounded distracted.

Charlotte walked from tree to tree, inhaling the fresh scent heavy with the promise of future pies, applesauce, and jelly. Bees buzzed among the branches, creating a low-level hum of busyness and familiar comfort.

The cycle of life.

She heard the sound of an engine and turned around in time to see a truck heading out to the field. Pete, she figured. Where was he going with Sam?

Anna kept glancing away from the garden. Charlotte guessed she wanted to find her girls.

As they walked toward the barn, the sound of crying reached them.

"What is that?" Anna stopped, cocked her head to listen, and then ran toward the barn. "Madison? Madison!"

Though Charlotte had on her sensible yard runners, she barely kept up with her daughter-in-law running in her treacherous high-heeled boots.

They both got to the door of the barn in time to see Madison sprawled on the floor and Emily coming down the ladder.

"Oh, my baby! What's wrong, baby?" Anna dove toward her daughter, completely disregarding the dirt smudging her dove-gray dress pants.

Madison screamed.

Toby, upset by the fuss, started barking.

While Charlotte reprimanded the dog, Anna grabbed

Madison before Charlotte could stop her. She shoved Madison's hair back from her face, checked her arms, her legs.

"What happened?" Anna cried, looking up at Emily. "What did you do to her?"

"I didn't do anything. She wanted to come up the ladder and I told her not to—" Emily glanced at Charlotte as if looking for support.

"Where were you, Emily?" Charlotte asked.

"Looking at the kittens. In the loft."

Just then Jennifer poked her head over the edge. "Is Madison okay, Mommy?"

Madison was still crying and Anna looked like she was about to join her. "Can you get up, baby? Can you walk?" Anna clutched the little girl close, rocking her. "Why didn't you take care of her?" Anna's accusing voice was directed at Emily. Then she turned her attention back to her daughter, who was trying to wiggle free.

"My head hurts, Mommy."

Anna touched her daughter's head and then started when she saw a smudge of red on her hand.

"Let me look at her." Charlotte peeled Anna's hand away from Madison, trying to find where the little girl was bleeding. Her hair was matted and sticky behind her ear and as Charlotte gently lifted the hair, she found its source. Blood trickled from a small gash above her ear.

"She might need stitches," Charlotte said quietly. "We'll have to take her to the hospital."

Charlotte pulled a hanky out of her pocket and pressed it against the cut. "Hold this against it," she instructed Anna, realizing her daughter-in-law needed a job.

She looked at Madison again. "Can you wiggle your toes?" she asked.

Madison stopped crying, then looked at her toes, wiggling them.

"Why isn't she wearing her socks and shoes? Where are they?"

"We took them off," Jennifer called out from above them, her face framed in the opening. "Emily said we could wash our feet. Emily has a phone like you do, Mommy, 'cept she can't talk on it here. She was trying to talk on it up here when Madison fell."

"You weren't paying attention to her?" Anna said, clutching Madison to her.

Charlotte felt her own anger rise when she realized how this happened. But she didn't have time to deal with Emily.

The sound of a truck engine distracted her and she looked back to see Pete's truck going past the door, Sam at the wheel, grinning, and Pete beside him.

She ran outside, waving at them to stop. Pete saw her and tapped Sam on the shoulder.

The truck lurched, then came to a sudden stop. Sam shut off the engine.

Pete hung out of the door. "What's up?"

"Where's Bill? We need to take Madison to the hospital."

Pete jumped out and went running around the back of the truck. Sam stepped out from behind the wheel.

"What happened?" Pete asked.

"Nothing desperately serious. She has a cut on her head that might need stitches."

"Last I saw Dad and Bill, they were looking over the seed drill. Bill figured he knows what's wrong with it."

She caught the cynical note in Pete's voice but didn't have time for petty family politics. "Go get him and tell him what happened."

Pete saluted, then ran toward the machine shed on the opposite side of the yard, dust kicking up from his booted feet. Sam followed Charlotte into the barn.

Anna still crouched on the floor, holding Madison, who now seemed quite pleased with all the fuss and attention.

"Am I going to the hospital?" she asked, reaching back to inspect the cut.

"Don't, honey. Just leave it alone." Anna was quieter now, but her pinched mouth betrayed her anger.

Though Madison seemed to be okay, Charlotte didn't blame Anna for being upset. The situation could have been much worse if Madison had been further up the ladder.

"What's going on? What happened?" Bill was at the door and inside the barn in record time. He bent over and lifted up Madison from Anna.

"Be careful, Bill. She's got a head injury." Anna adjusted the hanky she was holding against Madison's scalp.

"What?"

"Just a cut above her ear," Charlotte explained. "You and Anna should take her to the hospital."

Bill nodded, shifted Madison in his arms, and pulled the car keys out of his pocket. "Hurry and get your purse, Anna, and I'll meet you at the car."

Anna nodded, now the picture of calm, but her knotted mouth did not bode well for future visits.

"Where's my mommy going?" Jennifer called down the ladder.

"They're taking Madison to the doctor," Charlotte called up. "You and Christopher should come down here."

"But we're playing," Jennifer said, seemingly oblivious to her sister's pain.

"Jennifer found the kittens." Christopher's face appeared in the opening, his smile like a precious gift in the tension of the moment. "The mom had them hidden in a cubbyhole."

"So what's happening?" Pete came into the barn and stood by Sam.

"Is that kid gonna be okay?" Sam asked.

"What in the world is going on?" This came from Bob, who had now joined them as well. "Why is your truck parked outside the barn?" Bob glared at Pete.

"I was teaching Sam to drive," Pete said.

"Not when there's other kids around." Bob didn't sound pleased.

"He's gotta learn sometime and he did real good. The sooner he drives, the sooner he can go to school on his own."

"He's too young to be driving," Bob snapped. "I won't have it."

"I want to stay up here with Christopher, Grandma," Jennifer called out from the loft.

Charlotte felt her head spinning as the conversations slipped back on themselves, their words winding around her, demanding her response.

"Grandma—"

"Charlotte—"

"Mom—"

"Everyone, stop! Right now." She held her hands up to stop the onslaught as she marshaled her thoughts. "Bob, you and Sam move that truck out of the way. Pete, you get those two children down from the loft and keep them occupied for a few minutes." She took a deep breath and turned to Emily. "You come with me."

Emily paused as if she was going to protest, but Charlotte shot her a warning glance and Emily meekly followed Charlotte out of the barn.

The truck started up again, Bob driving, Sam in the passenger seat beside him.

Emily and Charlotte got as far as the house before Charlotte figured they had enough privacy. She walked to the porch and sat down on one of the wooden chairs; Emily sat across from her.

"I thought you weren't going to use your cell phone anymore." Charlotte kept her voice quiet.

"I didn't think Bekka would call."

"You had your phone on, so obviously you were expecting someone to call, and what was worse, you were talking on your phone instead of watching the girls."

"I told her to stay at the bottom." Emily bit her lip and glanced at Charlotte, her expression pleading. "I barely even talked on the phone. Barely said anything, Grandma! Madison didn't want to come up and see the kittens. She said she was scared."

Charlotte felt the beginnings of a headache. She wished she knew exactly how to deal with Emily. She had wanted to speak with her ever since she'd made that comment to

Anna at lunchtime, but for now, she had other things on her mind.

"We asked you to take care of the girls," she said, deliberately keeping her voice even. "And Madison got hurt because you weren't paying attention to her, because you were too busy talking to your friends." She took a breath, steeled herself, and held her hand out. "I think you best give me your phone."

Emily stared at her as if Charlotte were speaking Chinese. "What did you say?"

"First of all, the correct response is 'pardon me.' Second, we talked about your using your phone before and you had told me you weren't going to use it until we got the bill to see how much it costs you."

Emily pressed her lips into a thin line and looked away, her hands beating out a heavy rhythm on the arms of the chair, as if releasing her anger. "But my friends—"

"Can contact you through e-mail and that Facebook thing you and Sam were talking about."

"But it takes forever to load and Sam uses up all our computer time."

"Then we'll have to talk to him about that."

"But he's looking for—" Emily stopped there, looking suddenly guilty.

"Looking for what?"

She shook her head and averted her eyes, and Charlotte knew she wouldn't be getting more information from Emily. Brother and sister had their disagreements, but it hadn't taken long for Charlotte to realize that when outside forces intervened, they circled the wagons and protected each other.

And right now she was an outside force.

Charlotte still had her hand out and she knew she had to finish this. "I'd still like your cell phone."

"You can't do that, Grandma. You just can't." The anguish in Emily's voice surprised Charlotte, but she had to hold firm.

"I'm sorry, Emily."

"Please, Grandma." Her voice had toned down to a whisper and Charlotte wavered.

For a moment. "I'm sorry, honey. But we made a deal."

Tears sparkled in Emily's eyes as she reached into her pocket and pulled out the phone. She opened it, hit a button, and a chime sounded. "I'm just turning it off." She handed it to Charlotte, pushed herself away from the chair, and ran into the house.

At least she didn't head down the road this time, Charlotte thought, her heart beating abnormally fast. Tension, she decided, taking a few deep breaths to calm herself.

She looked down at the phone, still warm from being in Emily's pocket. Was the battle worth the cost?

She laid her head back against the wooden chair and closed her eyes.

Lord, I really need your help with her. I don't even know if I'm capable of handling all the stuff that comes with teenage girls. Look what a mess we made with Denise.

She felt tears prick her eyes and once again, forced them back. She had no room for tears. She had too much to do, too many people dependent on her holding it all together.

Chapter Fifteen

Charlotte parked her car downtown, then glanced at the list she had compiled before she left the farm this morning.

Hoses for Bob. Check. Clamps that Pete had warned her not to forget. Check. Case of oil from the Tractor Supply that neither of them had even mentioned but Brad had phoned to tell her had come in.

She had just dropped off the tractor part Pete had put in the back of her little car and was told it would be ready at eleven o'clock. This meant she had to waste an hour in town. Her stomach did a small flip when she thought of all the work waiting for her at home. At seeding time, keeping tractors and implements working was everyone's first priority. Housekeeping chores were relegated to second place.

I'll never catch up. May as well just get a cup of coffee at Mel's Place.

She stepped onto the curb and then jumped back as a couple of kids zoomed straight toward her, the wheels of their skateboards making a *clack-clack* sound on the cracks in the sidewalk.

Their hurried "Sorry, lady" drifted behind them as they swooshed off again, weaving and bobbing past other pedestrians who alternately got out of the way or frowned at them.

What were they doing out of school?

Then she heard one of the boys call out, "Hey, Slater, catch up."

Slater? Sam?

She turned her head and there, coming toward her at top speed, was her grandson.

"Sam! What are you doing?"

Sam swerved, jumped off his board, and stomped on it to stop it. Then he hit its tail with his foot, launching the board upward, and caught it all in one neat motion. He shifted his backpack on one shoulder and looked at her, his expression defiant as he ran his hands through hair, damp at the ends.

Charlotte felt her stomach fall. "Sam, why aren't you in school?"

A flush stained Sam's neck, and his mouth became grim.

"C'mon, Slater. Let's go." The other two boys had skated back, and now were hovering a few feet from Charlotte. "We're gonna be late."

"I gotta go, Grandma," he mumbled.

"No. You need to explain."

"Slater. Chop, chop."

Sam glanced from Charlotte to the other boys, then jumped on his board and left.

Charlotte stared at his retreating back as anger and frustration did battle in her mind. Even Pete, outspoken as he was, had never openly defied her like that.

She knew one thing. As soon as he came home tonight, they were going to have a talk.

She drew in a steadying breath to still her pounding heart, feeling as if she were suffocating. Too many things were piling on top of her. Emily had been sulking all week and this morning had come downstairs wearing some ridiculous outfit and declaring to Bob that she wasn't going to eat breakfast.

Poor Christopher had simply slunk down in his chair, eating the cereal Charlotte had poured for him while trying to make himself invisible to both his siblings.

"Hey, Charlotte."

Melody Givens, a pink, purple, and apple green patterned apron swaddling her ample figure, waved at Charlotte as she strode down the sidewalk toward her.

"How are you doing?" Melody asked, juggling the mail stacked up on her arm and the grocery bags suspended from her hand.

"I'm fine. I was just coming for a cup of coffee." This was a big, fat lie, but Charlotte wasn't about to dump all her struggles on anyone else.

Charlotte pulled open the door of the coffee shop for Melody and followed her inside.

"Ginny, here's the stuff you needed," Melody called out as she walked behind the counter and around the corner into the kitchen.

Melody had gone for the homey, country look in her coffee shop when she redecorated a couple of years ago. Patterned curtains hung at the windows, and each table had its own individual quilted table runner. Various antiques were displayed on the walls. Melody liked to change the art on her walls regularly, and she had hung groupings of pictures of pioneers from the area for now. One was a copy of a picture of Bob's grandparents that Charlotte had donated.

The clock on the wall showed she had three-quarters of an hour before the tractor part would be ready.

"There, that's taken care of." Melody returned, wiping her hands on a towel. "You look like you could use that cup of coffee."

"It shows?" Charlotte gave her a weak smile, wondering if taking care of the kids for only a few weeks was already aging her.

"Little bit." Melody raised her hand, her thumb and finger measuring off an inch to show Charlotte precisely how much. She pointed her chin at an empty table by the window. "Sit down. I'll be with you right away."

She disappeared into the kitchen behind the counter and returned with a pot of coffee and two mugs. "I thought I would join you," she said, setting the mugs on the table and pouring the coffee. "If you don't mind."

"No. Of course not. If you're not too busy."

Melody laughed as she settled herself into the chair across from Charlotte. "This place is as quiet as a teenager in an old-age home. Besides, I've been meaning to call you for the past few days. Ashley wants to have Emily over for a sleepover this coming weekend."

"I didn't think they spent much time together at school." Charlotte took the cup Melody pushed toward her and spooned some sugar into it from the bowl sitting on the table.

"I don't know if they do, but Ashley wants to get to

know her better." Melody took a quick sip of her coffee. "I know I'm pretty biased, but the little girl has a big heart. She knows that Emily's been having a hard time lately."

"That is kind of her. Emily hasn't been doing very well this past week." Emily had been downright cranky. Bob was all for grounding her, but how can you ground a girl who never goes anywhere except school and down the road?

Melody gave Charlotte an encouraging smile. "And how have you been doing? You've got those I've-got-teenagers-in-the-house worry lines on your forehead." Melody swept her own hair aside and pointed to her own forehead. "See, I've got them too."

"Well, I've already raised three teenagers, so these lines on my forehead may be permanent—" Charlotte's voice trailed off as thoughts she had kept to herself threatened to spill out.

"But this situation is completely different. And harder."

Melody stirred her coffee. "These kids come to you half-grown and unknown."

Charlotte felt as if Melody had given voice to her own doubts and, at the same time, given her space to let those doubts air. "Melody, I feel like I've jumped halfway into an ongoing movie," Charlotte admitted. "I only have seconds to find out what's going on, and while that's happening, the movie keeps running."

Melody took a sip of coffee, her elbows resting on the table, the cup suspended between her hands. "Ashley's been saying Emily is having a difficult time as well."

Her voice released something in Charlotte and she felt as if she could tell this woman anything.

"We had an accident the other day because Emily was using her cell phone instead of doing what she was supposed to. So I took it away."

"So, as well as missing her mother and feeling lost in Nebraska, she's going through some texting withdrawals."

Charlotte couldn't help but smile as she nodded. Melody's breezy attitude about such serious issues made her feel that the situation might not be as dire as she thought. "I feel like I'm second-guessing my decision, though."

"Except you feel sorry for her at the same time," Melody put in.

Charlotte nodded. Melody had put her finger precisely on Charlotte's problem. "I know how to be a mother, or I thought I did until Denise left. I love being a grandmother. But now I'm trying to be both and I feel like every step I take is wrong."

"You must feel some resentment too. I know I would. Usually grandparents are supposed to be the ones who spoil the grandkids, not discipline them."

And for the first time since Denise's death, Charlotte felt that the feelings she hadn't dared to voice had finally been given shape.

"That's it exactly, Melody! I want to mother them, but I don't want to be their mother. I don't want to be the bossy disciplinarian. I want to have the same relationship I have with Bill and Anna's kids, but I can't. Not when they keep pushing and pushing."

Melody leaned back and folded her arms over her chest.

"Teens push boundaries because their lives are so confusing; they want to find out what will hold fast. The only way to find out is to push. Sam, Emily, and Christopher's lives are more confusing than most, so they'll probably push harder. Besides, you and the kids hardly know each other. Yes, they are your other grandchildren, but I'm guessing you and Denise didn't visit each other much."

"Or write each other. Or phone—" To her embarrassment and shame, Charlotte's throat thickened. She didn't want to cry. Once she started, she was afraid she couldn't stop.

"Denise was a private person," Melody continued quietly, as if she hadn't heard Charlotte's voice break; as if she couldn't see the threatening tears in Charlotte's eyes. "I was pretty good friends with her back then, but sometimes she would take off and hide away, all alone."

"Just like Emily does."

"Yeah. Except Denise would really try to be alone. At least when Emily retreats it's because she's trying to connect with her friends back in San Diego."

Charlotte sighed. "And now she can't. She must feel so cut off."

"Don't start second-guessing your own good judgment." Melody waved the comment away. "Trust me on this. Kids have a ton of communication options through the Internet. Facebook, MySpace, IM, chat rooms. Too many choices, if you ask me."

"I still am completely in the dark about it all. Bob and I got the computer so we could do the farm books. Then Pete decided we needed Internet access. Now the kids keep complaining about how slow it is." Charlotte raised her hands in a gesture of surrender.

"I don't think you need to know everything about the World Wide Web, but there are a few things you should watch for. Kids, especially if they are lonely, can get into a lot of trouble on the Web. You should move the computer where you can keep an eye on what they're doing. Get Pete to help out if you're not sure what's going on."

"He might not want to help."

"Doesn't matter. You can't take care of these kids alone. You need backup."

Charlotte gazed out the coffee shop's big front window.

"Melody, what should I do about the muffins?" Melody's assistant, Ginny, stood by the waist-high counter separating the kitchen from the rest of the café. Her hair net, hanging askew on her head, and her flushed face told Charlotte this woman needed Melody immediately. "I think I'll need to make another batch."

Melody turned to Charlotte and rolled her eyes. "Crisis time," she whispered.

Charlotte set her mug aside and started to slip on her jacket. "I've taken up enough of your time."

"Hey, my time is not taken up. It's given. So don't you ever worry about stopping in here again." Melody pushed herself up from the table, laid her hand on Charlotte's forearm, and squeezed. "Remember, all for one and one for all."

Amen, Charlotte thought to herself.

And as she left Mel's Place, she felt as if she could breathe again.

"I DON'T THINK YOU should give Emily her cell phone back until she shows she can be responsible." Bob picked up the remote control of the television and dropped into his recliner. "I'm still angry over what happened to Madison."

"Madison shouldn't have climbed that ladder. She never had before." Charlotte sat curled up in the chair across from Bob, her book open on her lap. Emily and Christopher were upstairs, doing homework.

Bob glared at her. "Don't tell me you're taking the girl's side now."

Charlotte glared back. "That girl is *your* granddaughter too."

Bob's frown deepened, as if he had to process that information.

"I was thinking we need to pay them an allowance."

Bob harrumphed. "Never did with our own kids. Don't need to mollycoddle these."

Charlotte felt the beginnings of a headache. Lately she felt as if she was betwixt and between; Bob and the way they'd always done things on one side, these hurting and vulnerable children on the other side.

Hurting and vulnerable children that were testing her on every level, she reminded herself.

Bob clicked on the television and another unresolved conversation was over. He leaned back, put the remote down, and crossed his arms over his chest.

Charlotte started reading. Then reread what she had just read. Unable to concentrate, she put the book down.

On top of the nondecision about Emily and her phone, she still had to deal with Sam.

As soon as Sam came home from school, he had headed to the shop to help Pete put the part back in the tractor. Charlotte had been reluctant to bring anything up over supper, and immediately after that, Pete and Sam had decided Sam needed some more driving lessons.

Charlotte glanced at the clock. They'd been gone forty-three minutes now. What could be taking so long?

She got up and looked out the window but couldn't see a truck in the yard. Had Pete taken him down the road already?

She glanced at Bob, who was asleep now, then turned down the volume of the television. She straightened the pile of magazines on the coffee table, plucked a dead leaf from a plant, then went upstairs to check on her other grandchildren.

She knocked lightly on Emily's door then opened it.

"How are things going?" she asked Emily, hunched over the books spread out on her bed.

"Good." Emily kept twisting her hair around her finger and didn't look up. Charlotte didn't push the issue. She closed the door and walked to Christopher's room.

Christopher was reading, his mouth moving with the words. Charlotte had to smile. Pete always did the same thing.

"Do you want to read downstairs?" Charlotte asked.

Christopher shook his head. "Grandpa always has the TV on too loud," he said. He put his book down. "Why does Grandpa even have the television on? All he does is sleep."

"I think the sound puts him to sleep."

"It keeps me awake."

Charlotte went further into his room and picked up a sock lying on the floor. "Did you have a good day today?" she asked, setting the sock beside its mate on the dresser.

"I found the kittens again. The mama cat moved them, but I found them." Christopher shifted, getting to his knees, his hands punctuating his conversation as his smile blossomed. "And the one kitten was snuggling right up to me. I think he likes me."

Charlotte smiled at his enthusiasm. "He probably does."

"I named him Lightning. Could I bring him into the house?"

Charlotte sat on the bed, close to Christopher, and smoothed out a wrinkle in the quilt. "Those cats are barn cats. They're used to being outdoors."

"But one could get used to being in the house."

"We'll see." Charlotte knew exactly what Bob would say to that, but she was reluctant to extinguish the light of hope that shone in Christopher's eyes.

Christopher's smile faded and he picked up his book. "My mom always said that too. Usually that meant no."

His casual reference to his mother created an ache below Charlotte's breastbone. She got up and touched Christopher lightly on the shoulder.

"But sometimes it meant yes, right?"

Christopher just shrugged, then picked up his book and returned to his reading.

"Twenty more minutes, okay?" Charlotte told Christopher.

He just nodded, not looking up.

As Charlotte went downstairs she heard voices. Pete and Sam, she thought, relief slivering through her.

"It's an old truck. A few ground gears isn't going to kill it," Pete said as they went into the porch.

Charlotte glanced at Bob, asleep in his chair, surprised that Pete's booming voice didn't wake him up. She thought of what Christopher had said. Bob had been sleeping more often the past few weeks and Charlotte had presumed this was his way of coping with stress.

For a moment she envied him his escape as she steeled herself to deal with Sam.

"Hey, Mom," Pete said, sauntering into the kitchen. "Sam and I will move the computer for you now."

"Why don't you go and unhook it by yourself," Charlotte said to Pete. "I need to talk to Sam first."

Sam's frown told her what he thought of that idea, but Pete glanced from Charlotte to Sam and thankfully understood what Charlotte wanted.

"Okeydokey." He saluted and jogged up the stairs, two at a time.

Sam hunched his shoulders and shoved his hands in his pockets.

"We'll sit by the kitchen table," Charlotte said, glancing at Bob once more, envying him his oblivion.

"Sounds important," he said, but his tone held a faint mockery that set Charlotte's teeth on edge.

"So, you were skateboarding through town today."

"You saw me." His sudden defensiveness did not bode well for the conversation.

"I was wondering why you weren't in school."

"I was on my way back from swimming. For PE."

Charlotte considered this. The high school's physical education department did use the pool at the town's rec center for swimming classes.

"The pool is down South Main Street."

Sam's reply was accentuated with the shrug she was now well acquainted with. "I took the long way around. Just for fun."

"All right. But should you be riding your skateboards on the sidewalks? Your friends almost ran into me. Isn't there anyplace else you can go?"

"We're not allowed to ride at the school, or in the parking lot, or most anyplace that has any paved spots. So, no. There isn't. This podunk town isn't set up for skateboarders. Or anything else, for that matter." He plopped back in his chair, his hands shoved in the front pocket of his hooded sweatshirt, his lips pressed together.

"I'm gonna need Sam's help up here, Ma," Pete called down from the top of the stairs.

Saved by the uncle, Charlotte thought as Sam leapt to his feet.

Fifteen minutes later the computer was hooked up in its new location, Charlotte's table in the corner of the family room.

"Great," Sam said as he turned it on. "Now I have no privacy whatsoever."

"Why do you need privacy?" Pete said, punching him lightly on the shoulder. "You boldly going on the Internet where no sixteen-year-old should ever go?"

"No." Sam scowled at his uncle. "It's just, I don't need

people looking over my shoulder every time I'm on the computer."

Oh yes, you do, Charlotte thought, remembering all the times he was holed up in the upstairs room. She couldn't help but remember what Melody had told her about all the options available to kids these days.

She needed to keep tabs on her grandchildren; she needed to stay on top of things.

Chapter Sixteen

Emily sniffed and used the cuff of her shirt to wipe away her tears.

It had taken her more than an hour of walking away from the farm before she dared sit down on the side of the road and let herself cry. The sun beat on her head and she was pretty sure the back of her blue jeans were dirty from the grass and gravel she'd sat in.

Her life sucked.

She missed her mom. Her brothers seemed to be settling into the farm life. And her grandmother hated her. Grandpa, well, he didn't notice much. Just slept in his recliner when he wasn't working.

Emily sniffed again, the silence that had pressed down on her ears broken by the sound of a truck engine coming down the road.

She scrambled to her feet, her heart pounding as the truck came nearer. Thousands of scenes of horror movies raced through her head. Movies where the dumb girl is stranded out in the middle of nowhere and a strange vehicle stops. That's when the music always got creepy.

She shot a panicked glance around. Nowhere to hide. Nowhere to run.

Why did she think taking off to avoid helping Grandma plant the garden was a good idea?

She could be shoving seeds in the ground right now instead of seeing herself ripped into tiny shreds.

But as the old, rusted truck came nearer, Emily's heart slowed down and she took a calming breath.

The lady behind the wheel was Mrs. Carter. The woman who had come this past Sunday and brought supper. A most delicious supper too, Emily had to admit. Better than any restaurant her mother ever took them to.

Mrs. Carter stopped beside Emily and rolled down her window. Today Grandma's friend wore her hair pulled back into a ponytail and tied with some kind of chiffon scarf. Her white sweater looked baggy and worn, like she'd had it for years. She didn't look like she cared much how she looked.

Which, actually, made her look kind of comfortable. Easy to be with.

"Hello, Emily. How are you?"

Soon to be in trouble, once Grandma found out she'd taken off; that's how she was.

"I'm fine," she replied with a totally fake smile.

"Nice day for a walk."

"Yeah. It is."

"Are you going back to the farm?"

Emily stood on the side of the road, her hands shoved in the pockets of her blue jeans. "No."

"How long have you been gone?"

"I dunno."

"Does your grandmother know you're here?"

"I just decided to go for a walk."

"You should probably come back to the farm with me," Hannah was saying. "I know Charlotte is probably worried sick about you."

"I doubt that," Emily said. She'd been sitting here, on the side of the road, for the past two hours and Grandma hadn't even come looking for her. "I think she's still mad at me."

"Not Charlotte. Your grandmother isn't that kind of person."

Emily shrugged her comments off. Mrs. Carter probably didn't know about Madison.

Though it had happened almost a week ago, Emily still felt sick when she remembered how Madison looked, lying on the ground at the bottom of the ladder. She wished she could turn back time and do it all differently.

"Let me take you back to the farm," Hannah insisted.

"That's okay. I'll walk back."

"I'm heading there right now anyway. Brought your grandma and grandpa some baking."

Emily looked past her to the containers piled on the seat beside her. She caught a whiff of cinnamon and, even better, chocolate. Her mouth watered.

"And the sooner you come, the sooner you'll have a chance to taste my baking. Walking back will take you forever and a day," Hannah said.

"Just twenty minutes."

"Are you sure?"

"Yeah. I'm sure. Tell Grandma I'll be back in a bit."

"Okay. But don't say I didn't offer." Hannah gave her a smile, then slowly drove off.

A few seconds later, she stopped and reversed.

Now what did she want?

Mrs. Carter drove until she was alongside Emily again and rolled down her window.

"Emily, I know this is hard for you. Goodness knows you've had a rough time. But you need to know that your grandma and grandpa really care about you. They love you so much and missed you a lot. I often got to hear how Charlotte wished she could see you kids." Hannah gave her a quick smile. "Just thought I should let you know that."

Emily wanted to believe that her grandparents had missed them. "But why didn't they come then?"

Hannah pressed her lips together and sighed. "Truth to tell, it was hard for Charlotte and Bob to leave the farm. And, well—" she looked away, as if she wasn't sure whether she should say the next thing.

"Well, what?"

Hannah sighed. "Your mom didn't really encourage them to come. In fact, there were times she asked them not to."

Emily frowned. Why would she do that?

"I can see that you're not sure, but I knew your mom as a young girl. She could get kind of stuck on an idea and you couldn't budge her with a ten-foot pole." Hannah fluttered her hand. "And you never mind what I just said. I loved your mom. She was like my own daughter. So it's been hard for me too, knowing she's gone. I can't imagine how much it hurts your grandmother."

Emily wasn't sure about that.

"I better go. You really don't want a lift?"

"I'll be okay. Thanks."

Through the dust of Hannah's truck tires, Emily saw her

looking in her rearview mirror, as if making sure Emily was actually going back to the farm.

As if Emily had anywhere else to go.

She doubted that Bekka and her friends noticed that she hadn't been able to call them this week. They didn't chat with her on the computer, and it had been days since they put anything on her wall on Facebook, even though she wrote on theirs.

It was like she had dropped out of their lives.

She needed her friends so badly. They remembered funny little things about her mother, things that she wanted to talk about so she wouldn't forget what her mom was like.

She stopped, holding her stomach. She missed her mother so much it hurt. She couldn't tell Christopher because she didn't want to see him cry. And every time she tried to talk to Sam he got mad.

Even though Hannah said that Grandma and Grandpa missed her mother too, she wondered. She had never seen either of them cry. Not even at the funeral or since then. It was like they didn't even miss their own daughter.

Emily felt a sob hiccup in her chest and she swallowed and swallowed. She had to stop. She couldn't start crying again. Not way out here on this empty, lonely road so far from home.

She waited a moment, looked around as if maybe someone else might come along.

All she saw was an empty stretch of road.

So, with a sigh, she started back to the farm.

Chapter Seventeen

"She was just sitting on the side of the road?"

Charlotte tapped the carrot seeds into the furrow. Her hand trembled a little and she spilled a few extra seeds in one spot. With her forefinger she gently nudged them along the row. The chore she'd been meaning to do for weeks was finally getting close to being scratched off her to-do list.

She would have been done sooner if her granddaughter hadn't made a sudden and mysterious disappearance.

Hannah knelt at the other end, pushing dirt over the furrow and patting it down. "I told her I would give her a ride, but she said she would sooner walk."

"She was probably trying to get out of helping with the garden. I guess it's not her idea of a fun Saturday morning." Charlotte couldn't help the grumbly tone that slipped into her voice. When she found out that Emily wasn't with the horses or wasn't in the barn with the kittens, she had run back up to her granddaughter's room, just to make sure.

Her bed was neatly made, much to Charlotte's surprise, but her clothes lay scattered over the floor.

"Maybe she just wanted to be on her own," Hannah said.

"She didn't need to go two miles down the road to be on her own." Charlotte felt the beginnings of a headache.

Since she had started working in the garden, the sun had grown hotter, beating down on her unprotected head. She should have worn her hat, but she thought she'd be done by now and would have been if Emily had helped. Thankfully, Christopher was able to pitch in. He helped where he could and he did make the job go a little faster.

"I've marked the rows of beans, Grandma," Christopher said. "Now what?"

"You can make up some markers for the carrot rows." Charlotte hunched up her shoulder and wiped a stream of perspiration from her cheek, leaving a streak on her blue blouse. For just a moment she felt jealous of Pete, Bob, and Sam working in the air-conditioned comfort of the cabs of the tractors.

"Is Emily coming yet?" Christopher asked.

"Who knows?" Charlotte said, unable to keep the anger out of her voice.

"Christopher, honey, could you get me a drink of water from the house please?" Hannah asked.

Christopher jumped to his feet, brushed the dirt off the knees of his jeans, and ran across the yard to the house. To Charlotte's surprise, Toby got up and followed him.

Probably hoping she might finagle some extra food from the youngster, Charlotte thought.

Hannah glanced over Charlotte's shoulder, as if making sure he was out of earshot, then turned back to her friend.

"When I first saw Emily sitting on the side of the road, she had her head down on her arms. I'm pretty sure she was crying."

Charlotte sat back on her heels, her own emotions a confusion of frustration, anger, and sympathy for her granddaughter.

"I just wish she would talk to me about what's bothering her, not run off and make me bounce between feeling worried about her one minute and angry the next."

"She was headed home when I left her," Hannah said. "Do you want me to drive back and check on her?"

"No. She'll come back here eventually. She doesn't really have any other place to go." And as Charlotte spoke the words, the reality of Emily's situation suddenly struck home.

"Which, I'm guessing, is part and parcel of her problem," Hannah said. "Charlotte, I know I didn't have kids and I'm not in any position to give you advice, but I think she feels stuck in a rut she can't see her way out of."

"Well, unfortunately that's something neither Bob nor I can change." A hint of panic clutched her midsection at the immutability of the situation, both for Emily and them. "She has to accept that."

"Maybe just give her time and space. Love her like you can, and she will come around."

Was it really as easy as the words tripping so easily off Hannah's tongue? She loved her grandchildren fiercely, but love wasn't enough.

"What about putting on a happy face?" Charlotte said, hoping Hannah caught the faintly teasing note in her voice.

"Oh, that's important too," Hannah added, looking very

serious. "After all, as it says in Proverbs, 'A cheerful look brings joy to the heart, and good news gives health to the bones.' So you know that I'm right about that."

"Well, we could use some good news," Charlotte said. "And Bob could pay better attention to his health. After Denise..." She let her voice trail off. "I guess I'm just feeling more vulnerable and rather overwhelmed. Sam's been defying me, and Emily, well, you saw the result of that situation."

"You need to come back to prayer group. You could use the support."

"I hope to as soon as things slow down here." A sigh escaped Charlotte's lips

"Oh, my dear friend," Hannah said, shaking her head. "I wish I could take part of your struggles. All I can tell you is, 'Weeping may remain for the night, but joy comes before the morning.'"

"I've tried not to cry, you know," Charlotte confessed. "For the sake of the children. I want them to feel like there is some security in their life."

She wanted to say more, to explain how confused she felt at times, but then Christopher came back from the house carefully carrying a glass of water.

"Did you see? Toby came with me," Christopher said, his voice holding a note of pleasure.

"I did. I think she knows you take good care of her," Charlotte said.

"I do." Christopher beamed and stroked Toby's head, his face split by a happy grin.

In his presence Hannah and Charlotte's conversation

shifted to gardening and some community gossip, a topic Hannah never tired of.

They finished the garden, cleaned up the tools, and went into the house. Still no Emily.

Fifteen minutes later, Christopher was happily swapping gems in a noisy computer game called Bejeweled, and Hannah and Charlotte were buttering bread for sandwiches to take out to the men working in the fields.

The slamming of the porch door made Charlotte glance at the clock. Surely the men weren't coming to the yard for lunch?

But then Emily marched into the kitchen.

"There you are," Charlotte said, relief battling with frustration. "Just in time to help me and Hannah take lunch to the men."

"I'm tired, Grandma."

Charlotte was sure she was. The poor girl must have walked over four miles already this morning.

"You won't have to walk. We'll be driving out to the field."

"Can't Sam bring the lunch?"

"Sam is helping Uncle Pete and Grandpa." Charlotte forced herself to remember what Hannah told her. Her granddaughter's sorrow was as great as her own, if not greater. However, Emily needed to obey her grandmother. Charlotte needed to regain control of this household and the only way this family would work was if everyone did what was expected.

Christopher shot a worried look over his shoulder at the two of them.

"I can help," he offered, slipping off his chair. "Emily doesn't have to go."

Hannah gave Charlotte an imperceptible nod.

Though it bothered her to give in, she had to agree with Hannah. Then she looked back at Emily. To her surprise, a tear slipped down her granddaughter's cheek. The sight melted her determination.

"Oh, honey—" she said, reaching out to the lost and hurting girl.

Emily turned and ran up the stairs.

Charlotte was about to follow her, but Hannah held her back.

"Let her feel like she has some control," Hannah said. "It's like that one episode of *The Partridge Family*—"

Charlotte's frustration spilled out. "This isn't a television show, Hannah. This is my life. There's no writer putting together a happy ending. No director calling 'Cut' when the scene doesn't work. Life just keeps going and going and you have to deal with each thing as it comes, and things seem to keep coming."

She pushed her hair back from her face, but as soon as her anger settled, she wished she could take the words back. She had no right to disparage her friend's advice, regardless of the source.

"So if it keeps coming and coming, maybe this time around you can get by with a little help from the friends in your life." Hannah gave her a careful smile, as if unsure of her words' reception.

"What do you mean?"

Hannah dropped the bag of grapes into a colander and turned on the water. "I loved your kids like they were my own. But I never felt I could say anything about them to you. I never felt like I could give you or Bob advice about them, though I wanted to."

Charlotte glanced over at Christopher, who was once again engrossed in his game, then turned to her friend. "Things like what?"

Hannah pressed her lips together as if she wanted to hold back her next comment. But then she turned the water off and faced Charlotte head on.

"You and Bob were always so strict with the kids, especially Pete and Denise. I know you loved them, but there were times I thought maybe you could have eased off a little. Been a bit kinder and gentler. I remember Denise—" Hannah stopped then and looked away, holding her hand up as if anticipating Charlotte's question. "I'm sorry. I'm talking out of turn."

Her mention of Denise's name triggered the avalanche of doubts in Charlotte's mind.

"Hannah, you're my best friend. If you can't tell me what you were going to say and trust that I can hear it, then I'm not much of a friend, am I?"

Hannah's faint smile was encouraging and frightening at the same time.

"I'm sorry I got angry with you." Charlotte moved closer, lowering her voice. "I feel overwhelmed. Please tell me what you were going to say about Denise."

Hannah took a deep breath, fortifying herself. "Denise used to come over and complain. I never paid much attention to that because I know that—well, okay, just like in *The Waltons*, the kids would complain . . . but anyway, she wasn't always happy, and we would talk. She said that sometimes she felt like she never measured up. Like she always fell short."

"In what way?"

"Bill was so smart and he always did the right thing and Denise and Pete, they were their own persons and they, well, didn't. I knew where they were coming from. I had the same thing in my family. My older sister was so much smarter than me, so I knew exactly what Denise felt like. I wanted to tell you but she asked me not to. So many times I felt betwixt and between."

"So do you know why she ran away?"

Hannah shook her head as she wiped her hands on the towel.

"Could you guess? I promise I won't be offended." Charlotte wrapped her arms even tighter around her stomach. "I need to know. I feel like there are too many questions I'll never get the answers to. They clang around in my head and go around and around."

"You know, they say it's always darkest before the dawn. So maybe right now you're in that darkness. But the light will come." Hannah touched Charlotte on the shoulder and gave her a sympathetic glance.

"As for your daughter, Denise had her own problems. She wasn't an easy kid to raise. The problems you had with her weren't only because of you and Bob. She had her own issues too. I think she wanted to prove to you she could do something on her own and it backfired. I mean, look what that Kevin did to her. I'm sure that made her ashamed. She was a proud person."

Charlotte pushed back her hair from her forehead, trying to erase the haunting memories.

"You were a good mother, Charlotte. I'm sorry I made it sound like you weren't. What I'm trying to say is you don't have to raise these kids of Denise's all on your lonesome. People want to help. People like me. People like Melody and Rosemary. We all want to help you with these kids."

A curious warmth enveloped Charlotte. She and Bob did not have to be alone in this.

"Thanks, Hannah. That's good to know."

"I like these kids," Hannah said. "They can thank their lucky stars that you and Bob took them in. I think you'll be good for them." She gave a wistful smile. "And maybe this is a chance for you to do things differently."

"Our kids didn't turn out that badly," Charlotte protested.

"No. Of course not. I wasn't trying to criticize. Everyone, no matter how good a job they do with their kids, has some that turn out and some that don't. I never had kids of my own. But I loved your kids and I want to help you with these."

"Thanks, Hannah."

"And I suppose we better get these sandwiches delivered," Hannah said, her voice suddenly brusque and businesslike. "Can't let the boys miss their lunch. If they're anything like Frank, they're working with one eye on the sky, one ear to the radio, and their hands clenching the wheel."

"Not to mention the way they're always listening to the

grain reports," Charlotte added, thankful for Hannah's tactful switch to safer topics.

Hannah rolled her eyes. "Don't I know it! Frank is convinced that if he misses even one broadcast he might miss out on some vital piece of news that could change the face of farming."

As they packed up the lunch, the talk turned to the easier subjects of crops and yields and all the things that farmers' wives who are involved in the family business talk about.

But while they worked, part of Charlotte's attention was focused on the girl upstairs.

"Come on, Christopher. Time to go," Charlotte said as they closed the lid on the cooler.

Christopher slid off his chair and went running to the kitchen.

Just as they were leaving, Charlotte heard Emily's feet on the stairs. She stopped beside the pantry, her hands strung up in her back pockets. "Are you leaving?" she asked.

Charlotte nodded, but remembering what Hannah said, didn't extend the invitation again.

Emily's glance slid over to Christopher, who was shutting down the computer. "Are you going, Christopher?"

"Yeah. I want to see the tractors. Maybe Uncle Pete will let me ride in one too."

"Too?"

"Sam is riding in it now," Christopher said. "Uncle Pete said he could learn to drive one."

Charlotte could see Emily digesting this piece of information.

"Oh yea. That sounds like fun." Her tone was sarcastic, but Charlotte saw something else flicker in her expression. *Interest? Jealousy?*

"So, I guess I should come along too," she said, shifting her weight from one foot to another.

"It'll be fun. Mrs. Carter has some great snacks." Christopher beamed at the thought.

"Sure. Okay. Whatever."

"Here, you can carry the cooler." Hannah held out the scratched and beaten plastic container in one hand and a dark, delectable square in the other. "And as a reward for helping me, you can have a brownie."

To Charlotte's surprise, Emily took both the cooler and the brownie. She took a tiny bite of the iced confection, then grinned. "Whoa, that's yummy." She licked her fingers then wiped them on her blue jeans. She took Christopher's proffered hand and walked out of the kitchen.

As the door fell shut behind them, Charlotte released her breath, unaware she'd even been holding it.

"I think she'll be okay." Hannah gave Charlotte a careful smile.

"I hope so." Charlotte wished she could share Hannah's optimism.

But as they drove to the field, Christopher chatting in the backseat with his big sister who was responding in kind, Charlotte felt things might be coming together after all.

Chapter Eighteen

Did you enjoy yourself at Ashley's house the other night?" Charlotte rinsed a plate and stacked it on the drying rack for Emily to dry.

Today was Tuesday, and thankfully, Charlotte hadn't heard from the school in the past few days concerning Christopher. In fact, when he came home today, he was chattering about a friend he had made.

"Ashley seems like a nice girl," Charlotte added, in response to Emily's curt nod.

"Yeah. She's kinda cool."

That reply isn't going to generate much conversation, Charlotte thought, watching the suds bubble up as she immersed the stack of salad plates in the water.

Bob didn't think she should be helping the kids each evening with the dishes. Their own children had always washed and dried dishes by themselves, but after her conversations with Hannah and Melody, Charlotte had added her name to the chore list under "dishes." She thought the mindless work of washing and drying dishes would give her some one-on-one time with the children.

On Monday she and Sam had talked about skateboarding. She had found out more than she might ever need to know about trucks and wheels and decks and ollies. But Sam seemed pleased with her interest.

Her conversation with Christopher was a halting one about Toby and cats and kittens and how he'd love to have a kitten in the house.

Emily, however, had proven harder to draw out. Charlotte suspected the few altercations they'd had didn't help, but that conflict was precisely the reason she needed to keep trying.

"Did you want to have her over some time?" Charlotte asked.

"What's there to do here?"

"You could take the horses out."

"I don't know how to ride."

"I'm sure Uncle Pete could teach you."

More silence followed that suggestion, broken by the sound of the two boys hooting with laughter at some old computer game someone at school had given Christopher.

Charlotte was scrambling. She and Emily had the hardest time communicating. A feeling of *déjà vu* caught her by the throat.

"Have you managed to talk to your San Diego friends on the computer?"

Emily's only reply was a quick shake of her head.

"I thought you had that Facebook thing?" Charlotte pressed.

"Yeah. I post on their wall, but they haven't put much on mine."

"Wall?"

This question netted her a frown. "You don't know?"

"I know little about computers. Just enough to do the farm bookkeeping," Charlotte admitted with a quick laugh. "Pete showed me how to surf the Web, but the only place I go is a recipe Web site and one about quilting."

"So you know about Web sites?" Emily asked, taking a dripping plate from the drying rack.

"Yes."

"Well, Facebook is sort of like a Web site. You can set up your own page and invite friends, and only your invited friends can put stuff on your wall."

"And you have a site like that?"

"Yeah. All my friends do."

"Is that allowed?"

"Yeah. Mom didn't let me start my page until I turned fourteen, but some of my friends were on even younger."

"And now your friends aren't writing to you?"

Emily shook her head and for a few more minutes they worked side by side in silence.

The only thing that still needed washing was the pot that had held the potatoes. Charlotte reached for it, wondering how slowly she could wash it without looking like she was washing it slowly. She wanted to tell Emily what was on her mind and her heart. She wanted to tell her that she loved her, and that she mattered to her. But she didn't know how to broadcast those deep, serious thoughts across the chasm that yawned between them.

Then she heard a faint sniff and with a covert, sideways glance she saw Emily quickly swiping at her cheeks.

She took a chance.

"So what do you think of their friendship now?" she asked, keeping her voice low and her eyes focused on the pot in the sink.

Emily sighed as she reached for a cup in the rack. "Melody said they're not real friends if they can forget about me that quick."

Why did she feel this faint prick of jealousy at the thought of her granddaughter confiding in someone else's mother?

But she remembered Hannah's comments about people wanting to help her. She didn't have to do this all on her own.

"Well, Mrs. Givens—" She caught herself. "—Melody was right. I had some friends who moved away after high school. Some still send me Christmas cards. Others I never heard from again."

Emily picked up one of the pots and started drying it as slowly as Charlotte was washing hers.

"That happens, I guess." Emily sounded so casual that Charlotte wondered if she had imagined her granddaughter's sorrow.

"It doesn't have to happen that way. When you have good friends, they stay by you."

Emily just shrugged as she set down the clean pot.

"Hannah, for instance, is the kind of friend who has been a support to me the past few weeks. I'm just getting to know Melody better after all these years. I think she would be a good friend."

"So you're saying Bekka and my other friends weren't?"

Charlotte shot Emily a sidelong glance. Her granddaughter's lips were set in firm lines, as if she was challenging Charlotte to agree.

Charlotte set the last pot on the draining rack with a feeling of finality. Emily sounded like she was closing off to her again.

"No. I'm just trying to say that a good friend stays by you. Helps you. In my case, prays with me."

Emily grabbed the pot but then lowered it to the counter, as if it was too heavy to hold. Her breath eased out on a sigh.

"So am I a lousy friend?" Her voice held a plaintive note that created an answering hitch in Charlotte's heart. "Is that why they're leaving me alone?"

"Oh, honey. That's not what I meant." Charlotte ignored the water dripping off her hand, took a huge chance and put her arm around Emily's shoulder, bringing the girl to her side. "You tried very hard to stay in touch. I feel bad that I had to take your phone away—"

"No. I'm sorry." Emily gave an ineffectual wipe at the pot, looking down. "I shouldn't have been on the phone when I was supposed to be watching out for Madison. I still feel so bad about that."

"She's okay. Nothing bad happened."

"I know." Emily swallowed and then, to Charlotte's surprise and delight, Emily leaned closer to Charlotte and laid her head on her grandmother's shoulder. "I'm sorry, Grandma."

Love and joy blossomed in Charlotte's heart, and she put both arms around Emily, holding her close. "It's okay, honey. I forgave you long ago."

Emily's only reply was a muffled sniff.

"Grandma, can I have a cookie—" Sam's voice trailed off as he entered the kitchen.

Charlotte looked up in time to see Sam backing away,

his hands up as if in surrender. "I don't wanna know," he said. "If it's girl stuff, I just don't wanna know."

Emily sniffed once more, then laughed. "Sam hates it when he sees me and Mom crying." She sniffed again. "Actually, *saw* me and Mom crying."

"Most men don't know what to do around tears," Charlotte said, letting Emily's correction slip by. She stroked her cheek, then gave her a gentle smile.

Emily studied her as if waiting for something more, then she returned Charlotte's smile and went back to drying her pot.

They finished the dishes in silence again, but this time Charlotte felt the connection between them.

"Is it okay if I go upstairs?" Emily asked when they were done.

"Of course."

"I mean, you don't have any more work for me to do?"

"No. I think we're finished here. Thanks, Emily."

Emily paused at the entrance to the family room, then joined her brothers at the computer instead.

Charlotte finished wiping the counters, drained the sink, and glanced around the worn but tidy kitchen.

It was exactly the same as before supper, yet a different feeling pervaded the atmosphere.

It felt more like a home.

"WHAT ARE YOU LOOKING AT?"

Behind her, Charlotte could hear the crackle of pages as Bob lowered his newspaper.

Charlotte stepped away from the rain-streaked window. "Just checking to see if Christopher is coming."

The rain that had started Tuesday evening had continued all day today, effectively keeping Pete and Bob out of the fields and the kids in the house. Christopher had finally put on a raincoat and headed out the door, Toby in tow.

"Where is he?"

"Playing with Toby and the cat."

"In the rain?"

"No. He's in the barn."

"And the other kids?"

"Pete took them into town. Said something about taking Sam to take the test for his learner's permit so he can drive to school."

Bob harrumphed. "As long as he's the one to be teaching that boy to drive."

"You used to teach our children," Charlotte teased.

"I used to do a lot of things," Bob replied, then gave Charlotte a quick smile. "Things seem to be settling a bit, don't they? With the kids?"

Charlotte nodded. "I think the kids enjoyed youth group on Sunday. Emily and I had a nice chat over the dishes the other day." Charlotte glanced back at the potatoes cooking on the stove. "I feel like we're getting somewhere, though there are still things that will take work."

"That won't change," Bob said, turning the page of his paper.

Charlotte straightened a pillow, folded an afghan. "I wasn't just talking about the kids. I was also talking about us."

Bob lowered the paper, frowning at her. "Us?"

"I think we need to make a few changes in our life for the sake of these kids."

Bob's frown deepened. "We took the kids in and are raising them. What else could we do?"

Charlotte perched herself on the edge of the couch, thinking she could start with the easy things.

"Christopher would love to have a cat in the house."

Bob snorted. "Cats don't belong in the house. Nor do dogs," he warned. "Just in case he wants Toby in the house as well."

"Lots of people have cats for pets and some people even buy dog beds for their dog."

"You don't have a cat for a pet, a cat has you."

The line was an old one, but it always made Charlotte smile. "He always has to go to the barn to play with them."

"It gets him outside. He'd be in the house all the time, otherwise."

"That's not a problem. He goes exploring all the time."

"Well, I think it's silly." His stock reply told Charlotte she was making some headway. This also meant, from a strategic point of view, it was time to retreat to let him study the matter for a while. In a few days she would approach it again. Maybe from a different angle to throw him off a bit.

Right now she needed to save her energy for the next skirmish. "There's another thing we need to talk about."

Bob nodded, his eyes still on his paper.

"It's important."

"I'm listening."

She knew he was, but at the same time, for this conversation she wanted his undivided attention. So she walked over to his chair, sat down on the coffee table facing him, and gently pulled the paper down so she could see him face to face.

He shot her a questioning glance over his glasses, then admitted defeat and lowered the paper to his lap.

"Thank you." She bit her lips, praying for the right words to broach this delicate subject. "I want to talk to you about our devotional time after supper. If we are truly going to be raising these children and responsible for their spiritual well-being, I think we need to meet them where they're at. They're not used to a lot of Bible reading and I think maybe we could start with a story Bible."

"Story Bible." The intonation in Bob's voice told her as much as the faint snort he added to his comment. "The Bible was good enough for our kids and it's good enough for our grandkids."

"Why did I know you were going to say that?"

"Then why did you bring it up?"

Charlotte pressed back her irritation with her husband. "Because I think it's important."

"The Word of God is important. I'm not going to see that my own grandchildren get some watered-down version of it."

"We could read a devotional book with Bible verses."

"We're still reading some person's interpretation of the Word of God."

Charlotte stifled a sigh. "Isn't that what we get in church on Sunday?"

"That's completely different." Bob's gaze slid to his paper, finding refuge there.

"It's exactly the same thing." Exasperation with her husband edged her voice.

"Charlotte, we are not going to continue this conversation." Bob was growing angry too.

"Just because you say it's over doesn't mean it is."

He lifted his paper a fraction.

"Don't ignore me, Bob."

"Then don't keep talking."

"I don't like it when you don't pay attention to me."

"I always pay attention to you. I just did, didn't I?"

There. He had done it again. He had taken an important discussion and shifted it to the same old ground they always went to when they had a fight. She, once again, was silly enough to follow him along the rabbit trails he led her down.

Charlotte tapped her foot as she marshaled her defenses. She wasn't finished with this and was about to press on when the porch door burst open and excited voices filled the entrance.

Sam came into the house waving a small card. "I got it. I got it," he shouted, grinning from ear to ear, Emily behind him looking a bit jealous. "I got it first try."

As Charlotte got up from the couch, she felt as if time had tumbled backward and it was Bill coming into the house bursting with pride, his younger sister following him.

"Well, now. Let's see." She knew what was required of her.

She took the proffered card with its official-looking seal and the picture that made her grandson look like a criminal on the lam. "Would you look at that? Congratulations, Sam." She admired it a few moments, then handed back the card, his entrée into the world of internal combustion engines.

She wished she could get more excited, but after teaching three kids to drive, she knew what lay ahead.

White-knuckle moments inside a vehicle, and worrying moments outside a vehicle, watching as it left the driveway holding precious children. The hours spent praying that each would return home in the same shape they left.

"Good job, son," Bob was saying, also admiring the permit. "I think it took your Uncle Pete two tries to get it."

"Three, actually," Pete said, standing behind Sam and looking as proud as his nephew.

"Uncle Pete let me drive the truck home," Sam said.

Charlotte and Bob exchanged cautious glances. They were thinking the same thing. Pete's truck now. Their vehicle next.

"He did real good too." Pete clapped Sam on the shoulder.

Sam grinned at his uncle, who winked at him.

In that brief moment of connection between uncle and nephew, Charlotte caught a glimpse of what Hannah had been talking about. Letting other people be involved in taking care of the kids. Allowing others to take some of the burden.

"Well, I think this calls for a celebration," Bob said. "How about bringing out that pail of peanut butter chocolate explosion ice cream for dessert?"

"What?" Pete cried out. "Since when did we have ice cream in the house?"

"Funny thing about that," Charlotte said. "It was in the freezer when the kids and I came back from San Diego."

When she found it, she had hidden it away from Bob and his insatiable sweet tooth, hoping to find a time to sample it when he wasn't around. Obviously she hadn't hidden it well enough.

Bob caught her eye and winked. Somehow the wink annoyed her. She was still angry with him, but he seemed to think the argument they'd had a few moments ago was done.

Still, it was time for a strategic retreat, so she put a smile on her face. "Excellent idea."

After a nutritious supper of barbecued chicken, mashed potatoes, salad, and green beans, Bob plunked on the table a pail of sugar-saturated, trans-fat-loaded ice cream. With peanut butter swirls, no less.

And as Charlotte scooped up the ice cream and passed it around the dinner table, everyone got to hear yet again how Sam had almost missed two questions, but thanks to reading the manual and taking the practice test on the computer, he had managed to answer them properly.

As they all dug into the sinfully delicious treat, the mood around the table was upbeat and fun, and Charlotte wished she could catch it, bottle it, and save it.

She tried to catch Bob's eye when the last bit of ice cream was licked off the bowl and it was time for devotions. He was reaching for the Bible.

She saw his hand hesitate, but then he pulled the Bible off the shelf, opened it up and slipped his glasses on.

Charlotte sat back and crossed her arms. She wasn't done. Not by a long shot.

Chapter Nineteen

"Why can't he drive, Dad?" Pete stood beside the car Sunday morning, his hands on his hips as he faced his father. The bill of his cap cast a shadow over his face, but Charlotte read his frustration with Bob in the set of his mouth. "He drove home from town and he's driven the car around the yard and down the road a couple of times. What's the difference?"

"The difference is he'll have his grandmother, me, and his brother and sister with him." Bob spoke quietly, but his voice held a note that normally brooked no argument.

A few moments ago Charlotte had taken Emily and Christopher to the car, dressed for church, fully expecting to see Bob at the wheel, but instead they had come across this scenario.

Charlotte knew that when Sam got his permit this would be coming. She just didn't think it would happen this soon.

"So go slow. He wouldn't be any different from any other Sunday driver," Pete retorted.

Charlotte looked from Sam, standing beside his uncle, to Bob to Pete. The three of them formed a triangle of hope, reluctance, and stubbornness.

Bob shook his head, undid the bottom button of his suit jacket, and got in the driver's seat of the car.

"You've got to give him a chance sooner or later, Dad," Pete said.

"I know." Bob closed the door on Pete and, it seemed, the conversation.

A palpable tension filled the air as Pete lifted his hands toward Sam in a gesture of surrender.

Sam ducked his head and got into the backseat. Christopher and Emily followed suit.

"I don't know why Dad's being so ornery lately," Pete said to Charlotte, arguing Sam's case as Emily shut the door behind her. "Sam's a careful kid. Dad needs to give him a chance."

Charlotte shot a quick glance behind her to make sure the vehicle's doors were closed. She turned her attention back to her son.

"Pete, I'm not comfortable with Sam driving either. Not yet," Charlotte said quietly. She fought her natural inclination to reticence, remembering what Hannah said about letting other people in. "We're still feeling vulnerable . . ."

But she couldn't finish the sentence.

Pete scratched his temple with his index finger, adjusted the fit of his cap, then sighed. "Okay. I'll back off, for your sake. But sooner or later Dad needs to trust Sam. I know what it feels like." Pete stopped, then stepped back as if removing himself from what he just said. He thrust his chin toward the car. "Dad's getting antsy. You better go."

Charlotte gave him a cautious smile. "We'll take it one step at a time."

As they drove away, Charlotte watched her son in the side mirror of the car and wished, yet again, that he would come with them to church.

Half an hour later Charlotte and Bob were settled in their usual pew, taking up more space than they did before, but exactly as much space as they did when their kids were still at home.

Sunlight from the arched windows lining the white stucco walls poured in like a benediction on the moment.

We've come full circle, Charlotte thought, looking around the church, so familiar to her. She had helped Rosemary make the spring banner that hung on the wall behind the pulpit. The brightly colored stripes of the banner were overlaid with the words *I Make All Things New.*

Charlotte reread the words, yearning for their simple comfort as she glanced sidelong at the children sitting beside her and Bob. She felt as if so much of her life had been taken apart and broken down.

Please, Lord, help us rebuild. We need you to make our lives new.

And at the same time, as she saw her grandchildren sitting on the same wooden pew their mother had sat on, she felt a sense of rightness flicker in her heart. This is where the children belonged. Beside them, in church. She put one arm around Christopher and squeezed his shoulder. He gave her a shy, sideways glance and granted her a careful smile. Emily caught the movement and she too smiled at Charlotte.

God is faithful, she thought, allowing herself the joy of

the moment. She slipped her arm through the crook Bob's elbow made as he read the bulletin.

He didn't look at her, but the smile teasing the corner of his mouth acknowledged the small moment of affection and connection.

She looked around the church and felt as if their little family was slowly settling into their place in this community.

CHARLOTTE PUT THE COFFEEPOT on and glanced at the clock. The rain at noon had sent Pete and Bob home from the fields, so she expected them in any minute.

She put out a plate of cookies and cake, her guilt offering. The kids loved homemade baked goods, and Bob and Pete were always ready for sweets, even though Bob shouldn't have any. She had made up a plate of cheese and crackers for him.

The shrill ringing of the phone pierced the silence.

She wiped her hands on her apron and answered it. "Hello, Charlotte speaking."

"Is this Mrs. Stevenson?"

The voice was vaguely familiar, but Charlotte couldn't place it. "Yes. Who is calling?"

"Tonya. Tonya Beckson. I live in the same building as Denise and the kids did? They were staying with me?"

Was she asking her or telling her, Charlotte wondered. "Oh yes, I recognize you now. Hello. How are you doing?"

"Fine. I was just wondering how the kids are. I've thought of them lots and wanted to make sure they're okay. Can I talk to them?"

Charlotte glanced at the clock. "That's very nice of you. They should be home any minute now. Do you want to call back?"

Despite her offer, Charlotte was reluctant to let Tonya talk to the kids. While she was grateful for Tonya's help after Denise's accident, she'd also been glad to take the kids away from the woman's gloomy apartment. Even in the middle of the day, the curtains had been drawn over the windows, and the television blared from one corner of a living room full of scattered clothes and pizza boxes. The kitchen counters were barely visible under the piles of dirty dishes and pots.

"Nah. Just let them know I called. Tell them that if they ever want to come back, they can crash at my place anytime."

"Do they know your number?"

"Yeah, but you know what? I'll just send a text to Emily's phone. Then she can call me when she wants."

Charlotte was about to tell her that Emily no longer had her phone when Tonya unexpectedly hung up. Probably to call Emily on her cell phone, which now resided in a dresser drawer in Charlotte and Bob's bedroom.

"Is the coffee on?" Pete called out, the door slamming shut behind him. He came into the kitchen shaking his head. "I think we got company. Looks like the pastor just now drove into the yard."

Charlotte's hand flew to her hair. Pastor Evans? Now?

She should have figured on a visit sometime. He did mention on Sunday that he wanted to drop in. She only wished he had phoned in advance.

She heard voices, the door opening again. It was too late to go and change.

"We've got company, Char," Bob was saying as he stepped into the porch. "Best put on another cup."

If she'd known she was going to be serving their pastor, she would have used the good china. Instead she chose her best mug, pulled a few napkins out of a drawer and set them out by the plate of cake and cookies, hoping the presence of paper napkins was sufficient to dress up the snacks.

"Charlotte, sorry to drop in unexpected like this," Pastor Evans said as he came into the kitchen.

The overhead lights glinted off his glasses, showing his scalp through his thinning, brown hair.

"I was making a visit down the road and thought I would drop in." He laid his Bible on the table and gave her an apologetic smile.

"No problem at all," Charlotte said, indicating that he should sit down. "We were just going to have coffee anyway."

Pastor Evans eyed the plate laden with sweets and readily sat down. "So I imagine this rain is keeping you out of the fields," he said to Bob.

Bob nodded as he washed up in the kitchen sink. He pulled a tea towel off the stove handle and dried his hands. "We don't have many more acres to plant, so we should be okay."

A few minutes later they were all sitting down at the table, steaming mugs of coffee in front of them, an awkward silence settling around them.

Pete took another cookie, dunked it in his coffee. "So,

Pastor Nathan, how many souls did you save this week?" Pete asked.

"That's not really my job, Pete," Pastor Evans said, neatly parrying Pete's irreverence. "I just point people in the right direction. I let God take care of the rest."

"Well I guess God hasn't gotten involved in my soul yet," Pete commented.

Pastor Evans shrugged. "You might be surprised." He held Pete's gaze, but Pete just looked away.

Charlotte shot Pete a warning frown. He got the hint, took another piece of cake, and sauntered off to the family room, where he turned on the television.

The noise was distracting but not as distracting as Pete could be.

Pastor Evans turned his attention to Bob and Charlotte. "I've wanted to come and visit for a while but knew you'd be busy seeding. I have to tell you that all the way here I was trying to find the right way to talk to you about Denise. The right way to bring up her death. But you know, there is no right way. The death of such a young woman, a mother of three children, a daughter, it's an invasion. It cuts and it is painful and there is no way to make that pretty."

As Pastor Evans spoke, Charlotte saw Pete's head angled their way. He was listening.

"I know in your situation, I would have questions," he continued, his earnest gaze shifting from Bob to Charlotte. "I would wonder if God knew what he was doing."

Bob shifted sideways, his one elbow resting on the back of his chair, the other on the table. He tapped his fork lightly on his plate, marshaling his thoughts.

Finally he spoke up. "I know one thing that goes through my mind is, *why?*"

He stopped there, but Pastor Evans didn't say anything. He simply rested his hands on the table, watching Bob.

Charlotte waited as well, surprised at Bob's comment.

"I wonder why she had to die," he continued, his voice quiet, but firm. "Why didn't we get a chance to talk to her? I wonder where she was with God. I wonder why we had to lose our daughter and those kids had to lose their mother."

Charlotte was stunned at the length of Bob's comment and how accurately they mirrored her emotions. He had never said anything to her or given her any indication that these questions were bothering him.

"Questioning God is healthy and biblical," Pastor Evans said. "I can't answer your questions, but I can give you this. God wants us to talk to him. And part of talking is questions. Imagine a relationship where you are never allowed to question."

"But God is all powerful. Full of mercy. We can't question him," Bob said.

"But God is also our Father. And fathers want their children to talk to them, to be involved in the relationship."

As he spoke, Charlotte felt a space opening in her mind, allowing room for the thoughts, doubts, and questions she'd been pushing down. She glanced at Bob, thinking of their own relationship. What if she was never allowed to question him? To challenge him?

"I don't know," Pete called from the family room. "Some dads don't like their kids asking questions."

"Thankfully, God is not some dads," Pastor Evans said,

giving Pete a smile. He turned back to Bob and Charlotte as he opened his Bible. "I know my visit was unexpected, but I'd like to read you this passage, if I may. This comes from Romans."

He adjusted his glasses, cleared his throat, and began reading. "'For you did not receive a spirit that makes you a slave again to fear, but you received the Spirit of sonship. And by him we cry, "Abba, Father." The Spirit himself testifies with our spirit that we are God's children.'"

"The word *Abba* can also be translated as *Daddy*, a term of affection," Pastor Evans said as he looked up. "Daddy. That's not a word we often think of when we think of God. But that's how close he wants to be to us. So I think, asking questions of God, of our Daddy, is not disrespectful. It's allowed."

He looked from Charlotte to Bob, then turned back to the Bible again. "This is a passage I wanted to read as well. Romans 8:18: 'I consider that our present sufferings are not worth comparing with the glory that will be revealed in us. The creation waits in eager expectation for the sons of God to be revealed.'"

He looked up as if he were going to expound on that passage when the sound of the porch door slamming broke into the moment.

Charlotte got up just as Emily stormed into the house, down the hallway and up the stairs, her feet pounding on the steps.

Next, Sam came into the kitchen. "C'mon, Christopher," he snapped at his younger brother, who drifted behind Sam, dragging his backpack behind him.

"What's going on, Sam? Did something happen?" Charlotte asked.

His glare skipped over the adults gathered around the table, then he shook his head as if dismissing them all.

"Nothing. Nothing at all." His voice was edged with anger and another tone that sent a faint chill down Charlotte's spine.

He sounded exactly the same as he had when the kids first arrived at the farm.

Sam took Christopher's hand and together they went upstairs.

"And this is our happy home," Pete muttered from the family room.

AFTER THE AWKWARDNESS of the kids' abrupt arrival injected a strained note into the atmosphere, Pastor Evans said his good-byes and left.

Pete ambled back into the kitchen. "What do you suppose is those kids' problem now?"

"Who knows?" Bob sighed and pushed himself away from the table. "Always some crisis or drama, it seems with them."

Charlotte endured an instant of pain at the words that Pete and Bob used for the children, placing them at a distance from them. *Those. Them.*

"I'm going to be working on the tractor," Pete said to his father, then left.

Bob nodded, sitting back in his chair, his arms folded over his chest. He dragged his hand over his face and sighed.

Charlotte hesitated to ask, but he looked so weary. "What's wrong, Bob?"

He waited a moment, then without looking at her said, "Do you think maybe we shouldn't have taken this on?"

Charlotte felt as if someone had doused her with ice water. "Bob, what are you talking about?"

Bob kept his eyes straight ahead, as if unable to look at her. "Sometimes I think maybe we should have made more effort to contact Kevin's parents."

"But Denise's will named us as guardians." Bob's comments made Charlotte feel as if she had to catch her breath. "Are you saying you regret taking in our own grandchildren?" She could hardly believe what she was hearing.

Bob blew out his breath as if expelling his doubts and questions. "I dunno what I'm saying. I just know I'm tired of all the drama and fuss." He cut her a quick sideways glance. "And don't tell me there aren't times you feel the same."

Before Charlotte could protest, he got up from the table and strode to the porch, as if eager to get out of the house.

As they went their separate ways, Charlotte waited a moment, her head bent.

And once again, Lord, I need your help, she prayed. *I feel like I'm doing this all alone. I need you to help me be strong.*

Then she trudged up the stairs to try to understand what was happening with the children this time.

She knocked on Emily's door, and when Emily told her to go away, Charlotte hesitated. Should she ignore Emily's outburst? Reprimand her?

She met Sam and Christopher as they came out of

Christopher's room. They were both wearing older clothes. Christopher had his head down again, as if he didn't dare meet Charlotte's gaze.

"Sam, please tell me what is going on," she said.

"We're going out to do chores."

"I see that, but when you came home from school you were angry—"

"Talk to Emily about that," Sam said, walking away.

"Sam—" Charlotte let her voice trail off, uncertainty battling with the need to maintain order in the house.

But he kept on walking.

Christopher hadn't even looked at her, Charlotte realized as the boys walked down the stairs.

Charlotte turned back to Emily's door and gave it another knock but received no reply.

Things had been going too well, she thought, turning away from the door. She'd been too positive that the children were settling in.

And Bob. How could Bob have said what he did? How could he even question the decision they made?

She went to the porch and slipped on her jacket. She had to check on a calf she had treated yesterday for scours. On her return she heard the muffled voices of Sam and Christopher coming from the barn. She stopped outside the door, wondering if she should go in. Should she push them? Make them tell her what was going on?

She sighed, shoved her hands in the pockets of her jacket, and walked back to the house. She didn't have the energy right now.

Half an hour later, as she set the table, Sam and Christopher drifted in and went directly upstairs. Emily had stayed in her room the whole time.

"Where are those kids?" Bob asked, as he pulled out his chair.

"I tried calling, but they aren't answering." Charlotte put the casserole she'd made for dinner on the table. "Sam says he's not hungry and if Sam won't come Christopher won't. And Emily—" Charlotte ended the sentence with a barely discernible sigh. She had thought she and Emily had been making progress.

"Emily isn't talking to me," Charlotte finished.

"Well, then we eat without them," Bob said.

"And Christopher?"

"He has to learn too."

Charlotte glanced down the hallway, knowing Bob was right, yet the thought of sitting down at the table without the children seemed so cold.

The door of the porch slammed open again and Charlotte's heart jumped. Now what?

But it was only Pete coming to join them for dinner.

"That girl. She didn't come out to feed the horses," Pete grumbled as he slipped into his seat. "Why didn't you send her out?"

"She wouldn't talk to me," Charlotte said.

"So. Make her go out anyway."

If only it were that easy.

"Short of physically going into her room and hauling her downstairs, there's not much I can do to make her do something against her will." *And I've already taken away the one thing I might have used as leverage,* Charlotte thought.

"We're eating without them," Bob repeated for Pete's sake.

Pete shrugged. "In the immortal words of Emily Slater, whatever."

Their mealtime was no different than it used to be, but compared to the chitchat and quibbling that had been a part of their meals the past three weeks, the silence was deafening. Charlotte only picked at her food, her mind shifting between the children in isolation upstairs and her husband who wasn't sure they should even be here. By the time Bob closed the Bible and ended the meal with his usual prayer, her stomach felt like a hard knot.

Bob made a quick getaway to the family room once he was done.

"Tell Emily she had better show up to feed the horses tomorrow," Pete said before he left.

In spite of Bob's insistence that the kids live with the consequences of their choices, Charlotte made up a plate of food for each of them, just in case they did come down later.

When she was done with the dishes, Charlotte joined Bob in the family room, but he was sleeping, the remote still clutched in his hand. As she sat down on the couch and picked up her embroidery, she keenly felt the disconnectedness of her family.

She went through the motions. Her needle flashed in the muted light from the lamp beside Bob's chair. The television show's laugh track mocked her and after a few minutes, she got up and turned it off. Bob didn't even notice.

An hour later, Bob woke up and went to bed. Charlotte joined him.

As she lay in the dark, she looked upward. She began to pray, but she felt as if her prayers didn't go any farther than the ceiling.

Chapter Twenty

The next morning the sky was pewter with rain, mirroring Charlotte's mood. Her plans to work in the garden and weed her flowerbeds would have to be put off for another day.

Bob was quiet at breakfast time and ate his oatmeal without comment.

Pete hadn't even come in for breakfast, and she didn't blame him. The mood in the house was gloomier than the weather outside.

Christopher had come downstairs long enough to wolf down a few pieces of toast. Sam followed him just to make sure his little brother brushed his teeth and got his books ready for school.

Emily managed to slip out the door without Charlotte knowing, leaving her packed lunch bag behind.

Charlotte cleaned up her empty house. It took her forever to vacuum, dust, and change the bedsheets.

Finally she sat down to read her Bible, but she read and prayed by rote, going through the motions of spending time with God. Pastor Evans' words came back to her, but right now she wasn't sure she even knew what to ask God or how to talk to him anymore.

Charlotte felt everyone scattering, and the fragile control she had over this family seemed to be slipping out of her grasp. She needed to do something concrete. She put the Bible away and got up.

Emily had not only neglected to feed the horses, but Christopher hadn't collected the eggs as well. She hadn't told Bob because she didn't feel like having to deal with another mini-lecture about teaching the kids responsibility. Might as well do it herself.

The chill of the wet weather was a slap in the face. Charlotte huddled deeper in her jacket, bending over to avoid the stinging needles of rain.

The chickens didn't even bother to head out when she opened the door, but the egg pail was full by the time she left.

She walked past the corral and found Pete feeding the horses.

"Where's your father?" she asked as she set the pail of eggs down in the lee of a small shed.

Shania and Princess fought for their spots in line as Pete threw another forkful of hay over the fence. "Last I saw him he was heading toward the tractor shed," he said.

"Don't you need to help him?"

"Who wants to? He's as miserable as Emily."

She needed some advice and if Bob wasn't willing to talk, well then, she was going to head to town to see if she couldn't find someone there whose shoulder she could cry on. Maybe she'd go to Rosemary's shop. Engage in some retail therapy.

Half an hour later she pushed open the door of her sister-in-law's shop, the warm homey atmosphere drawing her in.

"Charlotte, hello again." Rosemary's smile was a welcoming beacon and Charlotte gravitated toward her.

"Don't tell me you're done with that table runner already?"

"I won't tell you, because I'm not." Charlotte perched herself on one of the stools that Rosemary had set up close to her cutting table and let the peace and tranquility of the shop surround her like the very quilts her sister-in-law had on display.

"I imagine the rain is keeping the men out of the fields?" Rosemary folded the material she had just cut into a neat triangle and set it in a long, rectangular box. Fat quarters, a quilter's addiction.

"Thankfully they don't have much more to do or I'm sure I'd have five grumpy people in the house, not including me."

"Who's grumpy?"

"Actually it's worse than that. Grumpy is too small a word to describe the tension in my house." Charlotte took a piece of fabric Rosemary had cut and meticulously folded it, then smoothed it out. "Bob has been even more stubborn than usual. Sam more surly. Emily came home from school yesterday completely out of sorts about something and she won't tell me what."

She couldn't tell her sister-in-law about Bob's doubts. She couldn't even process the idea herself.

"She's a young girl. She just needs guidance and discipline," Rosemary said.

And encouragement and understanding and a happy face.

The door of the shop swung open, barely giving the bell above it time to ring, and Melody strode inside. She wore a bright orange T-shirt tucked into pink capris topped with a white apron emblazoned with the words *Mel's Place*.

"Sorry to intrude, Rosemary," Melody said, sounding breathless. "But I saw Charlotte come in here and I really need to talk to her."

Charlotte clenched the cloth she held in her hands as her shoulders slumped. *Please, Lord,* she prayed, *let it not be about Emily or Sam or Christopher.* She couldn't take one more problem. But she also couldn't imagine what was so important that Mel had followed her here.

"Do you need some privacy?" Rosemary straightened as she clutched the tape measure hanging around her neck.

"No. No. You probably need to hear this too." Melody walked over to the table and dropped down on a nearby chair, catching her breath. "These may be made for walking but they're certainly not made for running." Melody lifted her foot, showing off orange clogs decorated with red hearts and purple flowers.

"Please, Melody, tell me what's going on," Charlotte said, her heart's rhythm slowly increasing.

Melody took another breath as she leaned forward. "I've been hearing some stuff going through the coffee shop. It's about Denise."

Charlotte frowned. "What have you heard?"

"I thought you needed to know in case it got to the kids. I overheard a couple of women chitchatting while they were having coffee. One of them was saying that she had heard Denise was leaving the kids when she was killed."

"What? How in the world—" Charlotte struggled to find the words to fit around the anger this created. "Who—why—"

"I did what I could to stop it. May have lost a couple of

customers, but I don't care. I know it's not true. Denise would never have done that to her kids. Never. I just didn't want Emily, Sam, or Christopher to hear it."

And suddenly everything became clear to Charlotte.

"I think they already have," Charlotte said quietly.

"I just wonder how it started," Rosemary said.

"Doesn't matter. We need to quash this." Melody shook her head. "I love this town but honestly. The gossip that can fly around here. It's like a secret is just information with a best-before date."

"I'm sure it all started innocent enough," Rosemary said, her tone assuring. "You know, two women wondering, thinking out loud. Then they wonder and do the same thing around someone else and it gets embellished. Just a bit. And on it goes."

"Well, I'm just disappointed anyone would repeat it in front of the children," Melody put in.

The phone rang and Rosemary excused herself to answer it.

"It probably went through the school." Though Charlotte was upset that people would talk about her daughter that way, she did feel relieved to find out what was bothering her granddaughter. "At least I know what I'm going to talk to Emily about."

"Charlotte," Rosemary held the phone out to her, "it's for you."

Charlotte took the receiver. "Mom?" It was Pete. "I'm calling from the hospital. It's Dad."

Chapter Twenty-One

"You've had a close call, but you're going to be okay." Dr. Carr set the chart he'd been holding on the metal rolling tray situated at the foot of Bob's bed. Bob lay on the bed, his grease-stained blue jeans a dark contrast to the pristine sheets of the hospital bed, as were his callused hands clutching the railing.

An intravenous tube, attached to his arm, snaked away to a bag suspended by a pole next to the bed. His other arm was anchored by a blood pressure cuff connected to a machine.

The pervasive scent of disinfectant and the metallic smell of medicine lent an air of gravitas to the proceedings.

Bob looked ready to launch himself off the bed and charge out the door as soon as he received the signal from the doctor.

"Part of that care—" Dr. Carr continued, slipping his pen in the pocket of his lab coat, "—is taking your medication on a regular basis and making sure you eat properly and stay away from sweets."

Guilt dogged Charlotte as she thought of the extra baking she'd done for the children.

"I'm sorry, doctor, but I'm still not sure what happened," Charlotte said.

"You forgot to set out my pills last night." Bob shot her an accusing glance. "So I took two this morning. Thought I could catch up."

"Which caused hypoglycemia. That means his blood sugar dropped dramatically," Dr. Carr put in. "We're giving him glucose intravenously. He should be okay in half an hour. We'll do another blood test, just to make sure."

"Any long-term damage?"

Dr. Carr shook his head. "No. He'll have a bad headache and will want to rest when he gets home."

"He doesn't have to stay overnight?"

The doctor shook his head again. "I'd like him to come in next week, though, just for a follow-up."

Charlotte released her grip on the bed rail and took a long, slow breath. "That's good. I'm glad."

Dr. Carr slipped his hands in the pocket of his lab coat and rocked back on his heels, looking at Bob. "I notice that you said Charlotte forgot to put out your pills. She shouldn't have to do this for you. You should be taking care of this yourself."

Bob frowned at Dr. Carr, but the man wasn't fazed by Bob's glower. "You're fortunate to have Charlotte's support, but I'd like to remind you that you need to take responsibility for your health. That way you'll avoid another incident like this."

Charlotte had to smile. She knew that wasn't going to happen very quickly. Bob was like most men of his generation. He was reared thinking the wife took care of the husband, and that was simply the way it was.

"Mom? Aunt Rosemary is here."

Charlotte heard Pete's voice from beyond the cubicle and she excused herself.

Rosemary stood in the waiting room with Pete and as Charlotte came near, she hurried to her side and gave Charlotte a quick hug. "How is he doing?"

"He's okay." Charlotte managed a smile. "We have to wait half an hour and then I can take him home."

"That's good. So he doesn't have to stay." Rosemary shook her head. "I'm so thankful it wasn't anything worse. I closed the store so I could come here."

"You didn't need to do that," Charlotte protested. "I could have called you to let you know what happened."

Rosemary shot Charlotte a frown. "Coming here to be a support for my brother, and for you, is not a burden, Charlotte. I want to help."

Her voice held the faintest sting of accusation, and her words underlined what Hannah had said to her when they were planting the garden, about letting other people in.

"Why don't we have a cup of coffee while we're waiting for Bob," Charlotte said quietly. But as Charlotte walked to the small cafeteria with Pete and Rosemary, her thoughts bounced between Bob in the hospital and the children who Bob thought he couldn't take care of.

So who was her first priority? Her motherless grandchildren or her husband?

"IS GRANDPA GOING TO BE OKAY?" Christopher asked as he dried the last of the plates.

Dinner was over. Bob was in bed. As the doctor had

predicted, he had come home with a bad headache. At suppertime he ate what he could, then went directly to their bedroom to lie down.

"He's going to be fine." Though Charlotte realized this fact, guilt over not watching Bob more closely nagged at her.

Christopher carefully folded the towel, hung it over the handle of the stove, adjusting it so it hung just so.

"Do you have any homework?" she asked him.

He shook his head. "Can I go out to play with the kittens?" he asked.

"Of course you can." Charlotte smiled at him.

"I wish I could have one in the house," Christopher said. "Then I wouldn't have to go to the barn."

Charlotte let out a long breath. "I'd like to come with you." She needed to get out of the house herself for a while.

The warm air felt good as they walked across the yard. When they got to the barn, she sat down on an old bale of straw while Christopher scooted in behind the wall to find the mother cat. After Madison's mishap, she and Christopher had moved the cat and her kittens to the lower floor and, surprisingly, the mother cat had been content with this arrangement. The musty smell of the barn brought back memories of times spent with her own children in this very place, playing games of hide and seek, telling stories, or simply sitting up in the loft.

Christopher came up from behind a stack of bales with two squirming kittens. "I got one for you, Grandma," he said, handing over the small orange, brown, and white kitten.

Charlotte let it nestle on her lap, stroking it gently, its

purring like a tiny rumble against her legs. Christopher settled onto the barn floor, playing with a brown tabby kitten.

He cuddled the kitten to his cheek, then turned it so he could look at it.

"Is that Lightning?" she asked, pleased that she remembered the name he had once told her.

"I call him Lighty for short," he said, bouncing it gently. "He's my favorite because he doesn't scratch me like the rest." His smile was like a much-needed beacon of light. She had an idea.

"Would you like to have a kitten in the house?" she asked him.

Christopher's head jerked up, his eyes wide. "Lighty? In the house?"

"That's what I said." Charlotte lifted the kitten she was holding to her cheek, rubbing her nose over the kitten's ears, making them twitch. "If you promise to take good care of him."

Christopher jumped to his feet, still holding the kitten. He gave Charlotte a big hug, then pulled back, as if embarrassed. "I would. I promise."

"Okay. Then that's what we'll do. I think he's old enough to be away from his mother."

"But would he get lonely?" Christopher asked, looking at the kitten Charlotte still held.

"You could bring him to visit every day," Charlotte said.

"Yeah. I could."

And that was that.

As they walked slowly toward the open barn door,

Charlotte prepared herself for what Bob would say, but it didn't matter. She was making this decision on her own and she would live with it. Too often they had denied their children the simple pleasure of a house pet. That was ending right now. The past few days had been an eye-opener for her. She was learning what was essential and what was optional.

Making a hurting little boy happy? Essential.

Doing things just because that's how they had always been done? Optional.

As they came out of the barn, they met Pete, leading Britney. "What's wrong?" Charlotte asked.

Pete stopped, stroking Britney's face. She snorted and shifted, pawing the ground. "I think she's going to have her foal any day now. I'm worried about her, so I thought I would put her in a stall."

"I'm getting a kitten of my own," Christopher said to Pete, holding up Lightning for his inspection.

"That looks like a good one," Pete said, nodding.

"He's the fastest one," Christopher agreed. "Can I go show Emily and Sam?" Christopher asked.

"You go ahead. I'll get a few things ready for you," Charlotte said.

Pete waited until he was out of earshot, which didn't take long at the rate Christopher was running. "What's Dad going to say?" he asked, shifting his hat on his head.

"Doesn't matter. I made this decision. Goodness knows we could all use the distraction right now."

Pete gave his mother a careful smile, then patted her on the shoulder. "You'll be okay, Mom. You're strong."

As Charlotte watched him bring Denise's old horse into the barn, she wondered if she really was. Right now she felt as if the smallest thing could knock her off her feet.

The kitten was a welcome distraction. And that night, as Christopher lay snug in his bed, the smile that had wreathed his face all evening was still firmly in place as he watched his kitten curled up in a box beside him on the floor. To her amazement, Lightning, or Lighty for short, didn't mewl or cry for its mother or littermates, and seemed quite content to be by itself in the box. Tomorrow, when Charlotte went to town again, she would pick up some cat litter.

Emily's door was shut tight. It was her way of saying keep out, so Charlotte did.

Downstairs, Sam was working on the computer.

"Time's up, Sam," she said, glancing over his shoulder to see what he was doing.

He shot a guilty look, then the screen flickered and changed. What had he been looking at? Not pictures, that much she had surmised.

And again, Charlotte didn't have the energy to ferret out information.

Sam turned off the computer, then pushed himself away from the table. "Good-night, Grandma," he said as he passed her.

Charlotte wished him a good-night back, then walked over to her chair and dropped into it. Her Bible lay on the table beside it, still open to the last passage she'd been reading. She covered her face with her hands as all the events of the past few days came crashing down on her.

Bob wasn't sure they should do this anymore. Other than Christopher, the kids were a mystery to her. She'd just had a bad scare with her husband's health.

She closed her eyes as she laid her head on the back of her chair. "Please, Lord," she whispered. "Please be with Bob. Please be with me. With us." She paused, drawing in a shaky breath. "I don't know if I can do this anymore. I don't know if I can take care of Bob and the kids. I don't know if I can give these kids what they need. I'm not strong. I'm weak and I need your help."

She stopped, not even realizing she had prayed aloud as the house seemed to creak in response to her cry.

"I HAVE TO TALK to the children about Denise," Charlotte said as Bob finished the last of his coffee. "I just thought I would warn you."

All weekend she'd tried to find a time to talk to the kids, to assure them that their mother loved them, that she would have never left them, but both Sam and Emily had been very creative in avoiding her.

Bob leveled her a steady gaze. "You telling me this in case you and the kids have another blowout?"

Charlotte swirled the dregs of her own coffee in her mug as her mind slipped back to their previous conversation. "I thought you might want to be prepared. I don't want you to end up in the hospital again."

"Me going to the hospital had nothing to do with the kids."

She and Bob glowered at each other across the table.

Bob made a noise in the back of his throat, then pushed

himself away from the table. "I'll be out in the machine shed."

He stepped onto the porch and a few minutes later she heard the door slam. He left just as the flashing lights of the school bus shone through the curtain of rain. The doors of the bus opened and three children spilled out, running past Bob, down the driveway to the house.

Charlotte put out the plate of cookies and poured hot water into the cups of hot chocolate powder she'd gotten ready twenty minutes ago.

The door banged open, announcing the children's arrival. She heard the rustle of wet coats and thump of shoes on the floor before they came into the kitchen. They stopped when they saw Charlotte waiting.

"Sam, Christopher, Emily. We need to talk."

Sam shot his sister a sideways glance, as if to gauge her reaction. Christopher hovered in the doorway.

"There's nothing to talk about," Emily said.

Charlotte ignored Emily's protests and decided to face the situation head-on. "I know about the rumor going around about your mother."

Emily swung her backpack back and forth, her face averted.

"You know it's not true," Charlotte said. "You know your mother would never do anything like that. She loved you. She would never, ever run away from you. She would never leave you."

The movement of Emily's backpack grew more and more erratic. Sam said nothing, and Christopher, picking up on his brother's and sister's mood, kept a low profile.

"How do you know?" Emily said finally. "You never talked to her. You never phoned her. You barely talk about her now."

"Emily, stop." Sam took a step toward his sister, but she moved away.

"Don't tell me to stop." Emily stared at her brother, and then dropped her backpack. "Stop telling me what to do. Stop being so bossy. I'm tired of everyone pushing me around and talking about me and pretending like everything is fine. It isn't fine."

"Emily—"

Her granddaughter turned on her. "Our mom is gone and we're stuck here. I don't want to be here, you know. I hate it here."

Emily stood in front of Charlotte, her hands clenched into fists as the angry words, loud and merciless, spun around the room, sucking any bit of happiness away.

"You and Grandpa don't care about us at all."

Emily's face grew suddenly pale, as if she now realized what she had said.

Then she turned and ran. The porch door slammed shut, sounding like a shot in the stunned silence she left behind.

Chapter Twenty-Two

"Emily, are you in here?"

The figure standing in the doorway wasn't Grandma or Grandpa or Pete.

Emily got up from behind the straw bales and walked toward her brother, Sam. "I'm here."

As she came closer to the doorway and to the light shining in from the barn's overhead light, she could see from his tight lips and hunched-forward shoulders that Sam was angry.

"What's the matter with you?" Sam shoved his fingers through his hair, wet from the rain, making it stick up in all directions. "Why are you making this so hard for all of us?"

"And why do you care?" Behind her she could hear Britney whinnying softly. She had come to check on the horse, to make sure she was okay. She felt guilty because she hadn't been taking care of the horses like she was supposed to. She knew Britney was going to have her baby any day. When she got here, Britney was standing up in her stall, but she wouldn't eat the hay Emily gave her, which made Emily feel even more guilty.

Sam stared at her as if he didn't understand her question. "I care because we've got no choice. My cell phone is dead and until I can afford to buy a new charger, we're here and that's that."

"We've got a couple of choices." Emily held out her cell phone. "I snuck this out of Grandma's bedroom."

"What?" Sam grabbed it away from her. "Are you nuts? That's stealing."

"It's *my* phone. That's not stealing," Emily said. "I needed to know if Bekka had left me a message." Emily released a bitter laugh. "She didn't. But Tonya did. Check it out."

Sam flipped through the buttons, then frowned as he read the text message Tonya Beckson had sent her a couple of days ago.

"So she says she talked to Grandma and we can come back." Sam frowned. "What does that mean?"

"It means, mister, that Grandma and Grandpa don't really want to take care of us anymore." Why was her voice going all funny? She didn't care, did she? She swallowed. Then again. "And I heard Grandma talking one night. I heard her say that she couldn't do this anymore. I heard her, Sam." Emily wished her voice wouldn't crack like that. "We need to get out of here. You need to find out where Dad is."

Sam gave her the phone back and shoved his hands in the pocket of his hoodie. "We haven't heard anything from him for a whole bunch of years. How'm I supposed to find him in a couple weeks?"

"Maybe you're not trying hard enough." Emily walked back to the stall where Britney stood, her feet mixing up the straw and dust on the floor. When they first came, she thought it stank. Now, it just smelled like a barn.

"I'm trying hard enough. But maybe he doesn't want to be found. Maybe he doesn't even care about us either."

Her tears started again.

Sam sighed heavily. "She's not coming back, Em. Mom's gone. Why can't you get that through your head?"

"Do you believe Grandma? Do you believe Mom wasn't running away from us?"

"Yeah. I believe Grandma. She was the one who talked to the police. And if Mom was supposed to be running away, why didn't she have any suitcases or anything with her?"

Emily hadn't thought of that.

"She wouldn't leave us, Em. She always said that."

"But she did," Emily said quietly.

Sam didn't say anything.

"I miss her so much," she said, her sorrow pushing away her anger. But behind the anger lay a well of tears. She felt them coming and swiped at her eyes.

"Please don't start crying again."

"Don't you care?" Emily said. "Don't you miss her either?"

Sam's mouth got tight and hard and when his hand came out of the pocket of his hoodie, his fist was clenched. "Don't ever say that."

And in that moment, Emily felt afraid of her brother. She took a few steps back, then a few more, and she turned and walked down the alleyway to Britney's stall. A few seconds later she heard Sam leave and she was alone again. She pushed the door of Britney's stall open and stepped inside. Britney neighed and Emily walked toward her.

"Hey girl. You know who I am?" she asked, reaching out to stroke Britney. "My mom used to ride you."

The horse shook her head and Emily stepped back, afraid. She had never known how big horses were or how big their heads were.

"I'm Emily, Denise's daughter." Emily felt a catch in her throat as she spoke the words. She moved to one side of the stall and slid down, her back against the rough wood, the door of the stall beside her.

And she started to cry. She cried the tears she had been holding back all day. Tears for her mother, for herself, for the friends who didn't call.

She didn't know how long she sat there, straw poking into her legs and Britney watching her.

She sniffed and Britney shook her head again, pawing the ground. What was happening? Was the mare okay?

Britney whinnied and walked around the pen, toward Emily. She seemed restless. Emily got up, wondering what she should do. Maybe she should get Uncle Pete?

Then everything happened at once.

Lightning streaked across the sky, lighting up the countryside for miles around, followed by a crashing boom that she felt in her chest.

She heard a frightened whinny behind her, and Britney burst out of the gate that Emily had left open. Emily jumped, her heart pounding in time to the sound of hoofbeats thundering off into the night. Britney was out.

And the only thing Emily could think of was it was her fault. She had to bring her back.

Chapter Twenty-Three

Something smells good." Bob rubbed his stomach as if anticipating a good meal.

"I hope it tastes good. Do you know if Emily is coming?" Charlotte asked Sam as he dropped into his chair. She tried to mask her concern and hurt with her granddaughter.

Charlotte glanced out at the rain pelting the windows. Emily had left the house an hour and a half ago. Surely she'd be back by now. "Christopher, run up and see if she's in her room, please," Charlotte said, trying to keep her annoyance with her granddaughter out of her voice.

Maybe Emily had snuck past her while Charlotte was praying. One thing she knew, the girl would not want to be outside in this rain.

Charlotte put the salad on the table, arranged the spoons beside the dishes, her heart starting that too-familiar thumping that was the first harbinger of anger. And worry.

She didn't want to be angry. She was tired of the emotional roller-coaster she'd been on since the kids had come into the house.

She'd had such good intentions when they took these children in, but she wasn't sure she could live with this stress anymore.

"She's not in her room, Grandma," Christopher called out as he came down the stairs.

Charlotte's breath left her in a heavy sigh. Then her heart kicked into high gear. "Did she leave a note?" she asked as Christopher came into the kitchen.

He shook his head as he slid onto his chair. "Nope. Nothing."

"I don't think she ran away, Grandma," Sam said, as if he could read her mind.

Charlotte pressed her trembling lips together and gave him a grateful smile. "Thanks, Sam."

"I think she's in the barn. I saw her there just before supper."

"Why didn't you say that before, son?" Bob asked. He must have caught Charlotte's anxiety as well.

Sam toyed with his silverware. "We had a fight. I thought she came back here afterward. But maybe she didn't."

"She's probably with Britney." Pete pushed his chair back. "I'll go check."

Charlotte looked at the casserole she had made especially because Emily had told her it was her favorite. It was to be her peace offering. A way of clearing the air between her and her granddaughter. A way of showing her that yes, she did care about Emily and Sam and Christopher.

"Should we start?" she asked, glancing around the table.

Bob shook his head. "We can wait." He looked at Charlotte, gave her a careful smile, then turned to Christopher. "That kitten seems to be adjusting." Bob hadn't said anything when Charlotte told him about Christopher's kitten, but she suspected he was softening toward the little thing.

Christopher's eyes lit up. "I took her to see her brothers and sisters, but she wanted to come back with me. That's good, isn't it?"

Charlotte thought the boy's smile would split his face.

The door to the porch flew open. Pete strode into the kitchen, his hair wet, his coat dripping water on the floor.

"Emily isn't in the barn. And Britney is out of her stall."

"Out?" Bob said. Both Charlotte and Bob were on their feet. "How?"

"The door to her stall is unbolted and the barn door is wide open. I told that girl to take care of her. Told her to watch out for her. I shouldn't have trusted her."

"Did Emily take off with Britney?" Charlotte asked, hardly daring to voice the question out loud.

"She doesn't know how to ride," Pete said. "And even if she did, Britney didn't have a halter on. Britney's probably ready to foal. Horses don't like spectators when they're foaling."

"So where did Britney go?" Charlotte asked.

"I'll head down the road with the truck," Bob said. "Pete, maybe you could saddle up one of the other horses. They might be able to find her quicker. Take the dog."

"Good idea." Pete ducked out of the kitchen and as the door slammed behind him, Bob turned to the rest of the family.

"Charlotte, you, Sam, and Christopher can take Pete's truck and go in the opposite direction on the road. Take an extra halter along, just in case."

Charlotte nodded and turned to Sam and Christopher.

"Put on some warm clothes and your raincoats. I'll meet you at the truck."

As the boys ran upstairs, Charlotte turned to Bob, feeling suddenly vulnerable. "What if we can't find them?"

"We haven't even gone looking yet, Char. Don't borrow trouble." Bob touched Charlotte's cheek and gave her a tentative smile. "I know you'll be praying. So will I. We need to do what we can and leave the rest in God's hands."

His quiet assurance calmed her jittery fears. "You're right, Bob."

"I better go." He bent over and brushed a light kiss over her forehead. "If you don't find her in half an hour, come back to the house and we'll come up with another plan. In this rain, we need to find her quick."

She nodded, watching as he walked to the porch. Through the open door she saw him put on his slicker, settle a cowboy hat on his head, and take a set of keys off the hook by the back door. He moved with quiet, steady efficiency, and she realized how much she depended on him.

"We're coming, Grandma," Christopher called out as he and Sam hurtled into the kitchen, out of breath.

"Let's go then."

A few minutes later they were driving down the road, peering into the night. The pelting rain absorbed the lights of the truck as the windshield wipers slapped back and forth, clearing the rain away for mere seconds at a time. Raindrops drummed on the roof, creating a cocoon of dark warmth.

"Can you see anything?" Charlotte asked, struggling to keep her own fears in check.

"Just puddles and rain." Christopher sat between her and Sam, watching.

Sam sighed, then leaned forward, his seat belt restraining him. "I'm sorry, Grandma," he said, his voice quiet. "I should have told you earlier about Emily. I thought she would come back to the house."

"That's okay, Sam. I'm sure you didn't think this would happen."

"I hope we find her."

Charlotte gave him a smile that held more assurance than she felt. "Someone will."

Charlotte came to a crossroad and stopped the truck. If Emily was following the horse and Britney had taken off across the field, there was a good chance they might have crossed this road. But what if the horse was long gone, with Emily following it? What if they missed her completely?

Charlotte stilled the nervous voices in her mind, trying to think rationally. It would take Emily some time before she got this far, walking in the dark through a plowed field. And she might not have even gone in this direction.

Charlotte made a quick decision, turned the truck right and slowly drove down the road.

"Sam, can you check the ditch on your side? Look for a broken fence or maybe even some beaten-down bush. Anything that will show if Britney or Emily might have passed this way."

"What's that, Grandma?" Christopher sat up straight and pointed.

"Slow down. I think that's Emily," Sam called out.

Charlotte eased off the accelerator, peering through the

curtain of rain. In the headlights of the truck she made out the figure of a young girl walking toward them, leading a horse.

Charlotte dimmed the lights and came to a stop. "Don't make any sudden movements, boys," she warned. "Britney could still be scared."

She reached behind the seat of the truck and pulled out the extra halter and lead rope they had picked up at the barn. Bracing herself, she got out of the truck.

Emily walked slowly toward them, favoring one leg as she held onto Britney's mane. Her shirt and pants were shiny with moisture and her hair hung in long, wet strands around her face.

"Are you okay?" Charlotte asked.

"I'm cold." Emily's voice quivered.

"Of course you are, honey." Charlotte moved closer. "I've got a halter here. Do you want me to put it on her?"

"No. I should do it . . . I have to do it." Emily's teeth chattered as she spoke.

Emily's hand was ice cold as she took the halter from Charlotte. Emily slipped the rope around Britney's neck, then reached way up to put the halter over the mare's head.

It took her a few tries to buckle it on, and Charlotte had to fight the urge to offer to help. This was something Emily needed to do.

When the halter was securely buckled, and Emily had the lead rope firmly in her hand, Charlotte went closer.

"Oh, honey. I was so worried about you." She took a chance and enveloped her granddaughter in a tight, hard hug. "I'm so glad you're safe."

Emily shivered in Charlotte's arms. The rain was slowly

seeping down Charlotte's neck as well, sending icy fingers slithering down her back. She became aware that Sam and Christopher were standing next to them.

"We need to get you inside the truck. Sam, you've got a raincoat on, could you lead the horse back home? I'll get Uncle Pete to come and get you with the stock trailer."

"Yeah. Sure." Sam approached Emily and held out his hand for the halter.

"I let her—get out of the barn. I should take—her home." Emily could barely talk through the chattering of her teeth.

"You already did your job, honey," Charlotte assured her. "Now let us help you."

Emily stroked Britney's neck, her hand shaking with the cold, then she handed the halter rope to her brother. "She's scared—of lightning and—thunder. Don't jerk on—the rope if she pulls back. Talk to—to her and she'll be—okay." Emily's words came out in staccato phrases as shivers wracked her body.

"Okay. I'll try," Sam said, taking a firm grip on the rope. Charlotte could see he wasn't comfortable, but she had no other choice. She couldn't let him drive the truck in this pouring rain and she had to get Emily warmed up as soon as possible.

"You'll be okay."

"I guess." He gave her a quick smile that she recognized as sheer bravado. "I'll see you back at the farm."

"Can I stay with Sam?" Christopher asked.

"You go with Grandma, bud," Sam said. "I'll be fine."

Christopher looked from Charlotte and Emily to Sam, and then back.

"Emily needs your help more," Sam said.

Christopher took up position on the other side of Emily and put his arm around her. Charlotte put her arm around Emily's shoulders and together they brought her to the truck.

As Emily was slowly climbing into the cab, Charlotte reached into the glove compartment, pulled out a flashlight, and took it back to Sam. "It's not very strong, but it will help you to see, and people to see you." She turned it on and handed it to him.

"Thanks, Grandma." He smiled as he saluted her with it, then shone it down on the road. "You should get going."

Inside, Charlotte wrapped Emily up in the old blanket she was glad she had thought to throw in. She turned up the heat. Emily needed to get out of her cold wet clothes, but keeping the cab warm was all she could do until she got her to the house. "Christopher, you rub her hands. Get the blood moving."

As she reversed the truck and Sam's figure receded into the rainy night, Charlotte felt as if she was deserting him.

By the time they got to the farm, Emily was hunched over, her entire body shaking. She couldn't even talk, she was shivering so hard. Christopher still rubbed her hands, his face twisted with concern.

Charlotte parked the truck right by the house and honked on the horn three times, just in case Pete was anywhere near.

Then she bustled Emily inside. She helped her take off her soaking-wet shoes, then brought her up the stairs to the bathroom.

"You sit here while I fill the tub," she instructed, setting Emily on the edge of the bathtub.

"So I'm in hot water—after—all?" Emily joked, wrapping her arms around herself, shaking as she spoke.

Charlotte smiled at her silly joke as she turned the taps on, testing the water.

"Do you need some help with your clothes?" she asked, straightening.

Emily shook her head.

Charlotte gently stroked her wet hair back from her face. "I'm so thankful we found you," she said quietly. "I was so worried."

"You were?"

"Of course I was."

"I'm glad I found Britney. Will she be okay?"

"Who knows? Maybe walking will help that baby come sooner."

The sound of a vehicle coming into the yard got her attention. "I better go and see if that's your grandfather," she said, pushing to her feet. "You get in that tub and I'll come and check on you in a few minutes."

As she hurried down the stairs she heard Bob talking to Christopher, who had been waiting downstairs.

"So you found Emily and Britney?" Bob asked as she walked into the kitchen. He still wore his heavy boots and water dripped off his coat onto the floor. "Where're Sam and the horse now?"

"I left them on the road and asked Sam to lead Britney back. I don't know how you want to bring the horse home."

"I'll hook up the horse trailer and go and meet him," Bob said, dropping his hat back on his head. "You want to come with me, Christopher?"

Christopher bit his lip and looked at Charlotte. "Will Emily be okay?"

His concern for his sister warmed her heart. Whatever people might have been saying about her daughter, she had done a good job with her children. Even though Charlotte, Bob, and Pete had their difficulties and tensions with the children, Denise had taught them to truly care for each other.

"I'll be watching out for her," she said.

"Okay." Satisfied with her answer, he trotted off behind Bob. Then the truck left the yard and Charlotte was left alone with Emily upstairs and a kitchen table set downstairs and waiting for people.

Charlotte wiped the floor where Bob had been dripping, tidied the porch, and finished cleaning up the kitchen. All the while she worked, she kept part of her attention focused upstairs. She wanted to be up there, to talk to Emily, but she sensed that the girl still needed some space.

A few minutes later, however, she saw headlights sweep across the yard and over the sound of rain battering against the window, she heard the unmistakable roar of the diesel pickup.

Bob was back with Britney and the boys.

Charlotte ran upstairs and tapped lightly on the bathroom door. "Grandpa is back. I'm going out to the barn."

"I want to come too," Emily called out.

"Are you sure?"

"I'm nice and warm now."

"Dress warm, okay?" As soon as the words left her mouth, Charlotte wondered if she should have told Emily what to do.

"I will." Emily's soft reply created a glimmer of hope.

"Then I'll see you in the barn."

Pete had arrived as well and was leaning against one side of the stall and Bob the other when Charlotte arrived. The light bulb hanging from the ceiling made their shadows dance over the wall and created an eerie backdrop to their murmuring voices. Christopher and Sam sat on some straw bales piled against the opposite wall. They looked scared. Charlotte heard a faint whicker coming from the stall. At least Britney was still alive.

"We'll need to do something, quick," Pete was saying.

Bob adjusted his hat, then blew out his breath. "I'll go call the vet."

"What's wrong?" Charlotte hurried toward her husband, alarmed at his simple statement. The last time Bob called a vet was when the milk cow was down with milk fever and his own basic doctoring wasn't working. That was over five years ago.

Bob gave her a cautious smile, as if he recognized how rare this was for him. "The foal was starting to come before Britney took off. Should have been born by now." Though he spoke quietly Charlotte caught the strain in his voice. He glanced toward Christopher and Sam, then spoke quietly. "I'm worried about Britney. She's pretty old to have a foal and all that running around could have caused some problems."

Charlotte's heart sat like lead in her chest. She knew how attached the kids were to this horse. She had belonged to their mom and in their minds Britney was a connection to her.

She also knew, though he would never admit it, how

much this horse meant to Bob. He and Denise had raised Britney and trained her together.

"We'll just have to pray things go well," Charlotte replied.

Bob squeezed her shoulder, then left the barn.

"So I guess we just wait." Charlotte took up a position beside Pete, resting her arms on the rough boards of the pen.

Britney lay on her side, her head extended. Now and again she lifted it, whickered, then lay down again as if even that small movement was too much work after all the walking she had done.

The sound of the rain on the roof narrowed down their world to this barn and the horse.

"How is she doing? Is she okay?" Emily called out as she came into the barn. She shook out the umbrella she had used and set it just inside the door.

"*Shh*. We need to be quiet," Christopher whispered, staying beside his brother on the bales.

Emily climbed up on the pen to see better. "She looks tired."

"She probably is. Having a foal is hard work."

"Is she going to be okay? She doesn't look too good." Emily searched Charlotte's face.

Charlotte responded to the note of worry in her voice by putting her arm around her granddaughter, as if to steady her. "Grandpa went to call the vet."

Emily closed her eyes and lowered her head. "I'm so sorry. It's all my fault. I should have checked the door better. I thought it was shut."

Charlotte squeezed harder, pulling Emily to her side.

Emily didn't resist. "Honey, you didn't do anything wrong, okay? She's here now, and when the vet comes, he'll help her."

She kept her fears to herself. They had never had to intervene with a foal's birth before.

The boys joined them while they waited for Bob to return. They hung over the boards as well, watching. The wait seemed endless as they watched poor Britney struggling, her legs thrashing the straw.

Finally Bob returned. "I caught Trask right on time. He was leaving Johnson's. Be here in fifteen minutes."

"I don't know if fifteen minutes is going to be soon enough," Pete said as he stepped into the pen. "If that foal doesn't get born soon we could lose 'em both."

To Charlotte's surprise, Pete's voice faltered and Charlotte felt an answering tightening of her throat.

Bob patted Pete on the shoulder and in spite of the sorrow of the moment, a tear slipped down her cheek at the sight of the two men, for this brief moment, in harmony.

Please, Lord, she prayed, *please let the vet come soon.*

Chapter Twenty-Four

The fifteen minutes slipped into twenty, but Charlotte and the children didn't move.

Britney was failing as they watched. Her legs moved slower and slower as her energy drained with each push.

Finally lights swept over the yard. A door slammed and Clayton Trask, the vet, rushed into the barn, rain dripping off his coat, his blond hair, and the large plastic box in his hand.

"Where is she?" he asked as he shook his coat off and set the box on the floor.

Bob led Clayton past Charlotte and the children as Britney found the energy to raise her head at this new disturbance.

Charlotte drew Emily and Christopher back and away from whatever was going to happen in the pen.

Emily resisted at first, clinging to the top board, but when Charlotte persisted, she allowed herself to be led back to the pile of bales against the wall. Close enough to hear but not close enough to see what the vet might have to do.

Charlotte sat down on the prickly straw, Christopher on one side, Emily on the other. Sam leaned against the wall, his hands shoved in his pockets.

Toby came over and dropped down at Charlotte's feet.

On impulse Charlotte put her arms around the two youngest, pulling them close. To her surprise, they rested against her.

The warmth of those young bodies pressed against hers raised a wave of maternal love so strong she thought it would knock her off the bales.

My dear grandchildren. Love, yearning, and the deep desire to protect them from pain swept through her as her arms tightened. How she had longed for moments like this all those years they lived so far away. How could she have thought she couldn't take care of them?

She pressed a kiss first to Christopher's head, then Emily's. Sam watched them, a wistful expression on his face, as if he wished he was sitting with them.

"Come, sit by my feet," Charlotte said.

And Sam lowered himself to the ground, putting himself between Christopher and Charlotte. After a moment, he leaned his head against her legs.

Please let this horse live, she prayed. *They've already lost so much. Please don't take this one last reminder of their mother away as well.*

On the heels of that prayer came another.

Thank you, Lord, for this moment with my grandchildren. For this time of being together. We can take care of them, she prayed. *But I will need your help and your guidance.*

And she would also need the help promised her by friends and community.

Toby yawned, stretched, and shifted herself. And when she lay down, she dropped her head on Sam's lap, as if completing the connection.

"Look, Toby is sitting with Sam," Christopher said. "Does that mean she likes him too?"

Charlotte smiled at the joy in his voice. "I think it means she knows you need her."

Sam laughed lightly, stroking Toby's head.

From the pen the vet's voice was a quiet murmur as he gave instructions to Pete, then Bob. Pete came out of the stall and dragged in a few bales of straw, then closed the gate.

"We've got to get her up so I can reposition the foal," the vet was saying.

"C'mon, Britney. C'mon, girl," Bob's quiet voice urged. "You have to do this, okay? You're my good girl. Help us out."

"Grandpa is talking to the horse," Christopher said, wonder in his voice.

"I thought Grandpa didn't like the horses," Emily said.

"Britney is special to Grandpa." Charlotte gave Emily another squeeze. "He and Denise watched when Britney's mother give birth to her in that very same stall."

"What was Britney's mother's name?"

"Two Bits. She was a lovely horse. Even tempered. She was the first horse your mom ever rode." She stopped there, remembering how that foaling had ended. The vet had come then too, but Two Bits had died giving birth to Britney. Denise had cried for three days. Even Bob had been subdued.

She hugged the children tighter, praying this wouldn't happen now. They couldn't take another blow like that.

"Your mom and Grandpa spent a lot of time with Britney," she continued, forcing a light tone to her voice. "They got her used to the halter, then taught her to lead. She was a quick learner and had the same quiet temperament her mother did."

Charlotte let the memories seep into her mind as she spoke. "I remember Denise had such big dreams for that horse. She was going to be a champion barrel racer."

"What's that?" Emily asked.

"It's a rodeo event. Three barrels are set out in a triangle shape a certain distance apart. The rider has to circle each barrel without making them fall over and yet do it as fast as possible."

"I'm guessing the dream didn't happen," Sam said, laying his head back against the bale. "'Cause she never told us about that."

"You're guessing right. She tried, but Britney didn't have the competitive drive necessary to be a good barrel racer." Charlotte laughed as a memory surfaced. "I can still see your mother on Britney, kicking and kicking that poor horse. Britney would carefully move around each barrel, like she was supposed to, but she never ran. I think your mom got her up to a trot, but that was as fast as Britney would go."

Charlotte could so easily picture her daughter at twelve, blonde braids flopping up and down, cowboy hat bobbing on her back, her small hand slapping Britney on the rump while the horse trotted through the cloverleaf pattern around some old fuel barrels Bob had cleaned up for his daughter.

"Did Britney ever gallop?" Emily asked.

"Once she was out in the open field, oh yes. Denise and her would run for miles and miles. Sometimes she would talk Uncle Bill into going with her."

"Uncle Bill rode horses?" Sam sounded incredulous.

"Oh yes. He wasn't born wearing a suit, you know. He and Denise used to make huts in the hayloft and fly paper airplanes across the yard . . ." Her voice faded. Behind the flood of memories came a pain, sharp and unyielding.

My little girl, she thought, then quenched the sorrow, swallowing the lump in her throat. She had to stay strong. These children needed her to be strong.

"Did they ever fight? Like Emily and Sam do?" Christopher's question elicited a poke from Emily.

"We don't always fight," Sam protested.

"You didn't at home. But you do here," Christopher said.

In the awkward silence following that comment, she heard Clayton's voice coming from the pen.

"She's presenting the wrong way."

Bob and Pete grunted and Charlotte suspected they were turning the foal, like they did sometimes with a cow that couldn't give birth.

"Will she have the baby now?" Christopher asked. His voice grew small. Charlotte was afraid the whole scene might be too dramatic.

"We should go to the house," she gently suggested.

"No. I want to stay here," Emily said.

"Me too." Sam nodded.

"Christopher, why don't you come with me?"

He shook his head and clung to Charlotte. "I want to stay here. With my mommy's horse."

Charlotte did too, so she sank back down, curving her arms around Christopher. On impulse she reached out and touched Sam's head. He turned suddenly, then he gave her a tentative smile.

They sat silently, listening to the quiet struggle going on in the pen. Britney groaned, then groaned again, and Charlotte prayed the foal would come soon.

"Tell us more about our mom," Emily said, leaning her head against the wall. "Tell us some stories from the farm."

Charlotte's mind reached back and plucked a memory. "One time your mom and Uncle Pete were going to run away. They were five and seven. I made them eat broccoli and they both hated it."

"I hate broccoli too," Emily said.

"Good thing I didn't plant any this year." Charlotte laughed. "Anyway, they got a big red handkerchief from Grandpa, put some of their favorite toys and some clothes in it and tied it to a fishing rod of Grandpa's. They marched down the stairs and gave me a note, then walked out the door."

"What did the note say?" Christopher asked.

Charlotte smiled at the memory. "It said, 'You stand at the window and cry. We are gone.' Except Denise spelled gone g-o-n. I think I still have that note somewhere. She took off a couple more times. For other reasons." Charlotte stopped there, her comment resurrecting the disappointed sorrow of that horrible day, the last time Denise ran away.

"Mom was eighteen when she left with my dad, wasn't she?" Sam said.

"Yes. She was." Charlotte choked out the answer.

"And I'm sixteen."

Charlotte wondered where he was going with that.

He glanced up at her. "I've done the math. I think I know why Mom left the farm."

Charlotte nodded, unable to say any more.

Sam frowned at her. "Grandma, are you crying?"

She sniffed and shook her head, blinking away the tears that warmed her eyes.

"You look like you are."

Charlotte swallowed once more and then, in spite of being strong, in spite of trying to shield the children the tears came.

First a faint trickle down her cheeks, then hot, thick, and heavy. She couldn't stop them. Her breathing became shaky and erratic and her chest quivered with sorrow. She had to stop or she would get the kids going.

"I'm sorry—" Her voice broke. She swallowed and tried again. "I'm sorry—I shouldn't."

Emily touched her shoulder, her eyes filling as well. "Do you miss her?"

"Oh, how I miss her!" She tried in vain to stem the tide of tears. "I miss her so much. I loved her so much."

And then, through the sorrow threatening to engulf her, she felt Emily's arms around her, holding her. Christopher pressed his face to her shoulder, his warm tears moistening her shirt as he threaded his arm through the crook of hers.

Sam laid his head against her leg, and she laid her hand on his head. She felt Toby push her wet nose against her hand as well, her dog offering what small comfort she could.

"I thought you didn't miss our mom." Emily's broken

voice was muffled by Charlotte's coat. "I never saw you cry."

"I missed her every day she was gone." Charlotte stopped, her voice thick with sorrow. Her chest heaved and then again as the sorrow she'd been holding back shivered through her.

"I wanted so badly to see you. I wanted to be a part of your lives. But you lived so far away and it was hard to visit as often as we wanted." She stopped and then, clinging to her precious grandchildren, she let the tears flow.

The children hugged her tightly, as if sensing that this time they needed to support her too.

Charlotte let her sorrow take over. Allowed the grief to spill out. Finally, as the storm subsided, she drew in a shaky breath, willing the tears away.

She kissed Christopher's head, then Emily's. She stroked Sam's head, wishing she could gather them all, like a hen gathers her chicks under her wings and protect them. She wanted to take their pain away.

They sat there, for a precious moment, united in their shared grief. Charlotte lifted her arm and wiped her tears away with the cuff of her shirt, then pulled Emily close again.

"We got the birthday cards you sent us," Emily said after a long moment.

"And the money," Christopher added. "Last year I bought a paper airplane book."

Charlotte pressed her cheek to his head. "I'm glad." Every time she sent a card, she got a thank you note from Denise with a short update of what the children were doing. Once in a while, Denise would call, but the phone calls, though chatty, were always too short, as if Denise was holding some part of herself back from them.

Was it shame, as Melody had intimated? Pride? Maybe a bit of both?

"I loved you children then, and I love you now," she said, giving them another squeeze.

"There she is!" Pete's excited cry from the stall caught their attention. "A little filly."

They all tried to get up at once. Charlotte almost fell, taking Emily with her. Sam got tangled up in Christopher's legs. Toby yipped as someone stepped on her tail.

With some laughter, they got themselves sorted out, then ran to the stall. Christopher and Emily climbed up the boards while Sam and Charlotte looked over the edge.

In the straw at the feet of the vet lay a shiny, wet little foal. Britney turned her head, her eyes red rimmed, and whickered gently at the baby.

The little creature lifted its head, but it flopped down. She tried once more and then again. Pete rubbed the foal with straw to dry it off.

"She's so cute," Emily said. "Look at her long legs."

They watched as the foal struggled to get up, its legs splayed. Finally she got to her feet only to take a few wobbly steps and fall to its side.

"Shouldn't we help her?" Sam looked back at Charlotte, concern clouding his eyes.

Pete rubbed her a bit more, then stood aside. "You have to let them figure it out themselves. Eventually they do."

"But the baby must be hungry." Emily frowned.

"She is. That's why she'll figure it out herself."

"But Britney isn't getting up yet either."

Charlotte shared their concern. Not only was Britney not getting up, her head lay stretched out, which was not a good sign.

"I thought horses shouldn't lie down very long." Emily leaned forward as if urging Britney to move.

"They can, for a while," Pete said. "But you're right. Lying down is harder on them. Puts stress on their insides. Makes it a bit harder to breathe." He pulled in one corner of his mouth, biting his lip, his concern mirrored by Bob and the vet chatting in the opposite corner of the stall.

Dr. Trask wiped his hands as he spoke to Bob, his voice low. Charlotte couldn't hear what he said, but she caught them looking from Britney to the baby filly. Charlotte didn't like the frown on the vet's face or the way Bob shook his head.

Finally Clayton walked over to Pete. "Keep an eye on the mare. If she's not up in an hour, try to make her get up. The foal is healthy so my biggest concern right now is for the mother. She's pretty old and I'm worried that the strain of birth might have been too much for her."

"Does that mean she might die?" Emily asked, panic edging her voice.

Charlotte tried to catch the vet's attention, but his attention was on Britney. "I wish I could say one way or another," was all he said.

Emily bit her lip and Charlotte laid her hand on the girl's shoulder to reassure her.

"For now, though, that foal needs to drink." Clayton pushed the rag he used to wipe his hands in his back pocket. "You got any colostrum?"

"Just what we kept from the last time the milk cow freshened."

"That'll do for now. Make sure you water it down though. I know we have some horse colostrum in the freezer at the clinic we could get you." Clayton looked over at the kids and smiled as he pulled out a small pad of paper. "Looks like you've got enough able bodies to help with the frequent feeds."

"How frequent?" Charlotte asked.

"Every two hours," Pete put in with a light sigh.

Clayton scribbled a few notes on the pad as Emily, Christopher, and Sam shared stunned looks.

Charlotte could identify. Even thinking about waking up that often exhausted her.

"I guess we'll be taking turns," Bob said, taking the paper from the vet when he was finished. "And I imagine we should start as soon as possible."

"Absolutely. The sooner you can get some food into that foal's belly, the better."

"I'll go warm up that colostrum," Charlotte said.

"Don't put it in the microwave," Clayton said. "You'll kill all the antibodies. Just warm it up in hot water."

BY THE TIME SHE GOT BACK with the warmed-up milk in a plastic bottle, Pete had forked some fresh hay toward Britney and had brought her a pail of water. She still lay on her side though, still looking distressed.

"If Britney doesn't get up soon, you're looking at a huge undertaking," Clayton was saying as Charlotte stepped into the barn. "It's going to require a lot of patience and a lot of cooperation."

Bob looked at the kids. "We're going to need your help."

"I guess," Emily said.

"There is no 'I guess' about it," Bob said, his voice firm, his eyes holding Emily's in an unyielding stare. "Saying 'I guess' isn't going to get that foal fed. It will be entirely up to us to keep it alive."

Charlotte wanted to tell Bob to tone down the rhetoric, but she also knew this was the reality. The foal was dependent on its caregivers and the children needed to have that made crystal clear.

"But, Grandpa. Every two hours?"

"You won't be doing it alone," Bob said. "We'll all take a turn."

Pete took the bottle from Charlotte and walked over to the foal. Pete held the wet foal between his legs, braced its head with one hand and tried to slip the nipple into the foal's mouth. She twisted her head, shaking it as she encountered the nipple, and then spit it out. Pete tried again, squeezing the bottle, letting a few drops of milk seep out.

Watching the process was almost as frustrating as actually doing it, Charlotte thought, leaning over the pen.

"What if it doesn't drink?" Christopher asked, a worried note in his voice.

"She'll eventually get hungry enough," Bob said.

"I've gotta go," Clayton said as he packed up the rest of his box. "If you have any questions, don't hesitate."

"I'll be dropping by tomorrow morning to get that milk replacer," Bob said, walking him out the door.

The rest of them stayed behind, watching as Pete struggled with the foal. It seemed as if every drop of precious colostrum coming out of the nipple dribbled out the sides of its mouth onto the ground.

Charlotte fought her innate urge to jump in, help, direct. She knew she would only be a hindrance, but it was so hard to simply sit back and watch.

"Is feeding going to be that hard all the time?" Sam asked.

"Not once the filly gets used to the bottle," Pete said, gently turning the foal's head back so he could put the nipple in again. The foal opened its mouth, showing off four blocky teeth—two upper, two lower. But when Pete put the nipple in her mouth she swung her head away and then fell over.

"Emily, why don't you come here and help me?" he asked as he gently lifted the foal up again.

"Are you sure?"

"Might as well learn right away, pretty lady."

While Charlotte watched, Emily and Pete tried again and again, surprising her with their patience as the filly alternately took the bottle, then spit it out.

"We're going to save the baby and Britney too, aren't we?" Emily asked as she slipped the nipple once more into its mouth.

Pete's only answer was to turn the still-slippery filly around and lift it up again. Charlotte understood his reluctance to assure her. While they all knew enough about feeding calves, feeding foals was an unknown journey. No one could predict how it would end. As for Britney, she was old. And the difficult birth had taken a lot out of her.

They watched for a while longer, then Bob yawned. "Bedtime for the rest of us," he said. "I'll take the next feeding in two hours. Charlotte, do you mind taking the one after that?" He looked at Sam. "And you can take the one in six hours."

Sam nodded, his eyes still on the foal, who had finally latched onto the nipple, only to spit it out again. "Will I have to do it by myself?"

Charlotte was about to offer her help when Pete spoke up. "I'll give you a hand."

Christopher dropped his head on the top board of the stall, his lip pushed out in a pout. "I want to help too," he mumbled.

Sam glanced at Bob. "Could he do some of the daytime feedings?"

"Of course. The more people help, the easier it will be for everyone."

"But I want to help at night," Christopher said.

"You need someone helping you, so that means they would have to get up twice in the night. That's too hard, okay?" Sam said.

Charlotte had been about to say the same thing, but she knew Christopher would understand things better if they came from Sam rather than her.

Christopher heaved a deep sigh, then gave a reluctant nod of his head. "Okay."

"So what's the filly's name?" Pete said as he once again guided the nipple into her mouth.

"How about Stormy?" Emily said. "Because she was born in a storm."

"Good name," Pete said. "I approve."

Charlotte glanced at her watch, then pushed away from the stall. "Bedtime for you, Christopher," she said.

She ushered him out, and Toby stayed behind with Emily and Sam.

Charlotte felt a gentle pang at the shift in Toby's allegiance, but behind that came a glimmer of joy. Toby was accepting the other kids as part of the family. She was their dog now too.

She and Christopher trudged carefully back to the house. Thankfully, the rain had stopped, but they had to skirt a few puddles.

They slowed down when they came to the patch of darkness between the yard light shining from the outside of the barn and the porch light of the house.

Christopher stopped and looked up. "I don't see any stars."

"The clouds are hiding them." Her coat was still damp from the rain and she shivered.

"At night, when I can't sleep, I count them." His grip on Charlotte's hand tightened. "I wonder if my mom can see me from up in heaven."

Charlotte felt a faint comfort in his words. She looked up into the sky, her yearning heart seeking God's comfort and presence.

"Are you praying, Grandma?" Christopher asked.

In the faint light cast from the porch, Charlotte could see his eyes looking up at her.

"Yes. I am."

"Can I pray with you?"

His softly spoken words brushed at the sorrow clinging to her heart.

"Yes, my dear boy. Of course you can." She gladly ignored the wet ground, the late hour, and the sleep clouding her mind, and knelt down beside her grandson, slipping her arms around his small body.

Christopher closed his eyes and lifted his head as Charlotte had. "Thank you, Lord, for my grandma and grandpa," he prayed, his young, innocent voice almost lost in the dark night. "Thank you for the baby horse, Stormy. Help her eat. Be with her mommy and don't let her die. Tell my mom I love her and miss her and help Grandma not to be sad either."

His poignant prayer encircled Charlotte's heart with a gentle warmth. She swallowed down the very sadness that Christopher had prayed she would be released from, then quietly added her own prayer.

"Thank you, Lord, that Christopher, Emily, and Sam can be here with us, even though I know they would sooner be back home. Help us to be a family and to love each other and help each other." She laid her head against Christopher's and waited a moment, letting the prayer settle. Then she said, "Amen."

"Amen," Christopher added. He sniffed and wiped his nose with the back of his hand then glanced back at the barn. "I'm going to keep praying for Britney," he said.

"I think that's a good idea." Charlotte slowly got to her feet then took Christopher's hand. "I think I will too."

Then they walked back to the house. Together.

Chapter Twenty-Five

"How was feeding?" Sam yawned as he dropped into his chair at the table.

"A little better." Charlotte had just come back from her turn at feeding the foal. "She's drinking a bit more than the last feeding."

"When I fed her early this morning, most of the milk dribbled out the sides of her mouth. That was so frustrating." Sam poured himself a bowl of cereal and dumped a few spoons of sugar on top. "But Grandpa said she had had a good feed before that so I guess it's okay."

"Grandpa was with you? I thought Pete was going to help," Charlotte asked as she rinsed the bottle and washed the nipple. She had drawn the early morning feeding and then had come in and set the table for the kids. Breakfast would be cold cereal and fruit until the foal either started drinking from a pail or Britney was feeling better.

"He was there, but Grandpa said Uncle Pete could go." Sam's voice held a note of surprise.

"You were okay with him helping you?"

"Yeah. I mean, I don't know much about feeding horses."

"But you're learning," Charlotte assured him, setting the bottle on a tea towel to dry.

"I'm learning," Sam echoed. "It's kinda cool. Seeing that little thing standing up on those long legs."

"Mornin', Grandma," Emily said as she entered the kitchen. She opened the refrigerator door and bent over. Charlotte cringed at the sight of Emily's tight pants and shirt, but at least she had covered them both with a loose sweater, so she said nothing.

Baby steps, she reminded herself.

"Hey, Sam, how did it go feeding Stormy?" Emily asked from the depths of the fridge.

"Good. I was telling Grandma about it." Sam bent over his bowl, reading his cereal box.

"I think I got half a bottle in her last night," Emily said returning to the table with a jug of orange juice.

As they compared notes, Christopher ambled into the kitchen, cradling his kitten. He sat down, nuzzling the cat with his nose.

"Christopher—" Charlotte began just as Sam spoke up.

"Hey, mister, put that cat down, go back upstairs, and wash your hands and face," he said, looking up from the box of cereal parked beside him.

"I'll help him." Emily downed her juice then held out her hand to her little brother.

"But I'm still tired." Christopher underlined his complaint with a wide yawn.

"We're all tired," Emily said. "C'mon. Let's go."

Christopher bent over and gently put his kitten on the

floor. As they walked back down the hall toward the stairs, the kitten weaving through their feet, Charlotte caught Sam's eye.

"Sorry, Grandma," he said. "I guess I'm just used to—"

"Taking care of your brother." Charlotte finished the sentence for him. "And that's good."

One day he would trust her and Bob to do the same, but for now she was thankful for small miracles. Emily and Sam were talking to each other again. Christopher was happy as a clam with his little kitten. Stormy was slowly getting better.

Charlotte clung to the hope that this family was coming back together.

"Morning all," Pete boomed as he burst into the kitchen. "What's for breakfast?"

"Cereal." Sam held up the box.

"That's all?"

"Fortified with nine essential minerals," Sam said, glancing at the side of the box. "Part of a healthy breakfast."

"But which part?" Pete groused as he sat down.

Bob was right behind him. "You could cook, you know," he said as he pulled his chair away from the table.

"Inconceivable," Pete retorted.

"Did you sleep okay?" Bob asked Sam as he reached for the box Sam had been reading from.

"Yeah. Thanks." Sam gave his grandfather a quick smile as he pushed the box closer, and for a moment, understanding flashed between them.

"What are you and Pete up to today?" Charlotte asked as she buttered the toast she had been preparing.

"I'm going to go finish seeding Jimmy's quarter." Bob dipped his spoon into his cereal. "Thought maybe Pete could go with the kids to school."

"Why would he want to do that?"

Bob shrugged. "Maybe Sam could get in some driving practice."

Charlotte almost dropped her knife. She glanced across the table at Sam staring at his grandfather.

"For real?" Sam asked.

"Yes." Bob's succinct reply said all Sam needed to hear. He jumped up from the table and ran upstairs.

"Where's he going?" Bob asked.

"Probably to do his hair," Pete said dryly.

Charlotte couldn't help but smile.

Epilogue

A young filly ran pell-mell over the grass, her dark brown tail straight up in the air, waving like a banner, her feet pounding out a joyful rhythm. She didn't go far. Inexplicably she stopped, then turned, as if curious at the movement she saw through the trees across the yard.

Her mother, a dun mare, stood in the late afternoon shade of a large willow tree, one foot crooked as she dozed. But then, she too seemed to sense what her filly was watching and she looked up.

"Stormy likes summer vacations too," Christopher said, standing up on the lower rail of the fence, his arms crossed over the top rail. His blue jeans had smudges of dirt on the knees, and his brown T-shirt sported a rip on one shoulder. His hair was liberally sprinkled with bits of hay from climbing on the new bales. "I wish they lasted longer."

"Yes, only a few more weeks and you're back to school," Charlotte said, wondering where the past few months had gone.

The children had been with them four months now, though at times it seemed shorter.

"I don't want to go back to school," Christopher said. "I want to stay and help Uncle Pete and Grandpa on the farm."

"I'm sure you'll find lots of new adventures next year again," Charlotte assured him.

"Maybe." But she could see he wasn't convinced. He straightened, looking at the colt. "What is Stormy looking at?"

"I wonder if she hears the other horses." Charlotte, glanced over her shoulder, brushing her hair back from her face. She listened carefully, filtering out the sound of the tractor piling up the bales.

Sam, Bob, and Pete had been busy all morning and part of the afternoon hauling the freshly baled hay from their land down the road. When they were done, Sam was appointed to stack the bales into neat rows because Pete had promised to take Emily out on the horses.

"There they are." Christopher was pointing at the bend in the road. Sure enough, Charlotte could see two horses coming toward them. Pete was in the lead on Ben, Emily behind him on Princess.

Charlotte smiled up at them as they pulled up beside her, the musky scent of the horses surrounding them. "Supper will be in half an hour," Charlotte told them.

Princess snorted and stamped her feet, as if eager to keep moving.

Emily gentled her with a pat on the neck and gave her grandmother a quick smile. "What's for supper?"

"Not tofu, okay?" Pete said. "We're farmers. We need protein we can chew."

"Chicken casserole," Charlotte assured him. "And some without meat for Emily. When you see Sam, tell him too."

Pete nodded, then with a gentle nudge of his booted feet, got Ben into a trot, Princess following.

"I'll go help them," Christopher said, jumping down from the fence.

"You make sure you all come back in time to wash up," Charlotte told him.

"I will." His promise floated behind him as he ran to catch up to his sister and uncle.

IT WAS EVENING. Once again the family was gathered around the table.

Supper was over and everyone had reported on the events of the day. The children's faces were flushed from being outside and Charlotte had to smile at the line of brown halfway up Sam's arm. *Farmer tan,* she thought, keeping the comment to herself.

"So how was the ride?" Bob asked as he wiped his mouth with a napkin.

"I was a little scared at first," Emily said, "but Princess is a good horse."

"She should be. I trained her," Pete said, sucking on the toothpick he had just used.

"Like you trained Sam to pile bales?" Bob asked. "I had to go and tell him to redo half that pile."

"I was just doing what Pete told me," Sam said indignantly.

"That's what I said, son," Bob replied.

"But if we do it your way, they won't shed the rain as easily."

"And if we do it your way, it will be too hard to pull the twines off in the winter when the snow melts and freezes again."

"When can I ride the horses?" Christopher put in, looking up from his plate.

"When we get a smaller saddle, you can," Pete said.

Emily chewed thoughtfully. "I'll be able to get my cell phone back next week, right Grandma?"

"When you make the last payment on your old bill, yes you can."

"Yea and again I say, Yea." She made two fists and held them up, then spun them around each other as if she was doing a little celebration dance in her chair. "I'll finally be able to text Ashley."

"I'm sure she's gonna be thrilled," Sam said wryly.

"You'll be thrilled when you can get your phone going again," Emily shot back.

"Ecstatic."

"I'm excited," Christopher put in. "I get a new backpack."

"Can we not talk about school?" Sam grumbled.

In spite of Sam's warning, the talk bounced from school, back to horses, to auctions, to trips, to town, and back to the impending school season. As she listened, Charlotte sat back, a feeling of contentment bringing a smile to her face.

Her thoughts cast back to the first time the children were at this table. *How far they've come.*

They had made it through this difficult time and they

were still all here. They were a family, and they were going to make it.

Bob sniffed and then half turned to get the Bible from the shelf. But before he pulled it off, he gave Charlotte a wry look.

Then he pulled down an old story Bible their children had received from Rosemary many, many years ago.

"I thought we would read out of this for a while," he said, placing it on the table in front of him as he adjusted his glasses. "The Bible starts with the words, 'In the beginning.' So we are going to start in the same place. In the beginning." Bob cleared his throat and began reading from the book that Charlotte had read to her children each night before they went to bed.

In the beginning.

And that was how she felt. They were making an entirely new beginning. They'd had their struggles, and she was fooling herself if she thought that she and Bob were finished.

But they had come through this darkness, the darkness of losing a daughter and mother. The darkness of rumors and half-truths. The darkness of change and new beginnings.

It's always darkest before the dawn. The phrase Hannah had so easily thrown out that morning returned to her.

Hannah was right, Charlotte thought looking around the table. As Bob's measured voice read the age-old story of the beginnings of the world, Charlotte felt as if they had come to a new day.

The dawn of a new beginning for their family.

About the Author

Kathleen Bauer is the pen name for a team of writers who have come together to create the series Home to Heather Creek. *Before the Dawn* was written by Carolyne Aarsen, a city girl who was transplanted to the country when she married her dear husband, Richard. While raising four children, foster children, and various animals, Carolyne's résumé gained some unique entries. She found out how to handle cows, to drive tractors, front-end loaders, snow machines, and ATVs, and to ride horses and train colts. She grew a garden and discovered pickling, canning, and preserving its produce. Somewhere in all of this, she also learned how to write. Her first book sold in 1997, and since then she has published over forty books. Her stories show a love of open spaces, the fellowship of her Christian community, and the gift God has given us in Christ.

A Note from the Editors

We hope you enjoy Home to Heather Creek, created by the Books and Inspirational Media Division of Guideposts, a nonprofit organization that touches millions of lives every day through products and services that inspire, encourage, help you grow in your faith, and celebrate God's love in every aspect of your daily life.

Thank you for making a difference with your purchase of this book, which helps fund our many outreach programs to military personnel, prisons, hospitals, nursing homes, and educational institutions. To learn more, visit GuidepostsFoundation.org.

We also maintain many useful and uplifting online resources. Visit Guideposts.org to read true stories of hope and inspiration, access OurPrayer network, sign up for free newsletters, download free e-books, join our Facebook community, and follow our stimulating blogs.

To learn about other Guideposts publications, including the best-selling devotional *Daily Guideposts*, go to ShopGuideposts.org, call (800) 932-2145, or write to Guideposts, PO Box 5815, Harlan, Iowa 51593.